For Tommy — My favorite rotten guy!

— Shae Connor

Sand & Water

SHAE CONNOR

Published by
Dreamspinner Press
4760 Preston Road
Suite 244-149
Frisco, TX 75034
http://www.dreamspinnerpress.com/

This is a work of fiction. Names, characters, places, and incidents either are the product of the author's imagination or are used fictitiously, and any resemblance to actual persons, living or dead, business establishments, events, or locales is entirely coincidental.

Sand & Water
Copyright © 2011 by Shae Connor

Cover Art by Reese Dante   http://www.reesedante.com

All rights reserved. No part of this book may be reproduced or transmitted in any form or by any means, electronic or mechanical, including photocopying, recording, or by any information storage and retrieval system without the written permission of the Publisher, except where permitted by law. To request permission and all other inquiries, contact Dreamspinner Press, 4760 Preston Road, Suite 244-149, Frisco, TX 75034
http://www.dreamspinnerpress.com/

ISBN: 978-1-61372-090-5

Printed in the United States of America
First Edition
August 2011

eBook edition available
eBook ISBN: 978-1-61372-091-2

Dedicated to my friends and family,
who support me even when they don't understand me.

A world of thanks to my editing team:
Dani, Dawn, Jackie, and Kat.
You've made this a better story and
me a better writer in the process. Love you!

Chapter 1

JOHN woke to another morning without Liz.

He blinked his eyes open and focused on the sheer curtain over the window, the soft, white folds drifting in the sea breeze. The vestiges of his dream clung to the edges of his mind, warmth and love and home. Liz smiled up at him, brown hair soft around her face, hazel eyes glowing, wrapped in his arms. Whole and happy and alive.

Today, he knew, would not be a good day.

"NO, TOM, it's the *third* dataset we want." John had been over this twice already, but for some reason it wasn't sinking in. "The first two are old data. Running those is a waste of time."

"But I already ran the second set."

John sighed, rubbing his forehead with his fingers. Days like this had a way of making him feel a lot older than thirty-two. "Well, then, you'll have to run it again on the third set." *Which you wouldn't have to do if you'd listened to me the other times I told you that.*

Silence greeted him, followed by something mumbled that he knew wasn't anything he wanted to hear. "Okay, I'll send it over later."

"I'll keep an—" The dial tone cut him off, and he punched the button on the phone to cut off the speaker. He leaned back in his chair, pinching the bridge of his nose and willing himself not to throw anything. "It's not that bad, it's not that bad," he muttered.

And it wasn't. Tom was a good worker. He did a good job. He just needed a little extra handling sometimes. In particular, he had a tendency not to read every e-mail all the way through, so he'd missed one of John's instructions for the data analysis he needed for his conference call that afternoon. *It'll get done*, John told himself. *Forget about it until after lunch.*

He scrubbed a hand through his hair, which needed a cut, the thick waves of soft brown getting unruly again. Letting out a long breath, he sat up straighter and turned back to face his computer, diving back into code.

Soft music floated from the speakers of the television in the corner. John kept it set on the "light classical" digital music channel, except when the Braves had a day game or he was watching Beth and changed it over to a children's channel for her benefit. Music with lyrics was too distracting when he was crunching numbers. When he was doing much of anything, actually. Part of it was that he had a tendency to sing along. Part of it was that too many songs reminded him of Liz, even now, five years later, when his life was back on track and he could feel his heart again.

A soft knock on his office door drew his attention. Meghan smiled at him, green eyes sparkling, as usual. "We're making sandwiches for lunch," she said. "Any special requests?"

John smiled. "No seafood," he said, watching her eyes roll.

"As if," she scoffed. Meghan, his aunt although only seven years his senior, owned a seafood restaurant on the beach, which meant that other than the occasional fish sticks for Beth's benefit, they never ate seafood at home.

Meghan rested the front of her shoulder against the doorframe, wrapping her hands on either side of the molding. A shaft of long, vibrant red hair fell forward across her other shoulder, the texture thick and wavy like John's. She ignored it. "Speaking of which, I have to go down to the restaurant this afternoon after all. Audra's got a doctor's appointment, and I couldn't find anyone who could cover her shift."

John frowned. "Is she okay?"

Meghan shrugged. "As okay as ever," she said. "She had an episode with her blood sugar the other day, so they're checking her insulin pump, making sure it's working right. Probably nothing, but better safe than sorry."

John couldn't help thinking about his Beth with a pump in her body supplying her with the insulin she couldn't produce, and he held back a shudder.

"Anyway," Meghan continued, "will you be able to watch Beth? I won't need to leave until around three."

John nodded. "Yeah, I have a conference call at two, but it should be over by then. If it isn't, I may start firing people, authority or no authority. So I think we can wrap it up in time."

Meghan eyed him for a moment. "You okay?"

John sighed, tipping his head against the high back of his office chair. "I had a dream last night."

Meghan's eyes softened. "Good or bad?"

John lifted one shoulder an inch and let it drop, a semblance of a shrug. "What's the difference anymore?" he asked. "But she was happy."

Meghan's smile was soft. "Then that's good," she said. "I know it's hard when you wake up either way. But that's definitely good."

She pushed off the doorframe. "I left Bethy in front of *Blue's Clues*, so let me go make sure she hasn't wandered off on a clue hunt again without telling anyone. We'll bring you lunch in a bit."

She walked away, and John blew out a breath and pushed his fingers under his glasses to rub his eyes. "Good dream," he murmured, picturing the smile on Liz's face. "Good."

The reassurances weren't doing much to help the deep ache in his heart.

JOHN jumped when Beth darted into the room, startling him out of his contemplation of the dataset Tom had finally sent. "Daddy!" she cried, running around his desk and taking a leap toward his lap. John caught her with practiced ease, laughing.

"Hey, sweetheart," he said as she threw her arms around his neck, hugging him tight. "What's got you so excited?"

She leaned back and smiled, and John's heart tripped in his chest. It was her mother's smile, dimples and all, and every time he saw it, he fell in love with both of them all over again. "Aunt Meghan said you're gonna take me to the park this afternoon!"

John raised an eyebrow and turned his head to where Meghan stood in the doorway, her expression exasperated.

"I said that *maybe* he'd be able to take you, Bethy," she said, stepping over to set down plates of sandwiches and carrot sticks. "Just because the weather's so nice. Your daddy has to work, you know."

Meghan turned away, to bring back drinks, John knew, and he shifted his attention to Beth. She'd arranged herself on his lap facing the desk, their usual position when they shared a lunch like this. "I'll try to take you, baby," he said, kissing the side of her head. "We'll see how this meeting goes. Okay?"

Beth nodded, still smiling. "Let's eat, Daddy!" she said. "I'm hungry!"

John laughed and reached for her plate first, handing her a triangle-shaped half of what he knew would be a peanut-butter-and-grape-jelly sandwich. A month ago it had been grilled cheese every day; a month from now, who knew?

Beth wrapped her small hands around the sandwich and took a bite right out of the center, tilting her head back against John's chest as she chewed. John reached for his own sandwich, which looked like ham and swiss. Meghan came back in carrying a tall glass of tea and a smaller plastic one with a lid, which would be filled with milk. "Here you go, kiddos," she said as she set them down within John's reach but not Beth's. "Enjoy your lunch! I'll be back to snag Miss Piggy in a bit."

Beth grinned and lifted one arm, wrapping it over the top of her head so her hand lay along the center of her face. She grabbed the tip of her nose with the tip of one finger, pulling it back flat so it resembled a snout, and gave a most unladylike snort.

John sighed as Meghan snickered. "I am so very sorry you ever taught her that," he said.

"Along with everything else like that I've ever taught her," Meghan agreed. "Sorry, Johnny. A kid's gotta do what a kid's gotta do."

She wiggled her fingers at them and disappeared again, and John took another bite of his sandwich. Beth reached toward her milk, a quarter of a sandwich still left in her hand, and John moved the cup closer and helped her wrap her hand around it. She used a regular plastic cup when they ate at the table, but after one near-catastrophe during an office lunch, she got a lid when she sat at John's desk even though she hated the "baby" cup.

"Daddy," Beth said once she'd had some milk, "do you think Jeremy will be at the park today?"

Beth had come barreling in a few days earlier after a trip to the park with Meghan, exclaiming about the cool new boy she'd met that day. John had struggled to understand what she was saying, but he caught that the boy was named Jeremy and he was "awesome," which seemed to be Beth's favorite word of the moment.

"I don't know, Bethy," John said. "I guess he might be." Right then he made a decision. "We'll go find out together, how about that?"

Beth wriggled and grinned up at him. "We can go?"

"We can go," he replied. "Work can live without me for an hour or two."

"That's awesome!" Beth raised both hands above her head in a classic victory pose, sandwich still clutched in one hand, and John laughed.

"All right, honey," he said. "First we have to eat our lunch, okay? And then later we'll go to the park."

"Okay!" Beth went right back to eating, and John could only shake his head. Even at thirty-two, sometimes he felt as old as Methuselah next to Beth's five-year-old energy. She was amazing and beautiful and the best part of his life, but boy, could she ever be exhausting.

JOHN put the conference call out of his mind as soon as it ended. Things had gone fine. They'd even finished up a few minutes early. One of the things he loved about Adam, his boss and friend, was that he hated long meetings, and that had paid off today. John had other things on his mind, like taking his daughter to the park.

She held his hand and half skipped down the sidewalk. John let her, just taking the time to soak up the sun and the salt air. Since he'd moved almost four years earlier back to Tybee Island, off the Georgia coast at Savannah, he'd gotten so accustomed to the warmth and sea breezes that he missed them when he went farther inland, even just into Savannah to visit his mother. The rambling old Victorian they lived in, which Meghan had bought not long after she opened her restaurant, sat only a quarter of a mile from the beach, so they spent plenty of time on the sand.

Today, though, they walked to the small play park two blocks in the opposite direction from the water. They came here often too, and Beth loved the swings and the big climbing set in the center that wasn't in the same universe as the monkey bars John had grown up with.

As soon as the playground came into sight, Beth tugged at his hand. "Come on, Daddy," she urged. "I wanna see if Jeremy's here!"

John laughed a little as Beth tugged him along. Once they were inside the park boundaries, John pulled them to a stop and squatted down to Beth's level.

"Remember, stay in the playground unless you're coming to where I am," he said, holding her gaze, knowing he was looking into eyes exactly like his own. "No going anywhere with anyone else, not even another kid, okay?"

John wondered if Meghan had taught Beth to roll her eyes too. "I know, Daddy," she said. "See ya!"

She ran for the swing sets, and John watched her for a minute or two, hands on his hips. He shook his head, smiling again, and crossed to one of the benches near the playground, where he sat and stretched his legs out in front of him, left arm across the back of the bench, face tilted up into the sun.

He didn't know how long he'd been there, but it couldn't have been long, because he'd only checked on Beth twice when a low laugh drew his attention. He looked up into a handsome face creased by a wide smile, white teeth shining in the sun.

"This seat taken?" the other man said, and John blinked in surprise for a moment before nodding toward the empty expanse of bench.

"Help yourself," he said, lifting his arm off the back and waving it toward the seat. He watched as the man settled in at the far end, taking up a similar position to John's but with his arms crossed over his chest. He had dark hair, cut shorter than John's but straight instead of wavy, and he exuded a charm that made John like him without hesitation.

"Which one's yours?" the man asked.

John looked over toward the playground and sought out Beth, who by then had moved to scrambling up the climbing set, a grinning boy about her age with her. Her honey-brown hair, pulled up into two ponytails, shone in the bright sunlight. "That's her on the climbing set," he said.

"Oh, with Jeremy?" The man grinned. "That must be Beth, then. Jeremy was crazy excited that he might get to see her again."

John chuckled. "Ah, young love." He turned in his seat enough to hold out a hand. "John McConnell," he said.

The other man glanced at him for a second before reaching out to shake. "Bryan Simmons."

Bryan quirked an eyebrow over deep brown eyes, and John smiled as they sat back. He returned his attention to the kids. "Looks like my daughter and your son really hit it off."

Bryan laughed, drawing John's attention back to him. "Oh, not my son. Nephew." He grinned. "My sister and her husband own the Sea Breeze." He named a bed-and-breakfast that was housed in an older house much like the one John lived in. "I'm helping them renovate the place, and I keep an eye on the munchkin for them sometimes."

John nodded. "I'm glad someone's doing that," he said. "I mean, I know the place wasn't exactly ramshackle before, but it was starting to look a little rough around the edges."

"Yeah," Bryan agreed. "Our cousins owned it. Our mom's cousins, actually. But they were ready to retire, and Davis—that's my brother-in-law—got a pretty hefty inheritance from his grandmother. So he and Karen bought the place, and they're fixing it up."

John nodded again, watching as Beth and Jeremy laughed and chased each other around the climbing set. Jeremy's short, curly hair was a riotous mess, reminding John of what his own hair did when he let it grow out. "Been on the island long?"

"Six months." Something in Bryan's voice made John look over at him, but he couldn't quite read the look in Bryan's eyes. "I was in Atlanta before that, but I had to…. I left. Needed to get away for a while."

Something in John's chest twisted. He recognized the tone of Bryan's voice now. He'd heard it from himself often in the past five years. "Bad memories?"

Bryan hesitated, but John had the feeling he needed to get something out. Finally Bryan gave a short nod. "Bad breakup," he said. "I mean, not like yelling and throwing things bad. More like having to break up for reasons neither of you can control. Having to choose between him and me."

It took a second for John to register the "him." He blinked. "You're gay?"

He winced immediately, knowing how the question sounded. Harsh. Accusatory. But he was only surprised, not put off. He opened his mouth to apologize, but Bryan's face had already twisted into a scowl.

"Yeah, I'm gay," Bryan challenged, glaring at John. "You got a problem with that?" He shook his head, starting to turn away. "Jesus, can't even go to the fucking park without running into some homophobe—"

"Hey!" John interrupted him with an upheld hand, and Bryan's face turned back toward him. "Not how I meant it, Mr. Jump-to-Conclusions. Not a homophobe, just surprised. I mean, not that many people are so casual about it in this neck of the woods. Trust me, I'm not bothered at all." He hesitated before taking the plunge. "Hell, the last person I dated before I met my wife was a guy. Okay?"

Bryan studied him for a moment before blushing and dropping his head. "Sorry," he mumbled. "I do tend to jump to conclusions sometimes. And a lot of guys seem to think I'm going to, I don't know, try to convert them or something."

John nodded. "Apology accepted." He shrugged as he relaxed against the bench. "I can understand it, really. A lot of people don't react well, especially in the South. But I'm not one of them." He shot Bryan a look out of the corner of his eye. "And even if I hadn't dated guys, I know that just because you're gay doesn't mean you're going to try to hit on every guy you meet."

Before he could say anything else, Beth and Jeremy came running up toward them. "Daddy!" Beth exclaimed. She never seemed to do anything at a normal volume. "Jeremy said his mom is baking cookies and wants me to come have some!"

John frowned. "Bethy, honey, you know you're not supposed to invite yourself over to somebody's house."

"I didn't, Daddy!" Beth was insistent. "Jeremy invited me!"

John threw Bryan a sheepish look just as Jeremy intervened. "Can she come, Uncle Bryan? Pleasepleaseplease?" He bounced up and down, and John had to laugh. He'd thought it impossible for another child to have more energy than his own, but Jeremy might just prove him wrong.

"We'll see, okay?" Bryan's voice was soft but firm. "We can't go back right now. I told your mom we'd give her an hour. But we'll see after that, okay?"

Jeremy nodded so hard John thought his head would bobble right off. "Okay!" He turned back to Beth. "Race you!"

They took off toward the climbing set side by side, and Bryan gave John an apologetic look. "Sorry again," he said. "We're trying to teach him to ask his parents or me before inviting someone else to do something, but it hasn't quite sunk in yet. He's a little impulsive."

John waved a hand. "Not a problem," he said. "I'm in no rush to get back, if the kids want cookies."

Bryan leaned forward, resting his forearms on his thighs and rubbing his hands together between his knees. "So where do you and your wife live? One of these great old houses?"

John's heart clenched at the question, but he pushed through it. "Beth and I live with my Aunt Meghan," he said. "She owns that seafood restaurant on the beach."

Bryan glanced over at John. "Let's Be Shellfish?" His voice was suffused with laughter. "One of the best restaurant names in history, I swear."

John almost grinned. "Yeah, it's certainly memorable," he said. "Anyway, when…. We moved down about four years ago. After…."

Damn. This is still so hard.

"After my wife died."

Chapter 2

"Oh God." The sympathy in Bryan's voice didn't make things any easier. Bryan turned to face John, drawing one knee sideways on the bench between them. "I'm sorry, man, I didn't mean to bring up bad memories."

"It's okay," John said, wishing it were more than a half-truth. He glanced over at the kids before returning his attention to Bryan. "She died in childbirth."

"Wow," Bryan said. "I didn't think that happened anymore."

John shrugged one shoulder. "It's very rare," he said. "She had eclampsia. Out-of-control high blood pressure. She had a seizure and then a stroke." He sucked in a breath and blew it out. "Beth was fine, but Liz didn't make it."

"Oh, man." Bryan was silent for a long moment. "So you've had to raise her on your own?"

"Not completely," John said. "We were in Atlanta then, too, but after a while I had to get away. Like you said. Meghan brought us here. I work at home, and she mostly works afternoons and evenings, so we both look after Beth." He shook his head and smiled, looking over at his daughter, now back on the swings with Jeremy. "I can't believe she'll start kindergarten in the fall. They really do grow up way too fast."

Bryan chuckled. "They do," he said. "Jeremy's such an awesome kid, but is he ever exhausting."

John laughed. "I was just thinking that about Beth earlier today," he said. "Where the hell do they get their energy? And can we have some of it?"

Bryan laughed. "I could sure use it when we're working on the house. Ripping plaster lath is a challenge even when it's already crumbling."

John winced at the thought. "Did you work in construction in Atlanta?"

Bryan paused before answering. "No, I... have a degree in architecture," he said. "But only undergrad. I couldn't go on for my master's then, and now I'm not sure I want to. So I'm helping Karen and Davis with the design, too, not just the manual labor."

John looked Bryan up and down a moment. "How old are you?" he asked. "I would've pegged you for barely out of college."

Bryan grinned. "Yeah, I get that a lot," he said. "But I'm twenty-seven, twenty-eight in September. Guess looking younger is more a bonus the older you get, right?"

John laughed. "Yeah, I guess so," he said. "I just turned thirty-two, and some days I feel like I'm over a hundred. Especially when I'm trying to keep up with Beth."

Bryan was silent again before taking a small breath. "You said your wife's name was Liz," he said. "Feel free to tell me to butt my nosey self out, but is Beth named for her?"

John nodded. "My mother thought I was crazy," he said, voice low, watching as Beth climbed up a ladder toward the slide. "But I needed to do something to, I don't know, mark her memory. Something tangible. I mean, not that Beth isn't tangible just by being here, but I wanted to be sure Liz was always with her. So I named her Elizabeth after her mom, but I call her Beth so it's not... not so hard."

Bryan shifted in his seat, drawing John's attention back to him. "My instinct after that is to, I don't know, give you a hug or something," he said with a small smile. "But I don't want you to think I'm hitting on any guy I meet."

John laughed, dispelling some of the tension, and felt himself relax. "I'm good," he said. "And I'm secure enough in my masculinity to let a guy hug me sometimes without having a big gay freak-out about it."

Bryan laughed, too, and they both settled back into a comfortable silence, watching the kids play. John let the sun warm him and the breeze cool him. Late May in Georgia tended to be much more sauna-like, but the summer heat had held off so far. Two weeks until June, and he could not only sit outside but even walk to the park without breaking a sweat.

"So what do you do?"

Bryan's voice broke into John's thoughts, and he smiled without opening his eyes. "Statistics," he said. "Consultant now. I work for Peachtree Home Improvement."

Bryan made a sound of recognition. "Pretty good company, from what I hear," he said. "All over the place too. A sea of orange as far as the eye can see."

"Peach!" John said, insistent but teasing, opening his eyes and turning his head to the side to send Bryan a mock glare. "It's peach, not orange. Get it right, now."

Bryan laughed. "And the claws come out," he said, holding up a hand, fingers curled. "Don't worry, Mr. Peachtree. That's where we get all our building supplies from. Those other places might be nice for the weekend fix-it people, but the serious ones know where to go."

John nodded once. "Damn straight." He paused. "Maybe I can get you guys a little discount now and then. We get employee and friends and family offers. I could pass those along."

"That would be great," Bryan said. "Every little bit helps. We've already gone over budget a couple of places. We've been able to make it up so far, but some breathing room will be nice."

"It's a date." John froze as he realized what he'd said, and Bryan bit his lip, clearly trying not to burst out laughing. "Er, it's a *deal*," John corrected. He laughed. "Not a Freudian slip, I promise. Still not freaked out."

Bryan did laugh then. "You know, it is okay to be a *little* weirded out," he said. "Or, I don't know, hyperalert or something. I'm kind of used to it by now."

John sighed and sat up, turning to face Bryan. "No, really, it's not a big deal," he said. "Yeah, I'll probably be oversensitive sometimes, even though I know that can be even worse. It's just how things have been before. Some people are really touchy about the subject. But I've always tried to think for myself and to judge people for their actions, not just because of who they are."

Bryan nodded. "Progressive thinking is always good," he said. "Did you grow up here?"

"On Tybee?"

Bryan nodded again.

"We lived here for a few years, but mostly we were in Savannah. My mom still lives there. She doesn't come out here much anymore. We were...." John hesitated. "When I was nine, my dad died in a car accident. It happened on the island, and it's just hard for Mom to be here."

"Oh, wow." Bryan leaned forward. "Now I really *do* want to give you a hug. Your dad when you were so young, and then your wife?"

John waved a hand. "It's okay," he said. "Yeah, it was a tragedy both times. But it's been a long time since Dad died, and Liz, well, it's fresher, but it's getting a lot better. Sometimes I can almost get through a day without thinking about her."

He crooked a small smile, and Bryan met it, eyes soft. "Well, the offer stands," he said. "I've always been a huggy person anyway. I guess that's my big contribution to stereotypical gay behavior."

John snorted. "Besides that whole dating men thing," he pointed out, and Bryan laughed. His laugh was infectious, John was learning, and he had to chuckle too.

As their laughter died down, Bryan shot John an appraising look. "So who do you look like?" he asked. "Your mom or your dad?"

"Both," John replied. "The hair is definitely from Dad." He ran a hand through the wavy brown strands. "I'm due for a trim," he said. "Gets crazier the longer it gets."

"Let it grow a little," Bryan advised, smiling. "Take it from a gay man. We know what looks good on other men. The curls—they just suit you somehow."

John felt himself start to blush, but running feet caught his attention, and he turned to see Beth and Jeremy coming toward them at full speed. "Daddy!" Beth cried, launching herself into his lap. "Can we have cookies now?"

Jeremy wasn't so calm about it. "Cookies cookies cookies cookies!" he chanted, bouncing back and forth from one foot to the other in front of Bryan.

John and Bryan looked at each other and cracked up. John couldn't remember the last time he'd laughed so much in one day, and most of it within the past hour.

"C'mon," Bryan said, standing up and reaching for Jeremy's hand. "Let's go crash Karen's kitchen and get some sugar into these kids."

John got to his feet and took Beth's hand. "I hope there's enough for the grown-ups too," he said. He was rewarded with one of Bryan's blinding smiles.

THE bed-and-breakfast was two blocks down and three blocks over, not far from John's house but a little closer to the beach. He and Bryan didn't have time to talk as they walked, not even able to keep up with the kids' constant babble about how much fun they'd had playing together.

"And then the swing went up *so high* that I 'most fell out, but I catched myself," Jeremy said, skipping and bouncing with every step. "But Bethy, she went even *higher* and didn't fall."

"But Jeremy climbeded higher than me on the bars," Beth broke in. "So it's okay. I'm gonna teach him how to swing better, and he's gonna teach me how to climb better."

"That's great, honey," John said as he and Bryan exchanged quick grins. "Just be careful while you're learning, okay? You don't want to fall and get hurt."

Beth bounced like Jeremy. "Maybe next time you and Mister Bryan can push me and Jeremy on the swings! We can go way higher then!"

John glanced at Bryan, who shrugged. "We'll see, sweetie," Bryan said, giving John a sly smile. "Your daddy may have to work."

John gave him a playful frown. "Hey now, not a workaholic," he said. "I'm headed from the park off to have cookies and milk on the spur of the moment in the middle of a workday. Work can handle itself sometimes."

"Point taken," Bryan said. "So, what, should we plan another date?" He grinned. "*Play* date, that is. Don't want to go all Freudian on you."

John laughed. "Sounds good," he said. "Work's a little slow right now. Maybe day after tomorrow? Same bat-time, same bat-channel?"

"You're on." Bryan looked down at Jeremy. "How about that, Germy? You wanna play with Bethy on Friday?"

"*Yes!*" Jeremy jumped in place as high as he could, throwing his free arm out with wild abandon.

"Yay!" Beth echoed Jeremy's celebratory outcry, tugging on John's hand in her excitement. Then she gave a sneaky grin that made her look just like her mother again. "But I dunno if I wanna play with somebody who's all Germy," she teased. "Germy Germy Germy."

"Stop it!" Jeremy hollered. "I'm not germy! I'm Jeremy!"

John pulled Beth closer and rubbed her head with his free hand. "Watch it, little girl, or I'll start giving away all *your* embarrassing nicknames." Beth looked up at him, eyes wide, and he nodded. She deflated.

"Okay," she said, solemn. "Sorry, Jeremy. I won't call you Germy if you don't want me to."

Jeremy looked at her and then smiled. "It's okay," he said. "You can call me Germy sometimes if you want."

John looked up and caught Bryan's eye again, finding him smiling. "Ah, young love," Bryan said, and John snorted out a laugh.

Bryan stopped and nodded toward the house in front of them. "Let's go around to the back," he said. "We're in the middle of fixing up the front parlor, so it's kind of a hard-hat zone at the moment."

John followed him across the grass and around the side of the house. "Parlor? I guess that's how you know it's a real Southern home."

Bryan shot him a grin over his shoulder. "That plus the plaster walls, the gingerbread trim, the high ceilings, the hardwood floors," he said. "All great stuff. Well, except the plaster. That's a nightmare."

John smiled. "I can imagine," he said. "Guess we're lucky that someone already took care of that at our place. It was drywalled when Meghan bought it."

Bryan looked at him again. "Oh, it's her place? I figured it was a family house or something."

"Nope, all Meghan's doing," John said. "She says all the time she's glad we moved in. I think she'd just rattle around in there if we weren't using the extra rooms."

They were at the back steps by then, and Bryan led the way to a screen door painted chocolate brown. "Hey, Karen, hope you don't mind we brought guests," he called out as he pulled the door open and nodded John through. John led Beth into the kitchen and stopped just inside, wide-eyed.

"Wow," he said. "This is beautiful." The design blended modern stainless-steel appliances with beadboard cabinets painted a pale cream and given a light antiqued finish. The walls were a soft sage green and the countertops a green-tinged material that John couldn't quite figure out.

"Thanks," Bryan said. "I designed most of it." He nodded down at Jeremy. "Jeremy, you take Beth over to the powder room and wash your hands, okay? No cookies until you're clean."

Jeremy's head bobbed up and down, and he dropped Bryan's hand, holding his out to Beth instead. "C'mon, Bethy!"

Beth looked up at her dad, who smiled back down at her and pushed her in Jeremy's direction. "You heard Mister Bryan, no cookies 'til you're clean!"

Beth grinned and darted over to Jeremy, grabbing his hand, and the two scampered down a short hallway. Bryan watched them for a second before turning back to face John. "So, yeah, this is mostly my doing, I'm afraid," he said. "Karen helped me pick stuff out, but I did the layout. The old kitchen was big, but *too* big. Felt like it took forever just to walk from the sink to the stove."

John looked around again. "It's very nice," he said. "It feels old, so it doesn't clash with the house, but it's got everything." He ran a hand over the countertop, which was smooth, not textured as he'd expected from looking at it. "What's this?"

"Recycled glass, believe it or not." Bryan touched the surface. "Mostly old Coke bottles. Seemed pretty appropriate for an old Georgia home."

John smiled. "Guess so," he said. "Did you guys do this room first?"

Bryan nodded, leaning one hip against the edge of the counter. "Seemed like the best move," he said. "We're trying to stay as open as possible during renovations, so we've been doing one room at a time, but the kitchen's pretty crucial to a bed-and-breakfast. We got it out of the way before we started taking in guests again."

Running feet caught John's attention, and he turned to see the two kids bursting back into the kitchen. "Hey, hey, slow down," he said, and the two stopped in their tracks and grinned a little before heading at a much slower pace toward the table by the bay window at the side of the room.

"Oh, we're used to that." The new voice came from the other entrance to the kitchen, and John turned to see a young blonde woman smiling at him. "Hello, I'm Karen Morrison," she said, walking toward him with a hand outstretched.

"John McConnell," he said as he took her hand. "Your brother invited my daughter and me for cookies and milk. I hope I'm not going to need to berate him for dropping surprise guests on you?"

Karen laughed, her eyes flashing as she stepped toward the refrigerator. "There's always a reason to berate Bry," she said. "But I think we can call a truce for cookies and milk."

"Cookies!" Jeremy's voice carried across the room. "Me and Bethy want cookies!"

"Keep it down to a dull roar, Germy," Bryan said. "Don't want to scare the ghosts."

Karen snickered. "Enough with the haunted house stuff, Bry," she said, holding out a plate loaded with a half dozen large chocolate chip cookies. "Here, you pass out the cookies while I get the milk." She smiled at John. "Milk okay for both of you? No allergies or anything?"

John shook his head. "Nope, we're good," he said. "Thanks for this. I know surprise drop-ins can be a bother sometimes."

Karen waved a hand. "Not like this," she said. "Show up looking for a four-course meal and we'll talk about being a bother."

John grinned and stepped over beside her. "Well, the least I can do is help carry the milk."

A couple of minutes later, John and Bryan were sitting with the kids, cookies and cups of milk in front of each of them. Karen set down the last cup in front of Jeremy and ran a hand over his curly hair, bending to plant a kiss on the crown of his head.

"Just the one, kiddo," she said. "Only a couple of hours until dinner." She straightened up and smiled at the two men. "Need to run to the bathroom," she said. "Baby's on my bladder again."

John blinked. "Oh, wow, I had no idea you were pregnant." He blushed as Karen lifted an eyebrow at him. "I mean…. Ouch, that sounded bad. Might as well have said, 'Oh no, I just thought you had a big belly.'" He crooked a half smile. "I just meant, your shirt"—he gestured with one hand—"is loose and I couldn't tell at all. But anyway, now that I've thoroughly embarrassed myself, congratulations!"

Karen grinned at him. "Thanks, and now I really do have to run!" She disappeared down the hallway toward the powder room, and John turned back to see Bryan with an evil grin on his face.

"Don't even start, Simmons," John said. "I *can* manage to get through a conversation without embarrassing myself. Sometimes. When I'm lucky."

He bit into his cookie and smiled around it, and Bryan smiled back, shaking his head. "I'll take your word for it," he said before taking a bite of his own cookie.

Chapter 3

COOKIES and milk devoured, John brushed crumbs from Beth's face and smiled over at Bryan. "We should get going," he said. "Meghan's at the restaurant tonight, so I'm on dinner duty. And we did *not* drop in on Karen for a four-course meal."

Bryan had a more intense cleaning going on with Jeremy and didn't look up. "She really wouldn't mind," he said. "She loves to cook and entertain. That's one thing that makes this place so perfect for her. She gets to be the ultimate hostess and make money doing it."

John pushed his chair back and stood, stepping over to help Beth down. "Well, if the rest of the place shapes up like the kitchen, you guys are going to have a real showpiece on your hands," he said. "Always nice to see one of these old places get fixed up. I hate it when one of them starts going to pot."

Bryan did look up then, smiling. "That's why I'm here," he said. "Satisfies my design drive and my home improvement urges. Plus I get to play with power tools!"

John laughed. "Well, thanks for a great afternoon," he said. He looked down at Beth. "Bethy, what do you say?"

"Thank you!" she crowed. "For the park and the cookies and the milk! They were yummy!"

John rolled his eyes. "Do five-year-olds ever do anything at less than full volume and full speed?"

"Not that I've been able to tell," Bryan said, finishing up with Jeremy and standing up. "Glad y'all could come. See you two on

Friday at the park?" He reached down to tug at one of Beth's ponytails, and she giggled and ducked away, grinning at him.

"Wouldn't miss it," John said. He looked at Jeremy. "Bye, Germy," he said, and he laughed when Jeremy pouted. Bryan laughed too, reaching to push open the screen door and waving a hand at him.

"Go on, get out of here before you set him off again," he said. "Tell that aunt of yours she's welcome to come by for cookies too, if she wants."

"Thanks, she'll love that." John smiled at Bryan one more time as he and Beth stepped outside, Beth turning back to wave as they headed back around to the front of the house.

"Did you have fun, Bethy?" John knew the answer, but he loved seeing her reactions when she was so happy.

"*Yes!*" Beth bounced and then jumped forward a big step. "I got to swing and climb and run and eat cookies and play with Jeremy! I want to do it again!"

John laughed. "We will, sweetie," he said. "We'll go back on Friday, and you can swing and climb and run and play with Jeremy, and maybe even eat cookies again."

"*Yayyyy!*" Beth crowed, a little too loud this time.

"Shhhh, honey, too loud," John said. "Don't want to scare our nice neighbors."

"Sorry," Beth said in a loud whisper. "I'm just so happy!"

John felt tears well up at the delighted tone in her voice, and he stopped and squatted down, catching Beth up in a big hug. "I know, sweetie," he said. "I know you are."

He wished, so hard, that he could have that kind of innocent happiness again.

NO MATTER what else he was doing, John tried to make sure he was the one to get Beth ready for bed and tuck her in. His consultant status left him with enough flexibility that it was rarely a problem, interrupted only by infrequent trips to Atlanta to visit the office in person. Tonight, he got Beth through a bath with minimum soaking of everything around her, including him, and into her favorite princess pajamas before settling her into bed, sitting on the edge while she said her prayers.

"And bless Daddy and Aunt Meghan and Jeremy and Mister Bryan and Miss Karen," she said, hands folded in front of her, eyes squeezed shut. "And thank you for cookies and milk. Amen!"

John smiled. "Amen," he echoed, leaning forward to press a kiss to her forehead. "Now you've had a really busy day, so lay down and go right to sleep. Daddy's going to be in his office for a while."

Beth nodded, her eyes already shut, arms wrapped around Maxie, the stuffed black dog she'd been sleeping with since she got it for her second birthday. "Night, Daddy," she mumbled, and John ran a hand over her head before pushing to his feet and walking out of the room, pulling the door almost shut.

He headed to his office, which was downstairs but right under Beth's bedroom. He kept a baby monitor around for times like this, so when he got to the office, he picked up the receiver from its spot on the bookshelf and flicked it on, setting it on the side of his desk.

He plopped into his desk chair and let out a long sigh. He'd had a pretty long day too, but it had turned out a lot better than he'd expected when he woke up. He'd even spent quite a bit of time thinking and talking about Liz, and while it did hurt, it was more of a distant ache. He hadn't talked about her often, but it always seemed to help when he did.

"Maybe I should do it more," he murmured to the empty room.

He thought about Bryan and smiled. He was a nice guy, and he seemed to love his nephew and sister like crazy. And he was a good listener. He hadn't judged John for still being in what amounted to mourning for Liz. He had encouraged John to talk about her, and his manner had stayed easy and open throughout.

Meghan had been urging John to get out more, meet more people, make more friends. He had some friendly acquaintances, guys he'd meet up with to have a few beers and watch a game at a sports bar. He had some friends back in Atlanta too, including Adam, but he didn't get back there often, and they rarely came to visit. Talking by phone or Internet had its limitations.

John sighed and shook off his thoughts, sitting forward and reaching out to wake up his computer. He and Beth would see Bryan and Jeremy again on Friday, and he'd just see how things were then.

For a fleeting moment he wondered what people would think about him being friends with Bryan. It was the South, so some people would always disapprove no matter what. Heck, some disapproved because he hadn't remarried and was raising his daughter alone. He knew he couldn't live his life based on what other people thought. It would drive him slowly insane.

Logging in to his work system, he focused his attention on that and left everything else to worry about later.

FRIDAY was about ten degrees hotter than Wednesday. Muggier too. John didn't much relish the idea of an hour at the park in much more typical Southern May weather, but a promise was a promise. He packed up bottles of water and slathered sunblock on Beth and then himself before they headed down the street. Beth was even bouncier than she'd been on Wednesday, which John hadn't thought possible.

He saw Bryan already sitting on the same bench as they approached, and Beth started pulling on his hand, trying to dart ahead. "Daddy, can I go?" she pleaded, and John laughed.

"Okay, be careful!" he said, letting her go and watching her run full-tilt over to the climbing set, where Jeremy greeted her with a loud shout and shared laughter.

Bryan was laughing, too, when John sat down and put the backpack he'd brought under the edge of the bench between them. "I remember being five years old," Bryan said. "All day long to do whatever I wanted, not a care in the world." He sighed. "Growing up sucks sometimes."

John chuckled. "Working for a living, paying bills, raising the five-year-olds of the world," he agreed. He stretched his legs out and leaned back against the bench, crossing his arms over his chest and closing his eyes. "But then you get an hour to just rest and relax and soak up a little sun, and it doesn't seem so bad after all."

"And a friend to do it with," Bryan agreed. John tilted his head in acknowledgement, and they sat in silence for a few minutes. John listened to the kids, not able to make out many words but catching the joy and excitement in their voices. He couldn't help smiling.

"You look like the proverbial cat," Bryan said. "Been swallowing canaries?"

John opened one eye and trained it on Bryan. "Can't a guy smile without another guy thinking he's up to something?"

"Not likely," Bryan shot back. "Or maybe that's just the pessimistic streak in me."

John rolled the eye and closed it again. "I know I haven't exactly spent a lot of time around you," he said, "but I took you for a glass-half-full kind of guy."

"Sometimes," Bryan said. "Most of the time, really. But there are bad days. Not often, but it does happen."

John shrugged but didn't move otherwise. "Happens to all of us," he said. "You just have to try to keep the good and let go of the bad as much as you can."

Bryan chuckled at that. "Yes, Sensei," he said. "What other pearls of wisdom do you have to share?"

"He who pokes the lion in his cage draws back a nub." John grinned, eyes still shut. "Which is to say, he who teases the sensei risks retribution, Grasshopper."

"Point taken." The bench shook a little, and John lifted one eyelid to see Bryan stretching out in a position very similar to his. "So then what should we talk about? How 'bout them Braves?"

John snorted, settling back into his comfortable spot. "Not if they keep getting hurt the way they have so far," he said. "It'd be nice for them to get through an entire series without having to pull someone for injury."

Bryan laughed. "I've never been a big sports guy—yes, I am a stereotypical homosexual in some ways—but baseball's different. Maybe it's the tight pants."

John smiled slowly. "Maybe so," he said. "I'm not afraid to admit I've taken more than one second look at some of those asses."

Bryan cracked up, sounding surprised, and John had to snicker a little at that. It wasn't like Bryan didn't know John had been interested in men in the past. "Why so shocked? I told you I wasn't totally straight."

"Yeah," Bryan said around a few remaining laughs. "But that's the first time you've said something that direct about it, so sorry if I was a little caught off guard!"

John chuckled. "Okay, you got me there," he said. "It's not something you can just *say* without people asking questions or getting all weird. But I know you're not going to get all weird about it." He shot Bryan a look out of the corner of his eye. "Well, except for the laughing. I assume that's out of your system now?"

Bryan waved a hand. "Yeah, yeah, I think I'm good now," he said. "John likes looking at guys sometimes, check." He tapped his index finger against his temple. "I'll be sure to remember that."

John harrumphed. "Okay, then," he said. "Baseball. Braves fan, I assume?"

"Of course," Bryan said. "Is there any other team?"

John rolled his eyes. "Unfortunately for me, my boss hails from New York," he said. "He never shuts up about the Yankees. Best club in baseball, all that crap."

"More like the Dark Empire," Bryan shot back. "Hell, anyone could win if they could afford to throw that much money against the wall and see what sticks."

John grinned. "I try to get up to Atlanta for a game at least once or twice a year," he said. "We should take the kids. They're getting old enough that they could probably behave decently."

Bryan laughed. "It's a *date*," he teased.

A sharp cry caught their attention, and they turned toward the kids to see Beth sitting on the ground, hand over one knee. John couldn't tell for sure, but she looked like she was crying. He jumped up and half jogged over to her, squatting down next to her. "What happened, baby?"

"I falled down," she said, her voice watery.

John reached for her hand. "Let me see, sweetie." He managed to peel Beth's hand away and saw a small cut with a larger red area around it. The ground under the playground equipment was sand, but a rock or something must have gotten into it.

"Here you go." John looked up to see Bryan standing next to him, holding the backpack. "I'm thinking maybe you have something in here?"

John smiled. "Yeah, there's a little first aid kit in the second pocket," he said, holding up his free hand to take the pack. Instead, Bryan squatted next to him and set the pack on the ground, zipping open the indicated compartment and reaching in for the kit. He flipped the lid open and held it out for John to take what he needed.

"Thanks." John picked through and found an antiseptic wipe. He turned back to Beth as he tore it open. "This is gonna hurt a little bit, honey," he said. "But it'll clean out the sand so it won't get infected or anything. Okay?"

Beth bit her bottom lip, a trait she'd inherited from her mom that never failed to send a rush of sorrow through John. He pushed it back and wiped across the cut.

"Ow!" Beth cried out. "Ow ow ow!"

Jeremy had run up to them by then and was watching with fascination. "That's cool," he said. "Does it hurt a lot?"

Beth ran a hand across her eyes to wipe away the tears. "A… a little," she managed, flinching as John finished cleaning her wound. "It's not too bad."

John shot Bryan a small smile. Jeremy was just the distraction Beth needed. John didn't think the injury was bad, and while he knew it hurt, he also knew focusing on it would make it worse.

He set the used wipe on the ground and reached into the box Bryan still held, extracting a bandage. "Sorry it's not princesses," he told Beth. "Just a plain one this time. We'll put some antibiotic cream on it and get you a princess bandage when we get home."

She nodded and watched as he applied the bandage over the worst of the injury. When he was done, he leaned down and pressed a kiss over it. "There," he said. "All better."

Beth threw herself into his arms, and John caught her, fighting to keep his balance and not fall over backward. A hand landed on his back, and he heard Bryan chuckle.

"Whoa there," he said. "Don't wanna cause even more injuries."

"Thanks." John braced himself and stood up, still holding Beth. He felt the strain in his lower back. "Ugh, I'm getting too old for this," he muttered, ignoring Bryan's snort of laughter. He glanced at the other man. "Would you mind carrying the backpack to the house for us?" he asked. "I don't know if we have any cookies, but I'm sure we can scare up some kind of snack."

"No problem." Bryan shouldered the pack and reached for Jeremy's hand. "C'mon, Germy, let's go check out Bethy's house."

John laughed a little as they started walking toward the house. "I don't know if I mentioned it, but Meghan's kind of a packrat. If Beth and I hadn't moved in, I think she would've filled the whole place up with the funkiest collection of stuff you've ever seen."

"I think Karen might do the same thing," Bryan replied. "Getting her to settle on fixtures and decorations for the kitchen was a major challenge. It's funny, because she totally goes for the streamlined in a lot of cases, but when it comes to home décor, she's the total opposite of minimalist."

"If only home décor were the only problem," John said. "Meghan and I have been taking an afternoon now and then to go through all the stuff that's stockpiled in the attic. It's full of old boxes of stuff from my grandparents that she's never gone through. She just had it all moved over here when my grandmother died and has let it sit." He laughed. "I've threatened to just bring in a Dumpster and throw it all out the window, but she knows I'd never do it. We've found some pretty cool things in there."

"Antique German bearer bonds?" Bryan grinned, and John laughed at the *Die Hard* reference.

"And sic Hans Rickman on my… on me?" Since Beth had gotten old enough to start to mimic what others said, John had gotten pretty good at on-the-fly self-censoring and managed to catch the "ass" before he said it. "Unfortunately, not much of value, although we did sell a couple of antique watches. Mostly it's family things, old photos and paperwork, my great-grandfather's service records from World War II, my grandfather's grade school report cards."

"Cool," Bryan said. "We lost a lot of our family stuff about twenty years ago. My grandparents had a house fire. They were fine, but not a lot of stuff made it out."

John winced. "Ouch, that's awful."

Beth had been quiet as they walked, curled into John's arms, but she spoke up then. "Are you hurting, Daddy?"

John smiled down at her. "Nope, just an expression, honey," he said. He pressed a kiss into her forehead. "How's your leg?"

She shrugged one shoulder. "It's okay," she said. "Hurts."

"I'm sorry, Bethy," John said. "Like I said, we'll get it all doctored up and get a snack, and then you can watch some TV before dinnertime. Okay?"

Beth smiled and smacked a kiss on his cheek. "Okay!"

Bryan laughed, and John rolled his eyes. "You sure do laugh at me a lot," he groused.

"Not *at* you," Bryan corrected. "*With* you. Just because you're Dexter Downer over there—"

"Shaddup, you," John said, bumping Bryan's shoulder with his.

Chapter 4

THEY were at the house by then, and John led the way up the stairs. He paused at the top and half turned toward Bryan. "Um, keys are in the outside pocket," he said, nodding toward the backpack.

"Oh! Okay." Bryan let go of Jeremy's hand and mock-glared at him. "Don't move," he said, and Jeremy froze in place like a statue, making Beth giggle. Bryan rested the backpack against his own thigh while he dug out the keys and handed them to John.

"Thanks," John said, shifting Beth to the side so he could reach the lock. He pushed the door open and nodded inside. "After you guys."

Bryan started in but then paused and looked back at Jeremy. He sighed. "Okay, you can move now," he said in a singsongy voice, and Jeremy bounced free of his artificial prison and dashed inside. "Slow down!" Bryan barked. "And don't touch anything, you crazy kid."

John bumped the door shut with his hip. "Kitchen's straight ahead down the hall," he said. "I don't know if we have any cookies, but I'll check. Let me get Beth taken care of and we'll be right back."

"Not a problem." Bryan grabbed for Jeremy's hand, which he was waving around for no discernible reason. "We'll see you there."

John carried Beth to the downstairs bathroom, setting her on the closed toilet seat. "You want some bubbly stuff?" he asked, and she frowned.

"Hurts," she said.

"I know it burns a little, but it's bubbly and cool," he said, reaching into the medicine cabinet to pull out the brown bottle of hydrogen peroxide, a box of gauze pads, a tube of antibiotic cream, and the promised princess bandages. *One thing about having a kid around*, he thought. *You certainly get in the habit of keeping plenty of first aid supplies on hand.*

Setting the items down on the edge of the vanity, John lowered himself to one knee and peeled the bandage off Beth's knee. The redness around the small cut had already started to fade, and the wound looked clean, but he wasn't going to risk it. He opened the bottle and poured a little of the liquid into the lid, using that to pour it onto Beth's leg.

"Ouch!" Beth jerked, but then she stared at her leg. "Bubbles!"

"I told you." He recapped the bottle and pulled out a gauze pad. "Let me wipe it off a little and put on some cream, and then you'll get your princess bandage, okay?"

Beth gave him a big, toothy smile. "Thank you, Daddy," she said. "You're making it all better!"

John had to swallow back the rush of emotion that hit him at her innocent words. "I sure am, honey," he said, finishing up his doctoring and applying the bandage. Once again, he leaned down to kiss the spot. "There, all done! Now let's go see if we can find some cookies or something in the kitchen."

"Okay!" Beth jumped down from the toilet and ran off down the hall as if nothing had ever happened. John shook his head, dropping the gauze and bandage wrapper in the trash can and leaving the other items to put away later. He had guests to feed.

FIFTEEN minutes later, the cookie search unsuccessful, John had the kids set up with glasses of milk and peanut butter foldovers, and a pot of decaf was just finishing up brewing for Bryan and him. Once again, Bryan was laughing at him. Okay, *with* him.

"Seriously, your aunt owns a restaurant but she doesn't bake?" he asked from where he sat at the table, turned in his chair to face John. "I thought that was kind of a given."

John leaned against the counter next to the coffee machine, waiting while it sputtered and popped out the last drops. "Cooking isn't baking. She hates having to follow a recipe that closely. Any baking that gets done around here gets done by me."

Bryan's eyebrows shot up. "Do tell," he said. "Cookies, cakes, pies...?"

"Cookies, sometimes cake, but usually from a mix," John said, turning to pour coffee into the two mugs he'd set out. "Every now and then I'll take a wild hair and do something from scratch. One of the things Meghan got from my grandmother was her cookbook collection." He carried the mugs over the few feet to the table, setting one down in front of Bryan and taking the seat next to him. "Some of the restaurant's menu items actually came out of those cookbooks. But the baking stuff, that she leaves to me. I can make a pretty mean pecan pie when I put my mind to it."

Bryan finished doctoring up his coffee with sugar and milk and took a sip, then grinned as he set his mug down. "I have an idea," he said while John stirred milk into his coffee. "Why don't you and Beth and Meghan come for dinner Sunday night? We cook out whenever the weather's good, and in the summer it usually is."

John opened his mouth, but Bryan held up a hand. "Before you start raising objections, it's never a problem to have extra people. We do probably half the time, and it's not any harder to throw a few extra burgers and hot dogs on the grill. Plus, you can pay for your dinner by making one of those famous pies for dessert."

John lifted an eyebrow. "Oh, so this is just a trick to make sure I'm telling the truth," he said. "Testing my pie abilities."

"Absolutely!" Bryan lifted his mug in a mock toast and took another sip. John had to laugh, and he realized he'd done a lot of that the past few days. It felt good. It'd been a long time since he'd felt like laughing so much.

Naturally, it couldn't last. A low crashing sound had them looking over at the kids, and Jeremy had a stereotypical guilty-kid look on his face.

"It fell!" he said. Bryan leaned back, looking down behind Jeremy's chair. His eyes fell shut, and he groaned.

"Well, good thing that was a plastic cup," he said, turning to grimace at John. "But now there's a veritable sea of milk on the floor over here."

John smiled and set down his coffee mug. "Not a problem," he said. "You get the cup, I'll get the paper towels."

Bryan insisted on doing the cleanup, and John poured Jeremy a little more milk, admonishing him to be more careful when he gave the cup back. He didn't want to put a lid on it. He knew Beth hated to be treated "like a baby," and besides, it was just a little spilled milk on a tile floor.

Spill cleaned, wet paper towels tossed, and milk replaced, John and Bryan sat back down and reached for their mugs in unison. "Almost wish this was high-test," Bryan murmured as he took another swallow.

"Probably would regret it when you were wide awake staring at the ceiling at one a.m." As soon as the words left his mouth, he knew Bryan would take full advantage of that setup, and he was right.

"Oh, I don't know," Bryan said in an idle tone. "That would depend on, er"—he paused, glancing at the kids—"on what else was going on at the time," he finished, giving a rueful grin.

John smirked. "Behave yourself," he said. "Tender ears."

Bryan's eyes widened in mock surprise. "Oh, I'm *so* sorry, I had *no* idea you were so sensitive!"

John snickered into his coffee, the sound of Bryan's laughter in his ears. It was soothing somehow. He liked it. He hoped he'd hear more of it.

BRYAN and Jeremy left twenty minutes later, with many thanks for the snacks and coffee and more apologies for Jeremy's little accident. John stood in the doorway holding Beth, who waved vigorously as they walked away, Jeremy turning halfway around to wave just as vigorously back at her. Once they were out of sight, John looked down at Beth and grinned.

"So what do you want for dinner, kiddo?" he asked, stepping back inside and setting her down before reaching to close the door behind her. "Chicken nuggets and carrot sticks?"

"Yum!" she said, bouncing on her toes. "And some peaches?"

John nodded. "I think we have some," he said. "If not, we have applesauce." He ran a hand over her head. "Why don't you go watch some TV while I see what we have for dinner. Okay?"

"Okay!" Beth was off in a flash, and as John followed, he heard the TV in the den next to the kitchen come on. He checked to be sure she was on the right channel—the TV had parental controls set, so she couldn't get much other than public broadcasting and the children's networks on her own anyway—and then stopped by the bathroom to put the first aid supplies away.

He was checking out the food situation in the kitchen when the phone rang. The caller ID said it was the restaurant calling.

"Hello?" He assumed it was Meghan but didn't know why she'd be calling.

"John, hi! Sorry to call in a hurry, but do you know the name of that little bed-and-breakfast down the street? I've got some customers here who want to stay on the island if they can find a room."

He chuckled. "Yeah, that's actually Bryan's family's place," he said. "The Sea Breeze. But I think he said they're booked up for the weekend."

There was a brief silence, and then Meghan spoke again, her words slow. "I think maybe there's something you haven't told me," she said, and John realized he hadn't. Meghan didn't know a thing about Bryan or their meetings.

"Um, whoops," he said. "Sorry. Beth and I made some new friends at the park this week. I'll tell you all about it when you get home if you're not too worn out."

"You're damn straight you will," Meghan said. "I'd berate you more now, but I gotta run. Thanks!"

"You're wel—" John stopped as the dial tone settled in his ear. He shook his head with a grin as he hung up. Much like Beth, Meghan rarely did anything at below full-tilt. It was why he hadn't thought to tell her about Bryan and Jeremy. He hadn't had a moment to think about it when she was home.

He turned back to his dinner prep. Maybe he'd get the baking going after dinner tonight, start the pie crust, at least. It was always better when it sat overnight before baking, and the finished pie was the same way. Making the perfect pecan pie took two days, so it was a good thing he had that much warning. Heck, maybe he'd throw caution to the wind and make two.

IT WAS after ten when Meghan got home that night. Beth was long asleep, initially curled up under the princess comforter she'd gotten for Christmas, but John knew she would've shoved it off within the first hour. Even with air conditioning, the weather was getting too warm for that.

He was sort of watching the late Braves game from Denver when Meghan walked in. "Hey, Johnny Boy," she said.

"Hey," he said, muting the TV and turning to look at her as she locked up. "You look tired."

"Gee, thanks," she shot back, dropping her purse on the table near the door and crossing to flop down on the opposite end of the sofa from him, the usual long braid she wore for work lying across one shoulder. "Crazy night," she said. "Busier than we've had in weeks. I don't know if people are getting a head start on the holiday or what, but if this is any indication of what the summer's going to be like, I might need to hire some extra help."

John smiled. "Great problem to have," he said, and Meghan nodded, conceding the point.

"Anyway," she said. "Really don't want to talk about work. Really want to hit the sack, actually. But what's this about some guy you met?" She waggled her eyebrows and grinned.

John rolled his eyes. "You're as bad as him," he said. "His name is Bryan, he's Jeremy's uncle—that boy Beth met earlier this week?" Meghan nodded in acknowledgement. "He was at the park with Jeremy on Wednesday, and we talked some. His sister and her husband own the Sea Breeze now, and he's helping them fix it up."

Meghan sat up straighter. "Oh, that's great! I was hoping someone would."

John nodded. "Yeah, that's what I said too. They're off to a great start. He and Jeremy invited us over for a snack, and the kitchen is amazing. You'd love it. Bryan designed it. He's got an architecture degree, so he's doing design work too."

Meghan nodded. "And?" she asked. "Single, married, gay, straight…?"

John rolled his eyes. "Single, and gay, as a matter of fact." He shot her a glare. "And don't you start. He's a nice guy, but he's just a friend. Okay?"

Meghan held up both hands as if warding him off. "I don't say a word," she said. Then she grinned evilly. "So when's your next date? Oh, excuse me, *play* date."

John sighed and Meghan cackled. "Just for that, I won't invite you to the cookout on Sunday," he said. "The Morrisons apparently grill out most weekends, and we're all invited if we want to come. And if you aren't working, of course."

Meghan shrugged. "I don't know, we'll have to see how it goes," she said. "If it's not weirdly busy like tonight, Kai can probably handle it for a few hours. And if it gets busy, it's only a few minutes to get back over there." She grinned again. "I gotta check out this mystery guy, after all. Make sure he's good enough for my nephew."

John glared at her. "Watch it," he said. "Or I'll start giving you grief about how Kai is totally head over heels for you and you won't do a damn thing about it."

It was Meghan's turn to roll her eyes. "He's too young for me and you know it."

"He's almost thirty and you're barely thirty-nine," John shot back. "That isn't even enough to make you a cougar."

"Oh God." Meghan groaned and buried her face in her hands. "Cougar. Is that what I have to look forward to?"

John chuckled and clicked the TV off before pushing to his feet. "C'mon," he said, holding out a hand. "Let's let our love lives alone, existent or imagined, and get some sleep. You know Bethy will have us both up at the ass-crack of dawn."

Meghan grabbed his hand and let him pull her up. "I'm glad we aren't open for breakfast," she said. "You guys wanna come out for lunch tomorrow?"

"Sounds good." John paused by the light switch as Meghan headed up toward her bedroom. "See you in the morning."

"Night," Meghan sent back, and John flipped off the light and followed her.

THE dream came again that night. He held Liz close, her hair floating around them, longer than he'd ever seen it in real life. He could hear children playing nearby and a deep, rich laugh that sounded familiar but that he couldn't quite place. They must have been on the beach, or near it, because he could hear the waves.

He woke up smiling. He couldn't remember the last time that had happened. Melancholy had become so much a part of his life that he hardly noticed it anymore. How long had it been since he'd felt happy?

He sat up, sliding one leg off the side of the bed, the other pulled up in front of him. He pressed his palms into his eyes, wiping away sleep and the wave of sadness his thoughts brought along with them. Dropping his hands into his lap, he stared out the window at the line of palm trees along the edge of the property line.

He knew he'd been marking time for five years. Well, four years, since the first was such a blur he didn't know if he could be sure which parts were real. The only reliable bright spot in his life since Liz had died was Beth. She made him happy just by existing. Meghan had been amazing, but she could be frustrating too. Like with her insistence that she was too old for Kai.

John smiled. He and Beth were going to the restaurant for lunch today. Maybe he could fight against the melancholy by playing a little game of matchmaker.

JOHN loved the beach. He loved the warmth of the sun on his skin, the cool offshore breezes, the juxtaposition of sand and water where ocean met coastline, smooth and hard land contrasting with turbulent and strong waves.

You know, Liz's voice said in his head, *for a statistician, you always did have the soul of a poet.*

John smiled. He'd always miss her, but every day got a little bit easier.

"Daddy!" Beth came running up from where she'd been building haphazard sand castles a few yards away. "I wanna swim!"

John gave her a look over his sunglasses. "How do you ask, Bethy?"

Beth schooled her face into a solemn expression and folded her hands in front of her. "Daddy, can we go swimming now, please?"

John smothered a laugh. He'd work on her English grammar skills later, but for now, asking politely would do.

"Okay, sweetie," he said, climbing to his feet and kicking off his shoes. He dropped his sunglasses on their beach blanket and stripped off his T-shirt, tossing it down beside the glasses. Reaching for Beth's hand, he let himself be pulled at full five-year-old speed across the sand and to the water's edge.

Beth had never shown a hint of being afraid of the water, not since the first time she'd been on the beach, when she was only sixteen months old and just walking was still a challenge. John had set her down on her feet, and she'd taken off toward the water as fast as her chubby little legs would carry her. John caught her in two long steps and hadn't let go of her on the beach again for over a year. Even then, he rarely took his eyes off her. She'd learned to swim the summer before, but a pool was not the ocean.

Now she led him into the surf, laughing as the water lapped at her legs. Once the highest swells reached above her waist, she turned toward John and held up both hands. John lifted her into his arms, settling her against his hip, her arms wrapped around his neck.

"Ready?" he asked, and Beth bobbed her head. John waded forward, balancing them as the intensity of the waves increased around them. The waters along the Georgia coastline represented only the tiniest fraction of the ocean's true power, but riptides and undertows were always a danger. John had never been one to take big risks, and he certainly wasn't taking chances where Beth's safety was concerned.

Beth laughed and flinched and squealed as the spray from the waves spun around them. John moved deeper, closer to the breakers, which were small even by East Coast standards. A few waves held together long enough to lift them up and drop them back down a little, never enough for John's feet to leave the ground. Beth gave a squeal of delight each time.

They stayed in the water for a while, John dipping them down until the water hit the base of Beth's neck and then popping back up again. Her laughter kept him smiling, and when his arms finally started to ache, he was sorry to have to head back in. It was getting close to lunchtime, though, and Meghan was expecting them.

"Time to head back, Bethy," John said, laughing as Beth gave him an exaggerated pout. "You could ride that bottom lip all the way to England," he teased, reaching up to pinch it lightly between his thumb and forefinger. Beth laughed again, and John started walking them back to shore. As soon as they were back on the wet sand where ocean foam churned, John set Beth down and took her hand again. "Let's run!" he said, and Beth took off again, pulling him back to their blanket, both of them laughing in the bright sunshine.

Chapter 5

Twenty minutes later, after a quick rinse under the showers at the edge of the beach to wash away the salt and a quick change into dry clothes in the public restroom nearby, John pulled open the door to Let's Be Shellfish and guided Beth inside. A chorus of greetings filled the air, one in particular rising above the rest.

"Pua!" Kai called out, stepping out of the kitchen, wiping his hands on a towel. "How's my little island flower?"

"Kai!" Beth ran toward Kai, who tossed the towel over one shoulder and squatted down to meet her. John grinned as Beth threw her arms around Kai's neck, and he looked up to find Meghan watching the two of them, too, a soft smile on her face. John raised an eyebrow just as she looked over at him, and the smile disappeared as she rolled her eyes.

"Shut up," she grumbled, and John laughed, leaning on the counter next to the register.

"Didn't say a thing," he pointed out.

"An eyebrow is worth a thousand words," Meghan shot back. She nodded toward an empty table nearby. It wasn't quite noon, so the restaurant wasn't quite busy yet. "You want one of your usuals, or are you feeling adventurous?"

John raised an eyebrow for an entirely different reason. "Depends," he said. He moved over to the indicated table, putting their beach bag on one of the empty chairs. "What's today's adventure?"

Kai answered before Meghan could. "Seafood crepes," he said, leading Beth over to the table. He kept talking as he helped her into her chair, while John sat down next to her. "Kind of stole them from that place on the wharf at St. Simons, but I lightened it up a little. Mixed seafood, mushrooms, baby spinach, cheese. White sauce and tomatoes on top. Side of pineapple slaw."

John grinned. "Bring it on!" he said.

Kai gave a quick salute. "Done and done." He smiled down at Beth. "You want grilled cheese?"

Beth nodded, smiling up at him. "Thank you!" she said, and Kai laughed.

"You're welcome. We'll get that right out for you," he added, glancing back at John.

"Thanks, Kai." The two men exchanged smiles before Kai disappeared back into his lair, also known as the kitchen.

John was just about to go looking for some of the crayons and coloring pages he knew Meghan always had on hand, but Meghan appeared with a blank piece of paper and a small basket of crayons in a multitude of colors. "Beth, sweetie, why don't you draw me a picture of the beach," she said. "Miss Audra's going to paint some pictures on the walls for us, and she needs your help coming up with some ideas."

Beth beamed and reached for the crayons, and John gave Meghan a skeptical look. "Seriously," Meghan said, holding up a hand. "She's going to do several different designs to make a mural on one wall, so she needs several different ideas. It'll be her senior project, and she's using it for her portfolio too."

John smiled at that. Audra's mom was the vicar at the Episcopal church John, Meghan, and Beth all attended. Between the low pastoral pay and the expenses for Audra's diabetes treatments, her family hadn't been able to save much toward college. Audra saved every penny she could from her job at the restaurant to help cover the costs of the art school she dreamed of attending.

John watched as Beth worked, drawing out brown and blue lines to divide sand from water from sky. She colored in each space diligently, adding white, fluffy clouds and, off on the horizon, the tiny outline of a ship, like the ones they often saw passing by in the distance when they were at the beach. She drew in a big yellow sun, rays reaching all the way to the edges of the page.

She dropped the yellow crayon into the basket and stared at her drawing for a moment, her small face serious. Finally she picked it up and held it out to John. "Daddy, is this okay?" she asked, sounding worried. "I want Miss Audra to have a good picture."

"It's beautiful, sweetie," John said, reaching out to cup her chin. "I'm sure Miss Audra will love it."

Meghan backed her way out of the kitchen door next to them, turning around with a plate in each hand. John gently took Beth's drawing and set it aside, and Meghan put down John's plate in front of him first. "Careful, plate's hot," she said, turning to put Beth's meal in front of her. "Mister Kai put some red berries on for you," she said, using the name Beth had bestowed on strawberries because "they don't look like straws, Daddy!" They were her favorite fruit by far.

Beth beamed. "Yummy!" She reached for half of her sandwich, which John knew would have cooled off sufficiently before Kai or Meghan let it leave the kitchen.

Meghan turned back to John, planting a fist on one hip. "So, let me know the verdict," she said. "Kai's been driving me nuts to get this on the menu before Memorial Day."

John bit back a grin. Meghan and Kai squabbled like an old married couple, had since she'd hired him almost three years earlier. Meghan refused to admit it, but John—and everyone else—knew damn good and well that Kai instigated most of it because he loved it when Meghan got all fired up.

John cut off the tip of a crepe with the side of his fork, spearing it and running it through the sauce that spilled onto the plate. He blew to cool the bite and popped it into his mouth. His eyes widened, and he chewed and swallowed so he could render his verdict.

"Oh, wow," he said. "That is really, really good. Everything blends together well, nothing overpowers it. You can taste all the components, but nothing dominates." He grinned as he cut another bite. "And I think I want this sauce on every meal I eat from now on."

Meghan grinned at him as he took his second bite. "Well, maybe now Kai will settle down for the summer," she said. "He got five new things on the menu for the season. Gotta cut him off *now*, so I'll have time to print up the new ones for the summer this week."

The front door opened, and about half a dozen people stepped inside, drawing Meghan's attention. "Off to play hostess," she said. "You guys enjoy!"

John did. The crepes were amazing, and he already loved the pineapple slaw Kai had created the year before, which had become a customer favorite. John wished he had some way to make Meghan see what she had in front of her. She talked a big game about loving her "free and easy" single life, but John knew her better than that. For all their differences, one thing they'd always had in common was that they both loved being in love.

The restaurant filled up as John and Beth finished their meals. Beth had started out chatting about their beach trip and the drawing she'd done for Audra, but by the time she finished eating (three-quarters of her sandwich and all the "red berries"), she was drooping, and John could empathize.

"C'mon, kiddo," he said, pushing to his feet and leaning over to help Beth out of her chair. "Let's go home and have a little rest, okay?"

Beth nodded as she took John's hand. "I'm tired, Daddy," she said in a near-whine.

"I know, baby, I am too. We'll be home soon." He bent over to pick up their beach bag and headed toward the door, shooting a smile at Meghan, who was just finishing up with customers at the register. "Tell Kai we said bye," he said. "I know he's swamped by now."

Meghan wiggled the fingers of one hand at them. "Will do. See you guys later."

John held the door for Beth again as they emerged back into the bright sunshine. The warmth hit John like a sleeping pill, and he almost stumbled. "Whoa," he said, pausing to steady himself, squinting against the light. He shook his head to dislodge the torpor and dropped Beth's hand to reach for the sunglasses in his pocket.

"You okay there?"

John turned his head to the left to see a smiling Bryan walking toward them. "Oh, hey!" John said, slipping on the sunglasses and sighing a little at the relief from the brightness. "Yeah, just let the munchkin here wear me out on the beach and then ate too much for lunch." He laid his hand on the back of Beth's head, and she sagged against his leg. John nodded back toward the door of the restaurant. "Try the seafood crepes. They're brand new and really awesome. Just be prepared for a long nap after you eat."

Bryan laughed. "I'll keep that in mind," he said. "I'm just headed back to the house now. You two want some company?"

Beth let out a big yawn. Both men looked down at her and then at each other, laughing softly.

"Sure, you can make sure both of us get home without passing out cold along the way," John said. "I'd carry her, but I'm just too out of it."

"No problem." Bryan stepped forward without another word and squatted down, wrapping both arms around Beth, pulling her away from John's side and lifting her into his arms. "Now let's get you two home," he said, shifting to settle Beth more securely.

John smiled at the picture they made, Beth's honey-colored hair fanned out across Bryan's broad chest, her arms around his neck. John's heart clenched, but he wasn't sure why. Maybe he just felt lucky to have made such a good friend in such a short amount of time. Not many friends would treat Beth with such tenderness.

JOHN had trouble getting to sleep that night. He and Beth had each slept for two solid hours after Bryan saw them safely home, and they'd spent the rest of the afternoon outside. Beth played in the backyard while John sat in one of the cushioned rockers on the back porch, ostensibly reading but mostly just relaxing and watching Beth. He had things he could be doing, things he *should* be doing. He just couldn't seem to muster up the inclination to do any of them.

After dinner, John got Beth bathed and off to bed, and she went with a minimum of fuss, still tired from her busy day. John knew the feeling, but his mind just wouldn't shut down. He made the crust for his pie, but when it was in the refrigerator to chill, he was still wide awake. He went back out to the porch and tried to read again, but he couldn't concentrate. He finally just set the book aside and relaxed against the cushions, tipping his head back and closing his eyes. He listened to the distant sound of the waves against the shore, felt the warm night breeze, breathed in the tang of the salt-tinged air.

He'd spent many nights like this when he and Beth had first moved back to Tybee and the wound from losing Liz had hung open wide and bleeding. Sleep often wouldn't come, and he'd find himself carrying on conversations with Liz and with God, some silent, some loud. He'd cried, too, but as time went by and he started to heal, his thoughts shifted to the happy memories and to what he still had left. Mainly that was Beth, and she was the primary reason he hadn't lost himself completely, hadn't lost his faith completely. He'd been angry with God when Liz died, but how could a cold, cruel, vengeful God have given him something as wonderful and perfect as Beth?

He rarely had nights like these anymore, when he felt the need to try to talk to Liz. He didn't know why he needed it now. But he was here, so he'd try, and maybe then he'd be able to sleep.

"Hey, Lizzy," he said into the night. "I miss you. I know I say that every time, but that's because it's always true." He smiled. "I miss seeing you, talking to you, holding your hand. I miss a lot of things. I wish you could be here to see Bethy. I hope you can see her from where you are. She's the best thing in the whole world, and I don't know what I'd do without her."

He paused and swallowed, not sure what to say next. An image of Bryan holding Beth earlier that day popped into his head. "Beth and I made some new friends this week," he said. "Beth's friend is named Jeremy, and my friend is his uncle, Bryan. They're both really great, and we've been having a lot of fun with them. Meghan and Beth and I are going over to their house tomorrow night to have dinner with their family."

He stopped. Somehow he felt like that was enough. "I love you, Liz," he said. "I'll always love you, no matter what. I hope you always know that."

He fell silent and stayed there, eyes closed, the island embracing him, until he felt like he could sleep.

"SARAH!" Beth bounced on her toes in her black patent Mary Janes when she saw the other girl walking toward the front of the church from the opposite direction. Sarah grinned and waved, her mass of blond curls matching those of her mother, Anna, who held as tight to her hand as John did to Beth's.

Beth turned her smile up toward John. "Daddy, can we sit with Sarah in church?"

John glanced up at Anna and shrugged. "If it's okay with her parents, sweetie," he said.

Anna smiled. "We'd love that," she said. "Keith's parking, so we'll just find a spot with room for all of us."

Church had been important to Liz, even though she hadn't been extremely religious, so John followed her wishes and took Beth most Sundays. The Episcopal church on the island was small and progressive, and both John and Beth enjoyed the services. They walked inside with Anna and Sarah, the girls chattering all the while, and John let Anna lead the way to a pew about halfway down. She nodded John in first, and he brought Beth behind him so the two girls could sit between them.

They were a few minutes early, and several people waved to them, a couple stopping by to say hi on their way to their own seats. The congregation was small but warm and relaxed, fitting in well with the island atmosphere. Audra sat with her dad and younger brother in a front pew, waiting for Audra's mom, Vicky—"Vicky the Vicar," she'd introduced herself with a grin when John and Beth had first visited.

Each service started with a selection of classic hymns accompanied by the grand piano at the front of the sanctuary. The hymns had always been John's favorite part of any church service. He was no great singer, but he could carry a tune well enough not to embarrass himself, and the familiar choices here were comforting.

Vicky emerged from a side door in her vicar's robes, and the morning's pianist moved to the piano. "Welcome, everyone," Vicky said when she reached the pulpit. "Thank you for joining us on this beautiful Sunday morning in God's house. Please join me in singing the first verses of numbers 48, 57, and 187 in your hymnal."

"Blessed Assurance," "Something Beautiful," and "Standing on the Promises," all ones both John and Beth enjoyed, the first among Beth's favorites. She sometimes sang it when she was playing, right along with the songs she'd learned watching television and movies. John held the hymnal between them, his finger following along on the words so Beth could keep up. Beth was reading very well for her age, but sometimes the strange ecclesiastical wording threw her off.

The service was quiet and brief, the vicar more subdued than usual but just as warm as always. After the benediction, John led Beth by the hand out into the small parish hall, where she joined a group of kids at a small table covered with boxes of crayons and stacks of coloring books. John walked over to get himself a cup of coffee and a doughnut from the weekly pastry tray and sat down next to Vicky and her family. He smiled at Audra, who had a small glass of juice and a few slices of cheese in front of her.

"How are you doing, Audra?" he asked.

She smiled back at him. "I'm okay," she said. "A little adjustment with the pump this week. They told me I'll probably have those every so often, though." She picked up one of her cheese slices and nodded toward his doughnut. "And I got the usual 'eat this, not that' admonishments."

John chuckled. "I should be doing the same thing," he said, breaking the doughnut in half. "I'm not getting any younger, and bad eating habits catch up to you sooner or later."

Vicky raised an eyebrow and lifted her cup to her mouth. "I don't see it stopping you," she teased, sipping her coffee, laughter dancing in her eyes.

John shook his head and grinned, unapologetic. "I'll start my diet tomorrow," he said, lifting one of the doughnut halves and taking a bite. Audra laughed and bit into her cheese.

They all sat and talked for a while longer, other parishioners coming by to say hello and ask about Meghan. John explained several times that she was busy getting the restaurant ready for the summer season, although most of them knew that. Meghan attended much less often than John or Beth did in general, but this time of year had her working even longer hours.

John and Beth said their goodbyes about forty-five minutes after the service ended and walked back down the sidewalk toward home. The sun was blazing hot, but a nice breeze coming off the water kept things from being too unbearable. Beth chattered about Sarah and the hymns they'd sung that morning, and John just let her talk, answering with encouraging words only when necessary.

Back home, John sent Beth to change out of her church clothes while he did the same before heading downstairs to make lunch. He kept it simple, sandwiches with carrot sticks and applesauce on the side. He grinned a little as he put two plates together for Beth and himself. Despite his joking at the church, he did eat pretty well overall. Watching out to be sure Beth didn't get too much junk kept him from having too much of it either.

Beth came running in, as usual, and they sat down to eat their lunch. "After we're done, Bethy, it'll be naptime," John said. Beth was not a fan of naps these days.

"But Daddy—"

"We're going to Jeremy's house for dinner tonight, remember?" John didn't let her finish her protest. "And we'll probably be up a little later. So you need to take a nap now so you don't get too sleepy tonight, okay?"

Beth huffed out a loud sigh. "I'm not a baby, Daddy," she said, and John bit his lip to keep from laughing at her exasperation.

"Being a baby doesn't have anything to do with it, honey," he replied. "I might even take a little nap myself. It's nice to just be able to lie down and rest in the middle of the day sometimes."

Beth didn't look convinced, but she didn't complain anymore either, so John counted it a victory. They finished eating, and John sent her off to brush her teeth while he took care of their dishes. He still had a pie to finish, so he didn't know if he'd get that nap in or not. While he was in the kitchen, he got out the rest of his pie-making supplies before going up to check on Beth.

He found her already curled up in her bed, arms wrapped around Maxie, down for the count. Managing not to laugh and risk waking her up, he pulled her door almost closed and headed back downstairs, stopping by his office to grab the speaker to the baby monitor.

An hour later, pie in the oven and kitchen cleaned up, he flopped down on the sofa and turned on the Braves game. Almost as an afterthought, he set his cell phone alarm to go off in half an hour, a few minutes before the pie should be done, just in case he dozed off. Naturally, he did, and once he took the pie out and set it aside to cool, he went right back to the sofa, resetting his alarm for 4 p.m. to give him plenty of time to get him and Beth ready for dinner. Letting out a soft sigh, he lay down on his side, a sofa cushion under his head, and within a few minutes, he was sleeping.

JOHN held tightly to Beth's hand and balanced his pie in his other hand as they walked down the sidewalk toward the bed-and-breakfast. Beth had woken up a little grumpy from her nap, and while she'd gotten over that, she still wasn't quite her usual sunny self. When they got to the house, John let Beth climb the stairs on her own, cautioning her to hold onto the rail, and then he helped her stretch up high enough to reach the doorbell.

After just a few seconds, the door opened and Karen smiled at them. "Hi, guys!" she said, stepping back to let them in. "We're just getting the grill going. Come on back to the kitchen, we're set up back there and on the back porch."

John smiled as he stepped inside, still holding onto Beth's hand. "Thanks for inviting us," he said. "Meghan's going to be over as soon as she can. She has to get the kitchen switched over to her backup for the evening first."

"She must stay really busy with the restaurant," Karen said. "We like it a lot, but we haven't been able to make it over there much. We're spending so much of our time and money on the house." She pointed up at the walls of the parlor as they walked through. "Bryan and Davis just barely got the drywall up this week. They'll be painting starting tomorrow, so it'll be in good shape in time for the holiday next weekend." She grinned and lifted an eyebrow. "Unfortunately, they'll have to do it without me," she said, running a hand over her swollen belly, more prominent under the fitted T-shirt she wore than the looser one she'd had on when John had met her. "I keep telling Davis I didn't get pregnant just to get out of the work, but I'm not really sure he believes me."

Just then, the door opened behind them, and they turned to see Bryan coming in. He wore snug shorts, a white tank top, and sneakers, and he was covered in sweat. "Hey, guys," he said, running the back of his wrist across his forehead to wipe away some moisture. "Sorry I'm back so late. Gonna head up and shower, and I'll be right back down."

John stood frozen in place. He couldn't seem to tear his eyes away from Bryan. From his body, to be specific: his glistening skin, his muscles in sharp relief as he moved. John's body liked what he was seeing. It liked it very, very much.

And John had absolutely no idea how to react.

He hadn't seen Bryan like this until just now. He didn't think he'd felt a bit of attraction toward him, just friendliness, but his mind replayed images of Bryan smiling at him at the park, teasing him over his "big gay freak-out," wiping away a milk mustache when they had milk and cookies with the kids, grinning at John over the edge of his coffee mug, and, above everything else, carrying an exhausted Beth home the day before. It all came together, and he finally recognized what his brain had been trying to tell him for days.

He liked Bryan, and as more than just a friend. He was *attracted* to Bryan.

And the thought scared the shit out of him.

Chapter 6

LATER, John couldn't remember what he said to Bryan, but it must not have been anything bad, since no one reacted strangely. The next thing he knew, he and Beth were out on the back porch, and then Beth was running into the yard, where Jeremy greeted her with a shout of joy. John smiled at that, then turned to face the man standing next to the gas grill on the small patio beside the back door.

"You must be John," the man said, giving him a quick smile as he watched the temperature gauge on the front of the grill's shiny silver lid. "Davis Morrison. I'd offer to shake, but...." He waved his hands, one wearing a thick oven mitt and the other holding a pair of tongs, and John laughed.

"No problem," he said. "Thanks for having us over. Beth and Jeremy sure have a lot of fun playing together."

Davis chuckled and turned out to look at the kids, who were already playing some combination of tag and hopscotch that reminded John more of the freewheeling Calvinball from the *Calvin & Hobbes* comic strip than anything else. "Jeremy can really be exhausting sometimes," Davis said, turning back to the grill. He shot John another look. "I guess all five-year-olds can be."

John smiled in agreement, bracing his hands on the back of one of the patio chairs. "Probably a good idea to let them wear each other out playing so we don't have to try to keep up with them."

"Or foist them off on Bryan," Davis shot back. "He doesn't seem to see it that way, though. He'll take Jeremy off our hands pretty much anytime we need, or even when we don't. I don't know if he'll get to have kids of his—"

He cut himself off, and John smiled and waved a hand. "I know he's gay," he said, trying to keep his tone casual. "Not a problem with me."

Davis nodded. "Good," he said. "I mean, I'll admit to having some reservations of my own at first. But Bryan's just such a great guy that none of that lasted very long. At least not for anyone we'd care to be around."

John nodded and moved around to sit down in the chair. "It's Georgia," he said. "You're more likely to get pushback than not, sad to say."

Davis shrugged. "Not always from homophobes, either," he said, something dark in his voice that piqued John's interest.

Before John could ask, the back door opened and the man himself stepped out onto the top step. He wore casual cargo shorts and a loose polo shirt now, and John breathed a small sigh of relief. At least maybe his libido would stay in the box he'd managed to shove it back into. He didn't need to deal with whatever this was tonight, before he'd even had a chance to process it.

"Hey, guys," Bryan said. "Karen wants to know if we're ready for the meat."

Davis gave a salute with his tongs. "Ready when she is."

Bryan shot John a quick smile and leaned back in. "Bring it on down," he called, letting the screen door close behind him as he descended the steps. He walked over and plopped down into the patio chair next to John. "How'd the naps go yesterday?"

John smiled. "Beth was down for the count about five minutes after I got her into her bed," he said. "I wasn't far behind. We slept a couple of hours, and even then Bethy went to bed at her usual time."

Bryan laughed. "Sounds like me just about every night this week," he said. "You saw we got the drywall done in the parlor?"

John nodded. "It looks great," he said. He glanced over at Davis as Karen emerged from the house with a tray of hamburger patties. "Oh, hey, I don't know if Bryan mentioned it, but I work for Peachtree Home Improvement. I'm sure I can get you guys some discounts."

Davis smiled as he opened the grill lid. "That'd be great," he said. "Anything we can do to save a little lets us do a little more to fix the place up."

Karen nodded, holding the tray for Davis while he transferred the burgers to the grill. "Bryan did mention that, I'd forgotten," she said. "That's really nice of you, John."

He shrugged. "Not a problem. We're glad any time one of the old houses here gets fixed up. So many have been left to rot over the years."

Bryan shook his head. "It's a shame," he said. "We spend way too much time on the latest-greatest thing and not nearly enough preserving what we already have."

John shot him a look. "Have you thought about going to graduate school for historic preservation?"

Bryan looked puzzled, so John clarified. "Your architecture degree would be great for that," he said. "I have a cousin who did it, and she oversees renovations now to be sure they're historically accurate. She's helped with work on a couple of houses in Millionaire's Village on Jekyll Island."

Bryan looked thoughtful. "Wow. That's—I never considered it. But that could be really cool. I'd probably have to take some history classes or something first."

John nodded. "Maybe. But it sounds like something you might enjoy."

Bryan gave John a sidelong glance and a soft smile. "Funny how you could figure that out about me in just a few days and I haven't been able to for the past four years."

John felt a hot flush run through him. He imagined his cheeks were turning red, and he knew it wasn't just from embarrassment. He shifted in his seat and tried to smile. "Just my uncanny insight into the human psyche," he said, happy to find he'd kept his tone light.

Bryan laughed and pushed himself to his feet. "I'm gonna check on the munchkins," he said. "Jeremy said something about mud pies earlier, and I don't entirely trust that he's going to listen to his mom's orders to stay away from the water hose."

John grinned and tried not to watch too obviously as Bryan moved away. He turned back to find Karen giving him an appraising look from where she'd sat in one of the patio chairs across from him. He forced himself to hold her gaze. "I don't think I asked, but when is your baby due?"

Karen hesitated but then relaxed and smiled. "Halloween," she said. "We don't think it'll actually go that long, though. Jeremy was a little early, and just based on the timing, my guess is the middle of the month instead."

John smiled. "That would be fun, though," he said. "Birthday on Halloween? Instant party every year, and all the candy you can eat."

Davis chuckled, flipping the burgers one by one. "Jeremy's birthday is April fifth, so it usually falls close to Easter," he said. "So we already have one sugar-rushed birthday every year."

"And they have more than enough energy already without that," Karen chimed in. She turned her head toward the yard, and John followed her gaze to where Bryan had sat down in the grass and appeared to be teaching the kids some elaborate hand-clapping game John didn't recognize. He smiled as he watched them until he felt eyes on him, and he turned back to see Karen giving him that look again.

He didn't know how to respond. He was pretty sure he knew what she was wondering—if his interest in Bryan was truly just friendly. He didn't understand what was going on yet himself, so it wasn't like he could offer either of them any assurances. He shrugged mentally and decided to just act as if nothing were going on.

"Do you guys need any more help with dinner?" he asked. "Setting the table or something?"

Karen's eyes narrowed for just a second, but then she smiled. "No, it's mostly done," she said. "We'll just get ketchup and ice for drinks and things when the burgers are done. Which should be...?" She directed the question toward Davis, who rolled his eyes a little as he flipped burgers again.

"Five more minutes, Mom," he half whined, sounding so much like a petulant child that John had to laugh. And then a pang hit him as he imagined him and Liz having an exchange much like that while she was pregnant with Beth. His mind drifted, and he lost track of the conversation for a minute or two.

A warm hand on his shoulder snapped his attention back to the present. He looked up over his shoulder to find Bryan smiling down at him. "I'm taking the kids in to wash up," he said. He lifted his gaze to meet Karen's but didn't move his hand. "Meet you guys at the table?"

That look was back on Karen's face, but John couldn't do anything about it short of shoving Bryan's hand away. And no matter what was going on with him, that would be rude, and he didn't want to hurt Bryan.

Bryan's hand slid away as he turned to herd the kids toward the door. John missed the warmth. He felt branded where Bryan's palm had rested, and he realized that was the first time they'd touched other than that initial handshake the first day and a couple of incidental brushes. Maybe that was why it had taken so long for him to recognize his attraction for what it was. In his previous relationships, he'd pretty much dived in with both feet, and touching was a big part of that. John might be reserved overall, but within a relationship, he'd always been very tactile. And in a flash, his mind filled with images of Bryan's large, warm palm on his bare skin, running down his chest, tangling through the hair below his navel and moving on to points south.

His face warmed again, and he had to yank his thoughts back in line. The last thing he needed to be doing was sprouting wood in front of Bryan's family, or Bryan himself, for that matter. He had to keep a grip on himself for the rest of tonight, at least. Then he could figure out what the hell was going on and maybe even what he was going to do about it.

MEGHAN arrived in a flurry just as they were moving to the table to eat, so they paused long enough for the rush of introductions to be exchanged. Karen especially gushed over Let's Be Shellfish.

"I don't know how you manage such wonderful food and still keep the place so relaxed and warm," she said. "Usually it's a choice between good food and a stuffy atmosphere or cookie-cutter food and casual."

Meghan smiled, pleased, but as John had expected she would, she shrugged off the compliment. "Having a great staff helps a lot," she said. "The place would fall apart without them."

John rolled his eyes and patted the empty seat next to him. He had Beth on the other side and really didn't want to deal with the possibility of Bryan sitting so close right then. "Sit down and smile and say thanks," he teased. "You know it's a great restaurant, and it's mostly because of you."

Meghan smacked him on the shoulder before sitting down where he indicated. "You'll have to let me help clean up, since I didn't get here in time to help set up," she said to Karen. "That's assuming we don't all eat ourselves into a stupor. Everything looks and smells amazing!"

Karen nodded at Davis, who was starting the platter of hamburger patties around the table. "Davis loves grilling out," she said. "The grill was one of the first things we bought when we moved in and started working on the place, and it's gotten a lot of use."

"Not just burgers, either," Davis put in, adding ketchup and cheese to his. "Anything that can go on a grill, I'll put on a grill. Planning to do some corn for next weekend."

"Oh, yeah." It was Bryan's turn to break in. "I don't think I mentioned it to you, John, but we're having a picnic and bonfire on the beach next Monday for Memorial Day. All of you are invited, of course, and everyone can bring whatever they want to eat. Davis is doing corn here to take over, and we'll have hot dogs and marshmallows to roast on the beach."

John grinned as he helped Beth dress her burger with ketchup, making sure it wasn't enough to drip onto her as she ate. "Sounds like we'll need chocolate and graham crackers." He glanced at Meghan. "Are you still planning to close early that night?"

Meghan shrugged and set down the mustard. "Depends on how busy it is." She smiled around the table at the others. "The restaurant is always crazy busy all weekend for Memorial Day until Monday night. I guess everyone heads home by then. Usually I close up by around seven, sometimes earlier."

"Great!" Bryan grinned as he picked up his burger. "We'll probably just be getting the bonfire going by then, so you'll get there just in time."

John told himself not to stare, but he kind of couldn't help it when Bryan stuck out his tongue and ran it around the edge of his burger where a little bit of the ketchup and mustard was trying to escape. He forced his gaze back to his own plate, concentrating on his hamburger and checking on Beth's process, and by the time he focused back on the conversation, talk had turned to home renovation.

"We're going to be on a tight schedule this week too," Davis was saying. "We just barely got the drywall up and the dust all cleaned out Friday before the first weekend guests arrived, and we didn't even have a full house this time. We're booked up next weekend, and on top of getting the rooms ready like usual, we really need to have the parlor painted and all the furniture moved back in."

Bryan shot John a grin. "So since Karen can't really be around much while we're painting, she'll be the one taking Jeremy to the park," he said. "I'm so sorry you'll have to miss out on my scintillating conversation."

John breathed a silent sigh of relief, not because he didn't want to see Bryan but because he did. A little too much. And he needed time to figure out how the heck he was going to handle it. He smiled. "I guess you'll just have to save up all your good stories for the picnic, then. And I'll just grill Karen for embarrassing childhood stories instead."

Bryan groaned, dropping his head into one hand. "And she'll do it too," he said. "I swear I think sometimes she was born a mom. She tells embarrassing kid stories like it's her job."

Meghan laughed at that. "Oh, don't think I don't have a few of those on John," she said. She grinned at Karen. "We should team up and take 'em both down. What do you say?"

Karen lifted an eyebrow and smiled slowly, looking more evil than John would've thought possible. "Sounds like a plan," she said.

"Watch it there, sis," Bryan broke in. "Or you'll lose your live-in babysitter."

"I'm not a baby!" Jeremy's exclamation broke everyone up. Karen shushed him and got him back to work on his burger, and John poured Beth some more milk. Meghan's voice in his ear made him jump.

"I think we need to talk, John-boy," she whispered, and he turned to find her giving him a knowing look.

He tried to keep his expression bland. "I don't know what you're talking about," he muttered back, knowing good and well she'd see through him but also that she'd keep her mouth shut about it. Until later, at least.

AFTER dinner, everyone started to help clear the table, but Bryan insisted he'd take care of it and shooed them all off. Karen took the kids into the small den off the kitchen to let them pick out a Disney movie, and Meghan started asking Davis questions about the renovations they were doing, which left John at loose ends. He thought about offering to help Bryan, thought that he really should, but he didn't know that being in such close proximity and doing something so thoroughly domestic would be the right move right now.

Instead, he snagged a beer and headed out back, sitting down on the top step leading from the porch to the yard, forearms resting on his thighs. The sun was just setting, the days nearing their longest, and the dying hum of cicadas was being overtaken by the throaty croaking of frogs. The warm breeze ruffled John's hair, and he closed his eyes, letting his beer bottle dangle from his fingers.

As it always did, the island night cocooned him in peace, helping him relax and let his mind wander. He wasn't surprised when it landed on Bryan. The other man had captured John's attention from the moment they'd met, but it had taken until tonight for his conscious mind to realize what his subconscious had been trying to tell him.

Trouble was, he didn't know if he was ready.

Sure, it had been five years since Liz died. But he'd spent seven years before that believing that he and Liz would be together for the rest of their lives. He'd devoted all of himself to her. And when she'd died, a part of him had died with her—a part he knew he'd never get back. It wasn't until now that he'd had reason to consider whether what he had left would be enough to give to someone else.

John had always been a romantic. With the exception of a dark few months not long after Liz died, he'd always dated one person at a time, and not that many overall. He'd had a high school sweetheart, a freshman fling that lasted a few months, and a boyfriend of eight months before he'd met Liz. Three months in, they were already talking marriage.

Twelve years later, he'd found the first person who made him feel something like he had when he'd met Liz.

He jerked when that thought coalesced in his mind. But it was true. He'd thought Bryan was handsome when they first met, just as he'd thought Liz was cute. He and Bryan had been able to talk and laugh and tease, same as he had with Liz. And while his attraction to Liz had been more immediately obvious, once he recognized it tonight, he could see how similar it was to how he'd felt about Liz. He didn't just want to fuck Bryan, like that string of near-faceless partners he'd gone through briefly during the year after Liz died. He wanted to hug him, laugh with him, watch him smile. Touch him. Kiss him.

And he felt so guilty for it.

Chapter 7

BEHIND John, the screen door squeaked open and fell shut, and he forced himself to pull away from his thoughts. He was pretty sure he knew who'd be coming outside, and he was right. Bryan stepped down and then sat on the opposite end of the same step, just a foot or so away. John wondered if he could feel the magnetic pull between them or if what he was feeling was all one-sided.

A beer bottle came into his line of vision, and he turned his head to look into Bryan's eyes. "Cheers," Bryan said. He was smiling, but his eyes were serious, and John saw in them that he wasn't alone.

"Cheers," he replied, bringing his bottle up to tap against Bryan's.

They each took a long drink, and John lowered his bottle back between his knees, one hand picking at the damp label. "This has been really nice," he said, keeping his gaze away from Bryan. "Karen and Davis are great. I'm glad we all met." He shrugged. "Even after living here for a few years, I haven't made all that many friends. I mean, there are a few guys I'll meet up with to watch a game at a bar or something sometimes. But there aren't a lot of people around our age, really, especially single people."

In his peripheral vision, he saw Bryan nod. His eyes were directed out toward some indeterminate point in the backyard. "Yeah, it can get lonely sometimes," he said. "Not that I don't love spending time with Karen and Jeremy. And, okay, even Davis." He flashed John a quick grin. "But it's not the same, you know? Most of my friends are back in Atlanta, and even with all the electronic communication in the world, it's not the same as having someone nearby."

The wistful tone Bryan's voice had taken on made John's stomach and heart clench, and his hands itched to reach out and touch him. He drew in a breath and blew it out. No. He wouldn't take a risk like that with someone who was becoming a good friend, not until he was sure of what he wanted. It wouldn't be fair to either of them.

Instead, he forced himself to relax and smile. "Well, guess we lucked out, then," he said, keeping his tone light. "At least, we haven't found anything to make us hate each other yet." He paused in contemplation and shot Bryan a mock frown. "You aren't a secret Florida Gators fan or anything, are you?"

Bryan's face lit up as he laughed, and John had to force his libido to shut the hell up yet again. "Oh my God, no," he said. "I may not be big into sports, but you know how it goes. I kind of have to be a Yellow Jackets fan, being that I went to school at Georgia Tech. But"—he leaned forward and whispered—"truth is, I'm a Georgia Bulldogs fan too. Root for them anytime except when they're playing Tech. And twice as hard when they're playing Florida!"

John lifted his bottle over for another toast. "Good man," he said, and he smiled as he took a drink. Whatever happened, he had to be sure to keep Bryan around, friend or otherwise. It had been a long time since anyone other than Beth had made him smile this much, and he didn't want to give that up.

MEGHAN and Davis joined them a few minutes later with their own beers, and with slices of John's pie for everyone. John had forgotten about the pie, which made him laugh at himself, considering the time and effort he'd put into making it. Could he help it if he'd been a little distracted by Bryan?

Meghan plopped down on the steps between John and Bryan while Davis dragged over the two rocking chairs from the sides of the porch, sitting in one of them. Meghan grinned at John. "You done good, kid," she said, holding up her bottle until John clinked his to it. He knew his face was puzzled, but Meghan just shrugged and drank. John's gaze drifted past her, and he watched Bryan's eyes crinkle a little around the edges as he smiled and took a sip from his own bottle.

Karen came out then, closing the screen door behind her, and took the empty seat in the second rocking chair. "The kids are fully engrossed in *Toy Story*," she said. "And under strict orders, under pain of severe grounding, not to go anywhere except the bathroom without coming out here to find one of us."

Bryan laughed. "Somehow Jeremy always seems to find some kind of loophole around things like that," he said, directing his words toward John and Meghan. "I don't know if that's Jeremy-specific or just a kid thing."

John grinned. "A kid thing. Beth's sure done it enough. 'But Dad, you said I couldn't have a cookie before dinner. You didn't say I couldn't have cake!'"

Karen snickered. "Bryan kind of seemed to have trouble with the concept," she said. Bryan gave her a dire look, but she waved him off. "Oh, I'll let you tell one on me. Anyway." She leaned forward to catch John and Meghan's attention. "Mom was going to some event or another, a ladies' club meeting or something, and Bryan decided that he just had to go. And he was begging and pleading and wheedling and everything he could think of. And Mom kept telling him no. And he finally got up a fine head of steam and clenched his little fists by his sides and declared, 'If you don't let me go, I'm not going to let you buy me any ice cream!'"

John laughed so hard that he snorted, which just set him off even harder. Which was fine, because everyone else was laughing, too, even Bryan, despite the high flush of embarrassment reddening his cheeks in the low light.

"All right, K, you've had your fun," Bryan said. "Shall I tell everyone about the time you dropped your slip in front of your preteen crush?"

Karen smacked him on the shoulder. "You don't want to get into a story war, Bry," she said. "I've been around longer than you, and I've been paying very close attention."

John shook his head at their sibling antics, but before he could say anything, Meghan spoke up. "So where did you guys grow up?" she asked. "How many years between you? Any other siblings? And all those other personal questions like that people ask when you first meet." She smiled at Bryan, and John watched her charm work on him as he smiled back.

"We grew up in Statesboro," he said, naming a small university town an hour and a half west. "Dad was a professor at the college, and once I was in school, Mom taught there part-time, too. Just the four of us." He nodded at Karen. "Big sister's five years older. And don't think for a second I will ever let her forget that."

Karen smacked him again, harder. "Ow!" Bryan rubbed the spot, looking petulant. "No fair beatin' up on me, now. I can't hit the pregnant lady."

John laughed and drained the last of his beer. Bryan reached out and grabbed the empty bottle before John could set it down, and John sucked in a sharp breath as Bryan's hand covered his for a split second. "I'm getting both of us another," Bryan said, standing up and turning to face Karen. He stuck out his tongue at her, and she returned the gesture, which made John laugh again.

Davis dropped his head back against the seat back as Bryan slipped inside. "I swear, some days it's like raising three kids around here," he said.

"And soon to be four." Meghan tilted her head back to grin at him upside down, but he just groaned louder.

Bryan came back out with a cold bottle in each hand. "Kids are still in front of the TV, but not so much with the consciousness," he said. "Jeremy's already out, and I think Beth's not far behind."

John smiled up at him as he accepted the beer. "Thanks," he said. "We should probably get going once this is done." He lifted both the bottle and the plate with his nearly finished slice of pie, and he watched out of the corner of his eye as Bryan settled back onto the step beside him. The soft cotton of his T-shirt stretched tight across his chest as he moved, outlining the muscles John had seen earlier when Bryan had come in from running. As Bryan lifted his bottle to take a sip, the muscles of his arm flexed, bicep and tricep standing out in sharp relief.

Strength, John thought, forcing his gaze to his own feet. He'd almost forgotten how that felt, to be with someone who was stronger than him, who could match him move for move. Who could hold him down if that was what John wanted.

John's body stirred, answering that question. Yeah. He wanted, all right. He just didn't know yet if he could handle it.

"Dammit!"

John caught his coffee mug—for the third time—before it tipped over and soaked everything on his desk. As it was, a wave of liquid splashed over the edge, landing on the spreadsheet he'd been trying to review.

For the past hour, his ability to concentrate had flown the coop. He hadn't slept well. Every time he'd fallen asleep, he'd dreamed of chaos. Running through storms without knowing where he was going, opening doors to a cascade of sand burying him, faceless fucking that he couldn't stop no matter how much it hurt.

He sat back and carefully sipped at his coffee, needing the caffeine but unwilling to risk catastrophe again. People used to take coffee breaks, right? He could do that. Until he could figure out how to hook up a caffeine IV, at least—

"John?"

A full-body jerk almost led to disaster, but John managed to keep from spilling the coffee. Again. He stared at Meghan where she stood in the doorway. "Hey, Meggie," he said, pulling out the nickname he'd used when they were kids. "What's up?"

"Apparently not you, all appearances to the contrary," she said. She crossed her arms over her chest and leaned sideways against the doorframe. "I was just going to ask if hot dogs were okay with you for lunch, but now you've got my curiosity piqued. What's going on with you? You were acting strange last night, and you were a million miles away when I came in just now."

John shook his head, draining the coffee mug and setting it on the coaster next to his computer. "It's nothing," he said. "Just got some things on my mind. You know me, work it out up here first." He tapped a finger against his temple, and Meghan's frown deepened.

"Yeah, not buying it," she said. "But I'll be nice for a change and not grill you for answers. Yet." She raised both eyebrows and pushed off the doorframe, turning back toward the hallway.

"Meggie?"

Meghan turned back at John's voice.

"Thanks," he said. "I know it sounds weird to say it now, like this, but thanks for—" He waved a hand. "All of this. Looking out for us. I know I haven't always been easy to deal with."

Meghan didn't move for a few long seconds, then shrugged one shoulder. "You had good reason," she said. "And that's what you do for family."

John rolled his eyes and offered a small grin. "You could just try 'you're welcome', you know," he teased.

Meghan stuck out her tongue at him and wheeled back around, heading down the hallway.

John sank back into his seat. Meghan's silly gesture had just served to bring back up the image from last night of Bryan sticking his tongue out at his sister. John wanted to have that tongue in his mouth, on his skin, in his—

Shit. He shook his head hard before his libido could get into the act. The one good thing about being so short on sleep was that it seemed to be keeping his body in check.

WHEN the phone rang mid-afternoon, John jumped what felt like a mile and a half. After lunch with Beth and Meghan—in the kitchen this time, John not trusting himself not to make a mess on his desk—he'd managed to focus on the report he was designing and had gotten most of it coded. After taking a few seconds to slow his heart rate from the jolt, he picked up the phone. "Hello?"

"Johnny Boy, what's goin' on?" Adam's deep, booming voice always made John smile, even when his head was a mess like it was today. John's boss, head of finance for Peachtree Home Improvement, had become a good friend in the almost ten years since John had gone to work for the company, especially during the year after Liz died, when John was adrift. Adam had taken care of the paperwork to get him time off with pay, and when John and Beth relocated to Tybee, he'd set John up so he could work remotely.

"Things are good here," John said, dropping his pen and leaning back in his chair. "A little crazy sometimes, but that's what happens when you have a five-year-old running around."

John could hear the laughter in Adam's voice. "I wouldn't know anything about that," he said. "Not like I didn't have three of them within three years or anything." Adam and his wife had twin girls a year older than Beth and a boy two years younger than her.

John smiled. "Well, I seem to have picked up a second one myself," he said. "There's a family nearby that has a five-year-old boy. He and Bethy met at the park, and it was best friends at first sight." He laughed. "Bryan and I can barely keep up with them."

"Bryan?" Adam's voice changed, and John could hear him shifting in his seat, like he was settling in for a long chat. That was just fine with John. He could use one, even if he wasn't sure he could articulate what he needed to say.

"Bryan is Jeremy's uncle," John said. "We all met at the park last week. He's a nice guy. Lives with his sister and her husband at their bed-and-breakfast and is helping them do renovations." He paused. "He's also gay."

He waited, knowing Adam would get the point. He knew John's history—all of it, the good and the bad. "So," Adam finally said. "Can I assume you haven't slept with him yet?"

John laughed, knowing it wasn't a serious question. "Geez, man, just because he's gay doesn't mean he hits on every man he meets," he echoed Bryan's words from their first meeting.

"I wasn't worried about *him*," Adam said. "The fact that you're bringing this up this way tells me *you're* the one I should be worrying about."

Chapter 8

JOHN'S smile fell away at Adam's words, and he bit his lip. Glancing at the open door, he stood and stepped over to push it closed. He didn't need Meghan to overhear this. Or worse, Beth.

"Okay, yeah," John admitted as he dropped back into his chair. "I mean, not the part about sleeping with him. I didn't even think about him that way at all until last night. And now I have not the foggiest idea how to deal with it."

Adam made an indeterminate sound in his throat. "Is it because he's a man?"

John tilted his head into an almost nod. "I think a little, yeah," he said. "It's different here from Atlanta. And I have Beth to think about. But that's not the main thing."

"It's Liz."

John blew out a breath. "It's Liz," he affirmed. "I know it's been five years, and I'm really not still grieving. Or really, I've accepted that part of me always will be. I'm always going to love her, no matter what."

"Of course." Adam's voice shifted. "Zo tell me about zee feelingz you are havink," he said, and John laughed at his bad Freud impersonation. Adam had studied psychology before going into statistics, but he'd always been careful not to try to analyze John unless he asked for it. Now John had, if not in so many words.

"Okay, well, I'm not sure how much of this you want to hear," he started. "So I'll spare the details. But we hit it off great, except for one little misunderstanding where he thought I was a homophobe."

Adam laughed.

"Yeah, I know, but he didn't. So I told him about college, and after that we were okay."

"Did you tell him about what happened five years ago?"

John knew Adam didn't mean Liz's death but what came after. "Not yet," he said. "I know if anything happens that I'll need to tell him. But anyway, we've gotten together with the kids a few times, and last night we went over to their place for dinner. Meghan too." He let his eyes fall shut. "I got a look at Bryan coming in after a run, and it woke up some parts of me I haven't really heard from in a while."

"Ahhhh, the shorts and tank top and sweat scenario," Adam mused. "I can see that. Works when it's a woman, too, trust me."

John laughed. "Oh, I know," he said. "Not gay, remember?" They fell silent for a few moments. "Anyway," John said, "I feel... I guess guilty? I suppose that's normal."

"Very," Adam replied. "I remember how much you beat yourself up after what happened five years ago. And this is different, because it would be more than just your body." He paused. "It *would* be more than just your body, right?"

John had to smile. "Don't worry, man, no more of that kind of thing," he said. "If anything did happen, yes, it would be more than just sex. I'm not about to do that to myself again, and I'm damn sure not subjecting Bethy to it."

"Good." Adam's voice was forceful, and John smiled wider. After Liz died, Adam had been pretty protective of Beth, not just John, and he'd never really stopped. There was a reason John had included him on a list of potential guardians in case something happened—with Meghan at the top, of course.

"Anyway," John said, shaking himself from his thoughts, "you didn't call to talk about my love life or lack thereof. So what's up?"

He could hear Adam shifting papers around on his desk. "It's the annual meeting," he said. "I need to get all the financials redone to check accuracy before they go into the annual report. I know we can't finalize them until our fiscal year ends in June, but if we can check the status to this point, that'll give us an idea how things are. After the clusterfuck last year...."

The year before, they'd had to fire an employee when they discovered she'd been using a company credit card to pay for personal purchases and altering expense reports to cover it up. That had taken months of work to resolve.

"Got it," John said, balancing the phone between his shoulder and chin and reaching for pen and paper. "When do you need me?" Almost all of John's work could be done remotely, but for major financial reports like this, being on-site was a big help.

"Well, if you can come, say, in two weeks? Then we can run everything and be ready to finalize once we run the fourth quarter numbers."

John scribbled a note and reached for the calendar he kept on his desk. Electronic calendars were great for making sure he didn't forget things like meetings, but he still preferred to have a hard copy on hand. "First full week in June, then," he confirmed.

"That's right," Adam replied. "We can hit the ground running Monday morning and should be able to finish it up in a week."

"Sounds good." John made another note. "I'll call Liz's parents, see if they're up for keeping Beth that week. She's supposed to visit them a couple of times over the summer anyway."

"Good," Adam replied. "I'll have Holly set up the apartment for you." The company had a deal with a local hotel for use of their corporate apartment space when needed. "Anything special you need?"

"Sweetwater!"

Adam laughed, as John expected, when he named a local Atlanta brewery whose beer had been one of their favorites for years.

"No, really, we'll come up on Sunday and I'll get some groceries," he said.

"Yeah, but you can't buy beer on Sunday," Adam pointed out.

"Then I'll pick that up after work on Monday," John shot back. He grinned. "Hey, there's another winning point for Bryan. He's a Sweetwater man."

"Oh, too bad," Adam said. "I was hoping we'd be able to pull out the initiation ritual."

"You are a sick, sick man," John said. "Let me go before you corrupt me."

Adam's laugh was loud and long. "I think it's way too late for that, man," he said. "You go do some work for me or something, and I'll see you in a couple of weeks. And keep me updated on your sex life, or lack thereof."

"In all the gory detail I can manage. Bye!" John hung up before Adam could respond. He shook his head, still grinning. Trust Adam to pull him out of his brain fog. He sure had plenty of practice at it.

JOHN and Beth went to dinner at Let's Be Shellfish Tuesday night. They usually ate there once or twice a week, but with the summer season coming up, John knew it would be busier than it was the rest of the year. They were careful never to take up a table that could be filled by paying customers.

Kai greeted Beth with the same huge hug and nickname as always, and this time Audra was there, too, smiling and taking her turn.

"Thank you so much for your picture, Bethy," she said from where she'd squatted to meet the little girl. "It's just exactly what I needed. I'm going to start working on my picture soon, so you'll have to come see me while I'm doing it. Okay?"

Beth's head bounced as she nodded. "Okay!" She looked up at John. "Is it okay, Daddy?"

"It's just fine, Bethy," he said, running a hand over her soft hair. "What do you want Mister Kai to make you for lunch today? Grilled cheese again?"

She shook her head this time and grinned at Kai. "Can I have macaroni?"

"Macaroni and cheese it is!" Kai grinned back at her and nodded to John before heading back into the kitchen. Kai's macaroni and cheese was just about the only kind Beth would eat that didn't come out of a blue box. John had no idea what his secret was, and Kai wouldn't tell; John had tried it himself and thought it was great but couldn't figure out the trick behind it.

Meghan came out of the kitchen, a light blush on her cheeks as she glanced back over her shoulder. She turned back to meet John's questioning gaze, and the blush deepened. "Crashing again, I see," she said. "Back for more seafood crepes?"

John lifted an eyebrow. "Don't think I'm letting that look go," he said. "We need to have a little talk, missy."

Meghan rolled her eyes, stepping behind the counter near the door and bending down to reach underneath. "You didn't answer the question. Crepes? Fish and chips? Lobster and arsenic stew?"

John laughed as he settled Beth into her seat and handed her the crayons and coloring page Meghan passed over. "How about scampi?" he said. "Haven't had that in a while."

"You got it." Meghan scribbled a note and passed it off to Audra, who was headed back to drop off an order of her own. Meghan looked at John, thoughtful. "You look a little better than you did yesterday," she said. "Got some things settled in your mind?"

John shrugged one shoulder, throwing a glance Beth's way, not wanting to get into it in public or in front of Beth. "We'll talk tonight," he said. "I think we both have some things to say."

Meghan nodded, reaching out to squeeze his shoulder. "Never a dull moment," she said, heading back toward the kitchen.

John watched her go and thought about the two men he knew they'd be discussing tonight. He wasn't sure why it was suddenly so important, but more than ever he wanted to convince Meghan to give Kai a chance. He knew she'd throw his words back at him, but somehow that didn't bother him. Maybe it'd be exactly the push he needed.

THE talk didn't happen that night. A late dinner rush kept Meghan at work an hour longer than usual, taking care of cleanup and prep for the next day, and John took one look at her when she came in and told her to sleep it off. She was so tired that she didn't argue.

Wednesday dawned cloudy and on the cool side for so late in May. John had planned to take Beth to the park that afternoon, knowing Karen would probably have Jeremy there, since she couldn't be in the house while Bryan and Davis were painting. John hoped it wouldn't rain and they could actually go. Beth would be disappointed if she didn't get to see Jeremy.

John was glad to find that he was able to concentrate better today than the previous two days. He got his report coded in the morning, stopped long enough to make lunch for both him and Beth, since Meghan had already gone to the restaurant, and then spent an hour afterward testing and fixing a couple of small bugs. By the time he was ready to break at two, he felt confident that it would work well when he and Adam started working on the year-end numbers in a couple of weeks.

Standing up from his desk chair, John stretched, hearing the pops and crackles from his back and neck. He laughed at himself. "Thirty-two years old, and you've got the joints of a senior citizen," he murmured. He needed to get back into a regular exercise habit. He used to swim and play tennis before Liz died, and he lived on an island that had beautiful weather nearly all year. He had no excuse for not getting out and enjoying it more often.

He walked out into the living room, where Beth was curled up on the sofa watching TV. She only got a few hours a day at most, and her viewing choices were very limited, but she preferred to play most of the time anyway.

"Found the clues yet, Bethy?"

Beth looked up and grinned, jumping down from the couch. "Are we going to the park, Daddy?" She bounced on her toes, looking so excited for something so simple that John had to hug her.

"We sure are, sweetie," he said as he let her go. "And I'm not going to promise because I'm not sure, but I think Jeremy might be there."

"Yay!" Beth bounced more, and John laughed as he pocketed his keys from the table by the door.

"Come on," he said, holding out a hand. "Let's go play."

DESPITE the cloudy skies, the rain seemed to be holding off. As they approached the park, John saw a woman who looked like Karen sitting on the bench where he'd met Bryan, and then Jeremy caught sight of Beth from his spot on the playground and started jumping up and down. "Beth!" he cried, and Beth grinned and waved before looking up at John.

"Can I go, Daddy?" she asked, and John nodded and let go of her hand, watching her run to join her friend. His heart clenched in his chest as he was hit by the images of all the times he'd have to let her go in her life. He'd tried so hard not to be overprotective, not to coddle her, but it wasn't easy, especially not when he still missed her mother every single day. A part of him was still terrified of losing the last tangible tie he had to Liz.

"John?" He looked up to meet Karen's concerned expression from where she'd turned on the bench to face him. "Are you all right?"

He nodded and forced himself to relax into a smile. "I'm good," he said, moving over to sit at the other end of the bench. "How are you feeling? Little one still plugging along in there?"

Karen laughed and ran a hand over her slightly rounded belly. "Doing just fine," she said. "I had a checkup yesterday, and everything's progressing nicely."

John smiled. "Do you know the sex?"

Karen smiled. "We do," she said. "But we aren't telling yet."

John laughed and glanced over at the kids, who were chasing each other around the climbing set, laughing and yelling. "Have you picked out names?"

"We have a few in mind. Family names, mainly." She was silent for a moment, then spoke gently. "You named Beth after your wife?"

John's eyes burned, more from the tone of her voice than what she'd asked. It reminded him so much of Liz. "Yeah, I did," he said. "I wanted her to have that piece of her mother, and selfishly, I wanted it too. I know Beth is part of her mother, but somehow the name seemed more tangible." He shrugged a shoulder. "But I couldn't stand calling her Liz, and Elizabeth sounded too big and formal. So Beth it was."

Out of the corner of his eye, he saw Karen smile. "I think it's a wonderful thing," she said. "Very thoughtful for all of you. I know things had to have been unbelievably hard for you."

John nodded, still watching Beth play. "I didn't handle it well," he admitted. "I did some things I'm not proud of. But I had friends and Meghan to help me, and I got through it. Beth and I both did." He turned to look at Karen. "Not that I don't still miss her."

"Of course you do," Karen said. "You love her."

John noted that she used the present tense and nodded slightly in acknowledgement. "Probably always will," he said. He took a deep breath. "That's part of why I haven't tried to date since then," he said. "Beth is a big part of it, of course. And I've been working on trying to move on, but I don't think I would've been ready anyway. Even now, anyone I did date would have to understand about Liz. I'm not going to let go of her. I think… no, I *know* I can love someone else. Maybe even just as much as I did Liz. But what I feel for her is never going to go away."

He felt a sense of relief at having gotten all of that out of his head and into someone else's ears. He didn't know if Karen was the right person, or if she'd figure out that he was talking about Bryan. But he did think that if anyone could understand how he felt, Bryan could. He had such an open, warm personality that John couldn't imagine him not having the compassion to share even a small part of John with Liz.

Karen's face shifted as John watched. Her eyes were trained on her hands, which were tangled together in her lap. "I shouldn't say anything. But we had something pretty bad happen a few years ago. It involved…." She trailed off, then looked up at John. "It happened to Bryan. And I can't tell the story. It's not mine to tell. I'm only saying it because we do understand. We've been through something pretty bad too."

Chapter 9

A CHILL ran down John's spine. He never would have guessed from his time with Bryan that he had any kind of tragedy in his past. He wasn't sure how to respond. "Is it.... Is everything okay now?"

Karen tilted her head to one side. "As okay as it gets," she said. "It's like you said. You move on, but you don't forget. You can't leave it behind completely. Something like that, it becomes a part of you. And you just have to learn to live with it."

John nodded in understanding. "If there's anything I can do—"

Karen smiled. "Just being a friend helps," she said. "I think it's something Bryan hasn't had enough of. He'd cut himself off, and I'm so glad to see him opening up again."

John smiled, but inside he was in turmoil again. Would he screw things up if he tried to move beyond just friends with Bryan? He'd been so focused on figuring out what he wanted and whether he was ready that he hadn't thought about Bryan's perspective. Bryan could well have demons of his own to battle, and John had to remember that. If a friend, and just a friend, was what Bryan needed, then John would do his best to give it to him.

JOHN was waiting when Meghan came home that night, on time for a change.

She paused just inside the door, regarding him with more than a little suspicion. "Lying in wait?" She closed and locked the door behind her, putting her purse on the table just inside.

John indicated the far end of the sofa with a nod. "Have a seat," he said. "We need to talk."

Meghan sighed as she crossed over to sit. "Look, John, I know what you're going to—"

"I'm attracted to Bryan Simmons."

He knew his statement would stop her in midstream, and it did. Her eyes widened, and then she smiled. "Well, I knew *that*," she said, lowering herself the rest of the way onto the cushions. "But I have to say I'm pretty damn thrilled to hear you admit it."

John rested his elbow on the back of the sofa and his head in his hand. "Took me a while to figure it out," he said. "Sometimes I need to be smacked upside the head. Which came in the form of him in shorts and a tank top, sweaty after a run."

Meghan's eyes widened. "Oh yeah, I think that would do the trick. He's a real cutie, and quite a body too." She let out a mock-exasperated sigh. "All the good ones really are married or gay, aren't they?"

"Not that the former stopped you," John said, gratified when he made her blush.

"That was different," she said. "His wife knew about it. Hell, she encouraged it, you know that." Meghan had spent almost two years in a friends-with-benefits arrangement with a man whose wife had a medical condition that left her unable to have sex. John didn't know the details, just that they'd only split up when Meghan had bought the restaurant and the house and moved from Atlanta to Tybee.

"Anyway," John said, shifting back to the original topic. "No, I don't know what I'm going to do about it. Spend some more time with him, I guess. Try to figure out if it's worth risking the friendship. And...." He paused. "And Karen told me today that something happened to Bryan a while back that affected him pretty strongly. I don't know what, but I think maybe I need to find out. Because if I do this, it's not going to be just some fling. I can't.... I *won't* do that, not to any of us."

Meghan nodded. "That's one of the things I've always loved about you, John," she said, so sincere that it almost brought tears to his eyes. "You don't pussyfoot around. You work through things so methodically and carefully." She grinned. "Okay, maybe sometimes a little too carefully."

John grinned back and nodded in acknowledgment.

"But you know me, too much by-the-seat-of-the-pants and not enough planning."

John sat up straight and lifted his eyebrows. "Which brings us to the second half of our conversation," he said. "You've never had trouble being impulsive before, Meggie. Why all the foot-dragging over Kai?"

Meghan closed in on herself, both figuratively and literally, pulling her feet up onto the sofa and wrapping her arms around her knees. "I don't know," she said. "I think... don't laugh, but I think maybe I'm scared." She almost smiled, her eyes wide. "You said it, Johnny. I'm all impulse, and look where that got me. A stupid marriage that was over almost before it started, a string of what amounted to one-night stands, and a relationship with a married man that never required anything approaching real intimacy."

John nodded. "And you think Kai would mean more than that," he said. "And that scares you."

Meghan laughed. "Listen to us," she said. "We sound like a couple of teenaged girls instead of two grown-ass adults in our thirties. What the fuck are we so afraid of?"

John laughed too. "That's easy," he said. "Getting our hearts broken. And that's harder now than it is at sixteen when you've got a crush on the captain of the football team." Meghan raised an eyebrow at him, and he nodded. "Yep. Didn't figure it out until college, though."

Meghan laughed. "So, what, we should get off our duffs and take a chance?" she asked. "And what happens when we fall right back down on them?"

"Pick yourself up, brush yourself off, and start all over again." John smiled as he quoted the classic song, and Meghan smiled back.

"So can we make a pact?" John asked. "I'll figure out if I'm ready for something with Bryan, and if I'm really interested. You seriously consider Kai as an option. You know he practically worships the ground you walk on, so his feelings aren't really an issue here."

Meghan nodded her agreement and unfurled herself, holding out a hand. "Secret handshake?"

"Oh crap, hope I remember it!" John stuck out his hand and grabbed Meghan's, the two of them going through a complicated serious of twists and thumb-bumps making up the handshake they'd developed when John was six and Meghan thirteen. They only fumbled once, laughing at themselves when they did.

"You know," John said as they dropped back against the armrests, still snickering a little, "I should teach that to Beth and Jeremy. I bet they'd love it."

"And Bryan," she said. "He needs to be in the club too."

"And Bryan," John said. He grinned wickedly. "Great chance to touch him in a completely appropriate way too."

Meghan rolled her eyes and pushed to her feet. "Men," she sighed out. "Always thinking with their libidos."

"You know it." John stood up as well. "And you love it too. At least when the libido's being directed toward you, you do."

It was Meghan's turn to grin. "That I do," she said. "Only what are we going to do if we both want to bring our guys back here at the same time?"

John pretended to ponder for a moment. "I wonder how well we could soundproof the bedroom walls?"

Meghan laughed and shoved at his chest. "Go to bed, you perv," she said. "Dream of pretty men, and I'll try to do the same."

John reached out farther to pull her into a quick hug. "Night, Meggie," he said. "Thanks for being you."

"You're welcome," she replied into his chest. "And ditto."

JOHN spent much of Thursday thinking about his next move. He'd see Bryan on Monday at the picnic, but he figured he should do something before then. Talk to him, spend a little more time with him, something. He considered and discarded a few ideas—dinner would be too much like a date for this point, but going down to the sports bar to watch a game wouldn't let them talk—before he settled on an idea he liked. He let it tumble around his brain for a while before deciding, and he waited until dinner was done and Beth off to bed before he picked up the phone. He didn't have a direct number for Bryan, a cell phone or anything like that, but he had the number to the bed-and-breakfast.

"Sea Breeze." John smiled at Bryan's voice when he answered the phone.

"Hey, Bryan, it's John," he said.

"John! Hey," Bryan replied. "How are you?"

"Good. Been having a pretty quiet week, for the most part. How goes the painting?"

Bryan blew out a breath. "Almost done," he said. "We'd hoped to finish up today, but we've got one more coat on the baseboards. We decided to knock off tonight and finish up in the morning. It'll have time to dry before the guests start arriving."

"Sounds perfect," John said. "We saw Karen and Jeremy at the park yesterday."

Bryan laughed. "Oh yes, Jeremy went on about it at length when they got home. *Great* length. *Five-year-old excitement* length."

John chuckled. "So you're saying he's still talking about it."

"In his sleep, yep." John could picture the wide smile on Bryan's face. "I'm betting you're dealing with the little girl equivalent over there."

"Definitely. Beth was bouncing off the walls all evening. Barely got her to sleep last night. And all she's talked about today has been going back again. Do you know if they'll be there tomorrow?"

"If it doesn't rain," Bryan said. Clouds had still been threatening that day, but not a drop had fallen. "So to what do we owe the distinct pleasure of a phone call?"

John braced himself. "I was wondering if you and Jeremy might like to have a play date this weekend," he said. "Have you ever been to the Marine Science Center?"

"Many, many years ago," Bryan answered with a laugh. "But I don't know if Jeremy has. Not that it matters. I'm sure he'll love it either way."

"Beth definitely does," John said. "She'll just stand and watch the turtles for hours if I let her. And sometimes, I'm tempted. When she's being particularly hyper and even SpongeBob won't hold her attention."

"I'd love to take Jeremy to the Georgia Aquarium sometime," Bryan said. "I went about a year and a half ago. Have you been?"

"Not long after it opened," John replied. "Some of the exhibits weren't up yet. I should go back sometime and take Beth now that she's old enough to appreciate it." He paused. "I actually have to go up for a week a couple of weeks from now. Maybe I'll take her then." He thought about inviting Bryan and maybe Jeremy along but stopped himself. *Too much, too soon*, he thought.

"Well, this weekend would be great for the science center," Bryan said. "I have something early Saturday morning, but I'll be done by around lunchtime. You want to meet up here, since it's closer? Maybe around one?"

"Sounds perfect." John smiled. "I hope your morning activity won't wear you out too much. You'll need to keep your energy up."

He put an undercurrent into the words on purpose, trying out a mild flirtiness that gave the words another layer of meaning. Bryan's pause before replying made him think that maybe the message got through.

"I think I'll be fine," Bryan said. "Although I might need a nap by the time we're done."

John's mind flashed on an image of a relaxed—and naked—Bryan stretched out on his bed, sleeping, sheets twined around him, covering only the most private parts. He had to blink hard to push the image away. *Holy crap*, he thought. *If he can do this to me and we haven't even so much as touched like that....*

"So we'll see you Saturday?" Bryan's voice pulled John's attention back.

"We'll be there," he replied. "Oh, and tell Karen if it rains tomorrow, she and Jeremy are welcome to come over here. One of the extra bedrooms is set up as a sort of playroom for Beth, so they'll have plenty to keep them occupied."

"Will do." Bryan's voice was warm, and he softened his tone for his next words. "Talk to you soon, John."

"Goodnight, Bryan." John found himself matching Bryan's gentle tone, and when they hung up, he found himself smiling just as softly.

WHEN John woke up from a sound sleep a few hours later, the smile was gone. He lay on his back, arms and legs spread wide, fingers clutched into the sheets as if holding a lifeline. His entire body felt strung as tight as a piano wire. His throat was raw as if he'd been screaming, and his dick was hard enough to drive nails.

He couldn't remember details of the dream. Bryan was there, and, off in the distance somewhere, Liz. He could feel phantom touches on his skin, burning like fire, and it was clear his subconscious remembered something, if his state of arousal was anything to go by.

He should *not* masturbate to mental images of Bryan. Not until he figured things out. But he didn't seem to have any choice. He was so close that he half expected to explode with just one stroke, but he managed to get his cock out of his boxers with one shaking hand and take a solid grip without losing it. He didn't tease himself, just stroked hard and fast, and in less than a minute he was coming, his mouth open in a silent groan, eyes pressed shut, Bryan's eyes filling his mind.

He collapsed back onto the mattress, breathing harsh, and tried to reassemble his brain.

Dammit, he thought once he could think again. He'd let the horse out the barn now, and keeping himself from deliberately jerking off to thoughts of Bryan was going to be a thousand times harder.

Sighing, he reached for the box of tissues on his bedside table, cleaning himself up and dropping the soiled tissues into the trash can nearby. He adjusted his boxers and rolled onto his side, staring at the window, which was cracked open a few inches as usual. A light breeze stirred the sheer curtains, and he watched them dance in the glow of the streetlight outside.

He didn't remember falling asleep.

Chapter 10

FRIDAY, it rained.

John sat in his office and listened to the drops hitting the old-fashioned tin roof that still covered that side of the house. A steady stream of water ran off the edge and dropped straight down to the ground below. Replacing the roof and adding gutters was the next big thing on their home fix-ups list, but they'd been told they had a few more years before it would become necessary, so they'd decided to hold off for now.

John found the sounds soothing. The house they'd lived in when he was a child had had a tin roof, and he remembered falling asleep to the low pinging the raindrops made as they hit the metal surface. It wasn't as peaceful as the sound of the waves he could hear off in the distance most days, but it was still comforting.

Beth had woken up that morning with a tummy ache and a low-grade fever, so he and Meghan had decided to keep her home and in bed. She'd fallen asleep again almost immediately, a sure sign that she really was sick, but when she woke up a few hours later, while she still didn't feel well, the fever was gone. John called to give Karen the bad news—neither of them wanted to expose Jeremy in case Beth was contagious—and before leaving to get the restaurant ready for the busy weekend, Meghan set her up on the sofa in the living room with a blanket and a Disney movie.

A big yawn split John's face wide. He'd slept well but not long enough, and all the caffeine in the world wasn't going to help. He stood up and stretched, walking out of the office and down the short hallway to check on Beth. She sat engrossed in *Cars*, one of her favorites, and John smiled and walked over to sit at the far end of the sofa to watch with her. After just a minute or two, Beth shifted and crawled across the cushions, climbing into John's lap and leaning back against his chest, like she used to all the time when she was a little younger. John's heart ached as he wrapped an arm around her to hold her in place, but it was a good ache.

They watched the rest of the movie like that, and John didn't think he stopped smiling the entire time.

JOHN slept like a log that night and woke up early Saturday morning feeling better rested and more refreshed than he had all week long. *Typical*, he thought. *The one day of the week I could sleep in, and I'm awake at dawn.*

Being up so early gave him a chance to do one of his favorite things: go down to the beach and watch the sunrise. Beth wouldn't be awake for at least another hour, especially since she was still recovering from whatever little bug she'd had the day before. Meghan would be up around eight to head into the restaurant, earlier than during the off-season.

Moving quietly so as not to wake them, John slipped into swim trunks and a T-shirt and pulled on socks and sneakers. Sliding his keys, wallet, and cell phone into his pockets, he headed toward the water under the lightening skies. The clouds from the day before had disappeared, and it promised to be a gorgeous day. Probably hot too, but they'd be in the air-conditioned comfort of the Marine Science Center part of the time. John planned to invite Bryan and Jeremy for a walk out on the pier and maybe along the beach once the kids got tired of the animals. The center was small, but Beth loved the touch tank, where crabs, small rays, and other marine life were available for kids to pet.

Crossing the last street at the edge of the island, John climbed the wooden steps leading across the dunes and onto the beach below. As the water came into sight, he could see two figures standing ankle-deep in the surf, boards under their arms, talking about something. After a few seconds, they both waded out farther, dropping the boards and climbing onto them, stroking out toward the breakers.

John smiled as he settled on the bottom step to watch. Surfing wasn't common at Tybee, since the waves weren't anything to write home about, but John knew Kai liked to go out sometimes. He couldn't tell who the two men were for sure—at least, from here they both seemed to be men—but one of them was about Kai's height and seemed to have his broad, muscular build. John had no idea who the other man might be but watched as he turned to catch a low wave, rising to his feet, gliding across the water. It wasn't a long ride or a fancy one, but it was smooth and steady, and he dropped back down to the board with an easy grace as it moved into shallower water. He slipped off the side and stood up, turning back to yell something to Kai before gathering up his board and walking up the beach.

Between the increasing light and the man's proximity, John could recognize then that it was Bryan. As he watched, transfixed, Bryan shook his head, throwing off droplets of water in all directions, then wiped his face with one hand. He bent to grab a sports bottle that sat in the sand next to a pair of shoes, and John's mouth went dry as the move stretched Bryan's swimsuit tight over his ass. Bryan came back up and tilted his head back to pour water into his mouth, and John couldn't look away.

"Holy hell, he is *hot*," John murmured.

Almost as if he'd heard him, even though John knew he was too far away, Bryan froze in place and then turned, catching sight of John where he sat staring. Bryan grinned and waved his free hand, bending to set his water bottle back down and then walking in John's direction. John fought for composure, but watching Bryan's muscles flex as he moved, bare chest still glistening with sea water, wasn't doing much to help him get himself under control.

"Hey!" Bryan said as he came within speaking distance. "Come out to take a surf lesson?"

He grinned, and John laughed at the unexpected question. "No, just woke up early and came to watch the sunrise," he said. He let his eyes run down Bryan's body and back up, just once and without pausing to take in any particular sights. "So this is your morning activity you mentioned?"

Bryan's eyes flashed just enough to tell John that he'd noted John's look. He glanced back over his shoulder to where Kai was just coming back onto the sand. "Yeah, I ran into Kai out here early one morning about two months ago," he said, turning back to grin at John again. "He's been giving me irregular surfing lessons ever since."

John nodded in Kai's direction. "Well, don't let me stop you," he said. "I'm just going to sit here until the sun's fully up and then go over to Tradewinds for coffee." He smiled at Bryan. "Still on for one?"

"Yep, wouldn't miss it!" Bryan flashed him another of his giant grins. "We'll get you on a board one of these days, Johnny Boy," he said, laughing as John rolled his eyes. Bryan turned to jog back toward Kai and their boards, and John watched him go, a small smile playing along his lips. Bryan always made him laugh. That was one of the things John loved about him.

His mind caught up with the thought he'd just had. "Love?" he whispered. *Holy shit.* He wasn't even sure he was ready to date the guy. He'd known him for a little over a week. No freaking way did he love him, not in any form.

He pushed the whole idea aside and turned to face the horizon, watching the sun rise higher in the sky.

AN HOUR later, coffee in hand, John stepped through the front door of the house and paused, listening. Not a peep. Meghan and Beth must still be out.

John knew just how to wake Meghan up. She might be the professional chef, but he'd learned a thing or two over the years. And one of them was how to make French toast that was to die for.

He gathered up the ingredients, glad to find they had part of a loaf of Italian bread, and pulled out the electric griddle. Whisking together eggs and milk while the griddle heated, John let his mind wander. His encounter with Bryan that morning had been unexpected but had helped him solidify what he wanted. The L-word turning up in his thoughts shouldn't have been a surprise. He'd always been one to fall hard and fast, and he knew that could get him hurt. But somehow he trusted Bryan. He didn't believe he'd do anything to hurt him on purpose, and if he did accidentally, he'd do what he could to fix it.

John dipped thick slices of bread into the egg mixture, giving them a light dusting of nutmeg before setting them on the griddle, where they sizzled a little as they cooked. He made six pieces, knowing Beth wouldn't be able to eat two, but he'd finish her second one. He poked around in the refrigerator as the toast cooked, coming up with a near-empty package of bacon. Sliding the toast to one side, he added the bacon strips, knowing if that smell didn't rouse Meghan, it might take an atomic bomb.

Sure enough, he heard footsteps on the stairs less than five minutes later, and Meghan shuffled in. She still had on her glasses, which meant she really *was* barely out of bed. She hated glasses, so putting in contacts was one of the first things she did in the morning.

"Morning, sleepyhead," John said. Meghan was a tea drinker most mornings, so he hadn't bothered making coffee, but he did reach over to turn on the burner under the kettle that lived on the stove. Meghan mumbled something that might have been thanks and fumbled a mug and a teabag out of the cabinet. She preferred loose tea, but morning wasn't always conducive to anything complicated, as John knew well from his own history of morning coffee disasters.

Meghan plopped onto a chair and yawned widely. "Bacon," she said, and John laughed.

"Yes, bacon," he said. "And French toast." He reached over with a foot to nudge hers. "You think you're awake enough to go rouse the munchkin? She and I have a play date this afternoon."

That got Meghan's attention. She gave him what would've been a wicked smile had she been awake. "With Bryan?"

"Bryan and Jeremy," John clarified. "We're taking the kids to the Marine Science Center."

"Love that place," Meghan said, pausing for another yawn. "The center itself may not be great shakes, but they do good work."

John nodded, flipping the toast. "We should see if they have something Beth could do this summer," he said. "We haven't gotten her signed up for any camps yet. Oh," he interrupted himself, turning back to face Meghan. "You don't have anything planned with Beth week after next, do you? I keep forgetting to ask. Adam wants me to come up and work on the year-end reports, and I thought I'd take Beth up to visit the Butlers, if they're free."

Meghan shrugged. "No plans," she said. Her kettle started whistling, and she got up and put together her tea. "Let me go get Bethy up. Does she know about the trip yet?"

"No, needed to talk to you and the Butlers first," John said, transferring the finished toast and bacon to the three plates he'd pulled down. "I'll get her some juice. You want some?"

"Sure." Meghan set her tea down at her usual spot at the table and disappeared around the corner toward the stairs.

John cut up Beth's toast and added just a little syrup, then set all three plates and the syrup bottle on the table. He grabbed silverware and napkins and poured juice for all three of them, finishing up just as Meghan returned, leading a groggy Beth by the hand.

"Morning, sweetie," John said, lifting Beth up for a hug and a kiss on her forehead before helping her into her seat. "Made you some French toast, and you've got juice too."

Beth just nodded and picked up her fork, sticking it into a piece of toast and lifting it to her mouth, chewing slowly. John frowned and reached over to lay the back of his hand on her forehead. "You feel okay, honey?"

Beth shrugged and kept eating slowly. Her skin didn't feel hot, though John knew that wasn't the best judge. But even just woken up, Beth was never this withdrawn unless she didn't feel well.

"I think maybe we need to stay home today, baby," John said, cupping his hand over the back of Beth's hand. "Just to be sure you're all better, okay? We don't want to go out and get you all sick again."

Beth did look up at him then. "But what about Jeremy?"

John almost regretted telling her about their planned play date today, but she'd been so happy despite being sick yesterday that he couldn't, even if he had to disappoint her now. "Tell you what, Bethy," he said. "I'll call Mister Bryan, and if it's okay with them—and if you feel better—then we'll go tomorrow. Okay? The crabs and turtles will still be there then."

Beth frowned but nodded slowly. "Can I watch Kermit?"

John laughed. "Yes, you can watch Kermit." He'd bought the first two seasons of *The Muppet Show* for Beth's birthday the month before, and while she didn't understand it all, she loved Kermit. And unlike a lot of the kids' shows and movies she liked, this one didn't grate on his nerves.

Meghan had stayed silent while they talked, working her way through her breakfast and finishing her tea quickly. "I need to get going," she said, more awake now. "I told Kai to be in early so we can get the crepe filling made. It takes a little longer than I expected."

John winked at her. "Maybe you could plan to take advantage of the alone time in a couple of weeks," he said. "Remember, we have a deal."

Meghan rolled her eyes as she set her dirty dishes in the sink. "Yeah, yeah, put up or shut up," she said. She stopped to drop a kiss on the top of Beth's head. "Feel better, sweetie," she said before heading upstairs.

John turned back to his own breakfast. "When we're done, we'll get you washed up and changed, and I'll put Kermit on for you," he said. "Then I need to call Mister Bryan. Okay?"

Beth nodded, picking at another bit of toast, and John watched her as he ate. He hoped this was just a holdover from whatever bug had laid her up yesterday and not something more serious. He knew kids got sick a lot, but that never made him feel any better when it was his kid who was feeling rotten.

THE call to Bryan had been quick, John apologizing and explaining, Bryan being understanding and funny as usual. John had hung up smiling after arranging to try their plans again on Sunday and then taken a few minutes to call Liz's parents and find out that, yes, they'd be "delighted!" to have Beth visit them. The exclamation came from Liz's mother, Jean, her father being much more stoic about things.

Now John sat in the small sunroom off the living room in an old, comfortable, overstuffed chair, legs propped on an equally broken-in ottoman, reading. Beth had watched three episodes of Muppets before dozing off on the sofa, and John had been checking in on her for the past hour, able to do so from where he sat just by leaning around the back of the chair.

Even so, he found it hard to concentrate, just as he had for most of the week. He still wasn't sure why he was so bothered by all of this. Yes, he had legitimate reasons to be uncertain. He hadn't had a real relationship since Liz died. He wasn't convinced he was ready to have one, but he also didn't know whether he'd ever be sure. He didn't want to start something and have it fall apart, not when the kids were already involved. He couldn't do that to Beth, or even Jeremy.

And then there was the gender issue. John had double-checked his personal feelings several times during the week, and he'd never found a trace of concern about being attracted to a man. What worried him were outer influences: how others would react. Not so much for himself, but because of Beth. Tybee was not Atlanta, and he knew he'd find much more resistance here than in the city. He didn't want Beth exposed to the kind of hatred that existed out there until it was unavoidable. But he also didn't want to live in fear. His personal life was his personal business.

John closed the book when he realized he'd read the same paragraph four times and couldn't remember a single word. He thought about trying a different book, or maybe a magazine, but he knew the reading material wasn't the problem. He just wasn't going to be able to focus all that well until he dealt with what was going on in his head.

He thought suddenly about Vicky. If Beth were better in the morning, they'd go to church as usual. It was one of Beth's favorite times of the week, between playing with friends and singing the songs she loved, so John hoped she'd feel up to it. And maybe he could get a few minutes with Vicky. He wasn't sure how he'd approach the subject without giving himself away entirely, which he didn't want to do before he had a chance to talk to Bryan. He knew he should feel comfortable confiding in his pastor, and he had in the past, but this felt different. Maybe because he didn't know how she'd react. The Episcopal church leaned liberal on gay rights, but individual pastors and congregations had their own opinions, and he'd never gotten much of an impression of how this church would handle it.

Not that it mattered. He wouldn't want to be part of a church that wouldn't accept him. If he had to leave, he would. But he hoped—

prayed, really—that it wouldn't come to that. He might not be the most religious person in the world, but he liked the church, and he didn't want to feel as if it was rejecting him.

He shook his head, trying to dispel his concerns. No sense getting the cart before the horse. He'd deal with this one step at a time.

He glanced at his watch and decided to throw together some sandwiches for lunch. Beth would be happy with PB&J, and maybe he'd do the same. It had been a while since he had, and he felt the need for some comfort food.

Chapter 11

THE parking lot next to the church was more crowded than usual Sunday morning, and John supposed tourists in town for the holiday weekend were the reason. He held Beth's hand tightly as they walked toward the door, keeping an eye out for people unfamiliar with the area who might barrel into the lot too fast for the pedestrians making their way toward the door.

Beth caught sight of Sarah and her mom at the same moment John did and began bouncing on her toes. "Can I go with Sarah, Daddy?" she asked, but John didn't let go.

"Wait until we get inside, honey," he said. "We'll see if we can sit with Sarah and her parents again like last week, okay?"

To his relief, Beth had woken up this morning her usual happy and energetic self. John could even admit that the relief was only partly because he worried about his daughter; the rest was that he wouldn't need to cancel on Bryan again.

The thought of seeing Bryan in just a few hours had his body on full alert. He kept trying to push everything back, but he was having a tough time of it. He hadn't been affected by someone like this in so long, really since he'd met Liz. That had been close to love at first sight, and they'd been nearly inseparable from then on. He'd never so much as looked at anyone else after that, except those few lost months after Liz died.

He found he enjoyed the feeling. The rush of anticipation, hopefulness. Imagining how Bryan might react if John made his intentions clear. *When*, he told himself. *You're going to do this. No ifs.*

Inside the small sanctuary, John settled in with Beth next to him and Sarah on the far side of her, her parents beyond. John glanced at the bulletin and smiled as he saw the list of hymns started with one of his favorites, "Morning Has Broken." The pianist started with the opening of the old Cat Stevens arrangement before moving into the straightforward version that was in the hymnal. It felt more like being at a concert than being in church.

John let the music wash over him as they sang, using one hand to help support the hymnal he shared with Beth. This was what he liked best about church services. His faith was personal, and he didn't like the way some people seemed to show off how often they were inside church doors, especially when they also didn't seem to carry out their beliefs in the rest of their lives. John was no zealot, but he believed in treating people well and doing the right thing by everyone as much as he could.

And that was why he had to talk to Bryan. Hiding his feelings would feel like a lie, and any friendship they might build would be based on that falsehood. *A house built on sand*, John thought as Vicky read the morning scripture. *Destined to fail.*

When the service ended and people started heading toward the parish hall, John took Beth's hand and followed, both of them greeting others as they walked. Once they were in the long, open room, Beth dashed over to join Sarah and her other friends where they were pulling out the coloring books and crayons again. John smiled as he watched them, then took a breath and walked over to the vicar.

"Good morning, Vicky," he said. "I don't suppose I could speak to you in private for a few minutes?"

Vicky smiled at him. "Of course, John," she said. She tilted her head toward the far wall. "Why don't we step into my office?"

Her office was a tiny room off to the side of the parish hall, down a short hallway from the main room, the separation making it more private. Inside, Vicky ignored the chair behind the desk and instead sat in one of the two chairs facing it, waving a hand to indicate John should take the other.

He sat and was silent for a few long moments. He finally blew out a breath. "I don't know what to say, so I'm just going to say it," he said. "I'm seriously considering starting a new relationship. And I haven't done that since my wife died, and that's a big part of why I'm struggling with the idea. But the other part is...." He stopped before plunging ahead. "The other part is that it would be with another man."

Vicky, to her credit, only let a flash of surprise cross her face. "Which part of that would you like to address first?"

John smiled. "I've pretty much come to terms with the second part," he said. "I've known since high school that I wasn't strictly straight. I even had a boyfriend for a while in college. Before I met Liz, of course." He shrugged. "I know it's not as simple here. A lot of people are pretty conservative, especially when it comes to homosexuality." He gave Vicky a look. "I'm not sure, but I don't think you or this church fall into that category."

Vicky shook her head. "No, not at all," she said. "I don't believe that Scripture forbids homosexuality. I've done a lot of reading and struggled with it, because so many people do teach that it does, but the words used in passages like the ones in Leviticus, if you go back to the original Hebrew, actually refer to homosexual *prostitution*, not homosexuality in general. The laws were written to forbid acts of pure sexual lust of any kind, between any partners." She smiled. "Only Paul specifically wrote against homosexuality, and in the same chapter he also stated that no one should ever have sex, for any reason. Not even procreation."

John raised an eyebrow. "So you're saying if early Christians had followed all of Paul's teachings to the letter, they would've died out within a generation?"

Vicky nodded. "Exactly. Although in Paul's defense, many of them also believed Christ's return would happen within a generation, so they felt no need to procreate." She leaned forward, folding her hands together on one knee. "I know you'll have some difficulty if you do pursue this relationship. It's probably inevitable. But it won't happen here, not through official channels. And if you have problems with other parishioners, please ask them to speak to me."

John nodded his agreement, and Vicky went on. "As to the other part of your concerns, how do you feel when you think about Liz and the possibility of a new relationship?"

John lowered his head, letting it hang loose on his neck. "A little guilt," he said. "A little longing. I do feel like I'd be betraying her, but I know that's not true, and it's not the focus." He lifted his head. "I'm concerned about making sure anyone I might have a serious relationship with understands that Liz will always be a part of me. I'm not going to forget her or stop loving her."

"And do you believe the man you're considering will understand that?"

John hesitated before nodding. "I don't know him all that well yet," he said. "But from what I do know of him, he's warm and thoughtful and very loving. I don't think that'll be an issue."

"But you never know until you try, right?" Vicky smiled, and John had to return it.

"You know, I'm glad I'm not Catholic," John teased. "Not just because this conversation would never happen, but because most Episcopal priests are married, so you get it."

Vicky laughed and patted his arm. "Nothing is ever certain," she said. "But you try, and if it doesn't work, you try again."

John nodded. "I'm going to try," he said. He smiled again. "I'll do my best to keep you from having to help pick up the pieces."

WHEN John and Beth got back home, John found a note on the refrigerator door from Meghan. *Chicken salad sandwiches in the refrigerator. See you tonight—I hope*, it read, and John laughed softly. He hadn't seen Meghan the night before, just heard her come in sometime after midnight. Holiday weekends were always busy at the restaurant, and the rest of the summer wouldn't be much calmer.

He got Beth changed out of her Sunday clothes and settled her at the table with a sandwich cut into quarters and a small pile of carrot sticks along with a glass of milk. He joined her a couple of minutes later with his own lunch, drinking tea instead of milk.

Beth swung her legs and grinned up at him. "We get to see the turtles today?"

John nodded. Beth loved the turtles more than anything else at the Marine Science Center. "And then maybe go out on the pier," he said. "We'll see what Jeremy and Mister Bryan want to do."

Beth nodded and turned her attention back to her sandwich. John watched her. Beth had no memories of her mother, of course, but John had been careful to tell her stories, show her pictures, make sure she knew as much as she could. He needed to be careful with her when it came to Bryan. He didn't want her to think that he didn't care about her mother anymore.

But that would wait until he knew if this would go anywhere. No sense starting things that might not even need to be dealt with.

The phone rang, and John swallowed the bite of sandwich in his mouth, washing it down with a swig of tea as he stood up. Crossing over to the counter, he picked up the phone hanging on the wall. "Hello?"

"Hi, John." Bryan's voice filled John's ear. "I just wanted to call and make sure Beth's feeling all right today."

John smiled, warmth spreading through his chest. "She's just fine," he said. "Back to her usual where-does-she-get-that-energy self."

Bryan laughed. "Back to a typical five-year-old, then," he said. "I wanted to be sure we were still on for today before I said anything to Jeremy. He's been known to get a major pout on before."

"We're good." John turned to watch Beth chew on a carrot stick. "We're having lunch, but we still should be over there by one."

"Great! We'll see you then." Bryan sounded awfully enthusiastic about their plans, and as they hung up, John wondered if Bryan was having some of the same thoughts he was. He couldn't help but hope so. It would make things a lot easier.

JOHN thought he'd be fine seeing Bryan today. He'd seen him shirtless and wet the day before, and nothing else could hit him as hard as that, could it?

Not so much, he thought when he caught sight of Bryan and his stomach started turning in circles.

Bryan sat on the front steps of the bed-and-breakfast, watching Jeremy as he ran around the grass in front of him, arms out to his sides, playing airplane. Bryan wore loose cargo shorts and a T-shirt, with sneakers on his feet, and he had a small smile on his face as he watched his nephew. Nothing special, nothing fancy, and yet he still looked gorgeous to John. To John's body, too, and he had to take a deep breath and concentrate to keep himself from getting visibly excited.

Bryan caught his gaze just then, and he smiled wide, nearly undoing every one of John's efforts to rein himself in. "Hey!" He stood up and ran a hand across his butt to brush away dust from the steps, and John forced his mind away from *that* image.

He summoned up a smile back. "Hey!" Beth was tugging on his hand by then, and he looked down and laughed before letting her run off to join Jeremy. He turned his attention back to Bryan, who stood a couple of steps up. His face was partly in shadow, so John couldn't see his eyes clearly, but he was still smiling.

"Ready to spend a little time with the turtles?" John asked, and Bryan laughed softly.

"I've heard conflicting reports about this place," he said, stepping down to where John stood on the sidewalk. "It's either a cool little place for kids to enjoy or the most overrated tourist attraction in history."

John grinned, shaking his head. "It's somewhere in between," he said. "If you're expecting anything like an actual aquarium, you'll be disappointed. It's small marine animals in basic aquarium tanks, with a few more interesting things like a touch tank with crabs. The kids will love it, but I doubt it'll last more than an hour or so." He paused. "I was thinking once they get tired of it, we could go up on the pier, if it's not too crowded. There's a snack bar, so we can get the kids snow cones or something."

Bryan raised a knowing eyebrow. "Somehow I get the impression it's not the kids who'll be wanting the snow cone." He shoved his hands into his pockets and seemed to lean forward a little, close enough that John could feel his body heat.

John felt his cheeks warm, and not from embarrassment. "Yeah, well, we all have our guilty pleasures," he shot back. "You gonna tell me you wouldn't get one yourself?"

Bryan laughed. "Only if they don't have Screwballs," he said. "Raspberry sherbet with a gumball at the bottom? Heaven in a plastic, cone-shaped cup!"

John's mind gave him an image of Bryan sticking out a tongue reddened by the sweet treat, and a hot flash ran through him. *Down, boy*, he ordered himself, taking a step away from Bryan under the guise of turning toward the kids. "Hey, guys, you ready to go?" he called, and Beth and Jeremy changed their path and headed straight for them at full speed. John and Bryan exchanged a quick glance before dropping into matching squats to catch the kids as they barreled into them. Despite their preparation, both of them were still knocked back into the grass, and the four of them lay there laughing for a few minutes before John could compose himself and sit up.

"All right, you crazed lunatics," he said, pushing to his feet. "Let's go while I still have the energy to walk over there."

Beth and Jeremy scrambled up, but Bryan just sat up and held out a hand. "Help me up?" he asked, and John could hear the challenge in his voice. Yeah, Bryan felt it. And it seemed he knew John did too.

John took the hand and tugged. He didn't do much to help Bryan up, but the charge of electricity from their joined hands was more than enough for him right then. Anything else and he'd be getting ahead of himself again. He grinned and gave Bryan's hand one tiny squeeze before letting go, and Bryan returned the smile.

John turned back to the kids. "Hands," he called out, holding one out as he headed in their direction, feeling Bryan close behind. "No letting go until we get there."

Beth took his hand and smiled up at him, then reached out her other hand to take Jeremy's. "We all hold hands!" she said, and John looked up to catch Bryan's eye. They smiled again, Bryan reaching for Jeremy's free hand, and the four of them headed down the sidewalk. They'd made it maybe ten feet before Bryan started… singing.

"We're off to see the turtles, the wonderful turtles of Oz." He swung Jeremy's hand and gave a little half skip as he sang. "If ever a wonderful turtle there was, the turtles of Oz are one because—"

John cracked up, and Bryan followed, unable to keep up the silly serenade anymore. He let Jeremy and Beth take over, making up even sillier songs as they walked along toward the beach.

THE shift from bright sunshine to low lighting left John blinking and waiting for his eyes to adjust when they stepped inside the Marine Science Center. The center's main purpose was research and education about the kinds of marine life that lived along the shore, so the small animal displays weren't a primary focus. Bryan had paid for their admissions before John could even protest, shooting him a quick grin.

"You can get the next one," he said, and John's heart pounded a little faster as he thought that maybe the "next one" would be an actual date, not a testing-the-waters pseudo-date under the guise of a play date for the kids.

He and Bryan followed Beth and Jeremy through the rooms of the center, pausing to let them point things out or exclaim over something they found *terribly* exciting. More than once the two men exchanged knowing smiles or even eyerolls as the kids chattered. After their third trip to the touch pool, though, they started to wind down. Beth stopped in front of a tank of turtles and watched them crawl for a few minutes, her fourth such visit since they'd arrived, but soon she turned to John and reached for his hand. "Can we get ice cream, Daddy?"

John grinned over at Bryan. "At this point, any kind of cold dessert is ice cream," he explained. "She knows the difference, she just doesn't bother."

Bryan nodded and grinned as he looked around. Jeremy stood with his face close to a tank full of tropical fish, and Bryan walked over and bent down to say something to the little boy. John's gaze drifted over to Bryan's backside. He thought about what it would look like naked and had to quash that line of thinking fast.

Kids corralled, the two men stepped back outside into the bright sunshine, squinting against the light and reaching in tandem for the sunglasses they had hung on the necklines of their T-shirts. John nodded toward the steps to the pier, which sat only a few yards away.

"Brave the hordes?" he asked. He could see from where they stood that the whole area was busy, people milling around on the pier and walking by on the beach beyond.

"Lead the way." Bryan waved a hand to indicate John should go ahead, so John crossed the pavement to the steps and climbed up slowly, one hand on the rail and one holding Beth's hand, hearing Bryan admonish Jeremy behind them to hold on to the handrail.

The open area at the top of the stairs was wide and octagonal, rows of picnic tables on one side and a snack bar built into the shape of the space on the other, with open windows for service. John headed over there, getting in line behind the handful of people who were waiting their turn. Bryan and Jeremy joined them a few seconds later.

"Not too bad," John said, nodding toward the line. "I've been out here when there were dozens in line. You should see it on the Fourth of July, especially when it's on a weekend."

The people around them wore dozens of variations on summer beach gear, some holding ice cream or other items from the snack bar, some loaded down with chairs and bags and coolers, but most just seeming to be meandering with no specific goal in sight.

John caught Bryan's eye and smiled. "We're pretty spoiled, living so close to the beach," he said. "Tybee might not have the nightlife of Atlanta, but it's got its charms."

If he hadn't been looking at Bryan so closely, he might not have noticed the change in his expression when he mentioned Atlanta's nightlife. Bryan's eyes dimmed, as if clouds had passed over them. "Yeah," Bryan said, his voice a far cry from his usual bright optimism. "Sometimes quiet can be really good."

Chapter 12

JOHN remembered what Karen had said about Bryan's past, and he wondered what had happened to put that look on Bryan's face. He wanted to know. He wanted to know everything about Bryan, not just how he looked naked or what he felt like against John's body.

He caught Bryan's eye again. "Hey, you okay?"

Bryan gave a half smile. "Yeah," he said. "Just… some bad memories. Don't worry about it." He nodded toward the line, which had been inching forward. "You're up next."

John frowned as he turned to help Beth pick out her snack. He'd known that he needed to talk to Bryan, but it seemed Bryan needed to talk too. Whatever was going on with him, it wasn't nothing.

Beth chose a snow cone, as John suspected she would, and he got one of his own, blue raspberry to her bright red cherry. He turned and nodded Bryan and Jeremy ahead. "I'll get these, since you got the admission before," he said, and Bryan's face brightened as he smiled.

"Snow cone!" Jeremy bounced on his toes, and John snickered.

"This kid has springs in his feet like Tigger has in his tail," he said, and Bryan laughed as he gave his order. Turning his head back toward John, he nodded down at the little boy.

"I'd start calling him Tigger, but I think that would just encourage him," he said. He turned back and accepted the rainbow-colored snow cone from the server, handing it down to Jeremy. "Now be careful with that," he warned. "No second chances if you drop it."

John handed over the money for their snacks and led the two children over to a picnic table a few feet away to get them settled with their treats. He sat next to Beth, Jeremy across from them, and a few seconds later Bryan joined them, holding the promised Screwball and smiling widely, looking like his usual happy self again.

"Told you," he said, tipping the frozen treat up as if toasting with it. "If it's not a Screwball, it's a Rocket Pop."

John laughed. "I guess you go for the Pop Rocks or those candy sticks with the flavored powder too."

Bryan smiled wider and nodded, peeling off the lid and digging into the surface of the sherbet with the little wooden spoon that came with it. "All this newfangled sour and gummy stuff, you can have it," he said firmly. "It's all about the classics for me."

"Good man," John said, lifting his snow cone in a mock-toast of his own.

They fell into comfortable near-silence as the four worked on their treats, each of the men having to pause to wipe up syrup spills and occasionally warn the kids to be more careful. John expected Beth to stop eating before she finished hers, since the cold usually got to be too much for her. Sure enough, two thirds of the way through, she swallowed and sighed loudly, holding the paper cup toward her dad.

"I'm stuffed," she said in an affected tone of voice that made John snicker as he took the remaining snow cone from her.

"Wait here and let me throw these away," he said, down to the dregs of his own cone. He stood up and stepped over the few feet to a trash can, tossing the remains of their snacks and pausing to wipe residual syrup off his hands with a napkin, throwing that out as well. He turned to find Bryan standing just a couple of feet behind him, and he sucked in a surprised breath. He'd done well at controlling his reactions, but he hadn't expected to find Bryan so close to him, and his body responded automatically. He felt a pull so strong that he almost gave in and touched Bryan the way he wanted to. He saw Bryan's eyes darken, his pupils widening, and that nearly broke his resolve.

Giving himself a mental shake, he took a step back and waved a hand toward the trash can. "All yours," he said, half of him hoping Bryan wouldn't hear the slight tremor in his voice. The other half still wanted to pull Bryan into his arms right then and there, but he couldn't let that happen.

He moved back over to the table where the kids sat jabbering back and forth about the turtles, and sat down, straddling the bench next to Beth. "You guys want to walk on the pier or the beach?"

"Pier!" Jeremy threw his hands up in the air, and John grinned at his never-ending exuberance.

"Okay, but gotta hold hands, okay?" John said. He stood up and helped Beth down from the bench, not looking at Bryan as he did the same with Jeremy. He took Beth's hand and a deep breath before glancing over at their companions. Bryan's eyes were shuttered again, guarded, and it made John's stomach clench to see it. He hated the thought that he'd put that look in Bryan's eyes, but he needed a little more time. And privacy.

He hoped he'd be able to get that soon.

AFTER letting the kids run around on the pier and then the beach for a while after that, John grabbed Beth around her middle as she passed by and turned her upside down, her ponytails hanging toward the sand. He caught Bryan's gaze and smiled. "We really need to get going," he said.

Bryan glanced at his watch, and his eyes widened in surprise. "Wow, I didn't realize it was after five already," he said. He reached out and snagged Jeremy in much the same way John had Beth, but instead of flipping him over, Bryan wrapped one arm around Jeremy's waist and spun them around in a circle. "You ready to head back to the house, Germy?"

"It's Jeremy!" Jeremy howled around his giggles, and John smiled as Beth cried out "Germy Germy Germy!" and then dissolved into giggles of her own when John flipped her back upright and got her on her feet. Bryan set Jeremy down too but grabbed for his hand immediately. He smiled at John, and John was glad to see the light back in his eyes.

"So I guess we'll see you guys for the cookout tomorrow?" he asked.

John nodded. "Any particular time?"

Bryan shrugged one shoulder. "We usually start setting things up around six, eat around seven," he said. "So any time in there is fine." He grinned wide. "You bringing pie again?"

John laughed. "Pie doesn't fare so well on the sand," he pointed out. "But I'll figure something out."

The four of them started heading toward home. They'd walked far enough along the beach that going back by Bryan's would be out of the way, though, so they parted ways at the first cross street.

"Say goodnight, Jeremy," Bryan said.

"Goodnight, Jeremy!" the boy yelled.

John snickered. "Please tell me you saw that one coming," he said.

Bryan was laughing too. "I swear, I didn't teach him that," he said. "I'm betting we can thank my sister for that one."

Still smiling, John looked down at Beth. "Tell Jeremy and Mister Bryan goodnight," he said, choosing his words more cautiously.

"Goodnight, Jeremy! Goodnight, Mister Bryan!" Beth waved her free hand wildly, and Jeremy waved back the same way, Bryan more sedately. Bryan shot John one more brief smile, lingering for just a moment longer than usual before turning and walking toward the house. John watched him go. He was getting tired of watching Bryan walk away from him. He'd much rather see him moving in John's direction.

MONDAY morning found John in the kitchen, searching through the pantry and refrigerator for inspiration. His exchange with Bryan the night before had him wanting to bake something to take to the picnic, but basic cookies or cupcakes just seemed too bland. On the other hand, no one could turn down a good old chocolate chip cookie.

He decided to ask the expert.

"Beth," he said, leaning across the table where she sat eating a bowl of cereal, "I'm going to make something sweet to take to the picnic. Like cookies or something. What do you think I should make?"

Her eyes widened. "Can you make those cupcakes? The chocolate ones?"

John started to ask which ones she meant when he remembered. A few months earlier, he'd tried making brownies in a mini cupcake pan, to make them work better as finger foods for a church function. They'd turned out beautifully, and Beth had loved them.

"You are so smart," he said, tousling her hair. "I'll do that. I think I might even have all the stuff."

He started going through the pantry again, pulling out flour, sugar, and cocoa powder, and then got out a bowl and the mini-muffin pan. When Meghan dashed through a few minutes later on her way to the restaurant, she paused and surveyed the items on the counter. "Feeling bakery-ish today?" she asked, and John smiled a little sheepishly.

"For the picnic," he said. "Bryan asked if I was bringing dessert again."

Meghan lifted one knowing eyebrow but, to her credit, didn't say a word. She just gave Beth a quick tickle and waved before heading out.

After breakfast, John got Beth dressed and set her up at the kitchen table with coloring books and crayons. He mixed up his favorite brownie recipe from memory, spooning the batter into the muffin pan. While the first pan baked, he sat down with Beth and, at her insistence, started coloring his own masterpiece.

Three batches of mini brownie muffins and a lunch break later, John searched for a plastic container big enough to hold them all, finally unearthing a rectangular one that he thought used to belong to his grandmother. It fit most of the brownies, and he left the remaining few behind for later.

With hours left to go before they were expected on the beach, John felt at loose ends. He hadn't worked out what he wanted to say to Bryan, but he had some general ideas. He decided to try to turn his mind off until they left, so he pulled out *The Muppet Movie*, something he knew would hold his attention as much as it would Beth's. They settled down on the sofa to watch it together, Beth curled into his side. John let the warm contentment wash over him, a feeling of peace that he hoped he could take with him that night. He might just end up needing it.

JOHN caught sight of Bryan the second he and Beth reached the top of the walkway over the dunes to the beach. It didn't hurt that he was shirtless, wearing only swim trunks, and laughing at something Davis was saying as they spread out a blanket on the sand, weighing down one side with a cooler and the other with their shoes. A small pile of equipment sat nearby, including two boxes with pieces of wood sticking out of the top and a shovel and bucket that John assumed were to dig out a spot for a fire pit and then douse the fire afterward. Fires were allowed on the beach, but they had to be a certain distance away from the dunes and any structures, such as the pier, and they had to be doused completely afterward.

Truthfully, the fire they'd have wouldn't qualify as a bonfire, John knew. More like a campfire. But it would be enough for atmosphere and marshmallow roasting.

Jeremy ran up, shouting for Beth to come play, and John looked over to see Karen and Anna sitting in lawn chairs off to one side, with Sarah and a couple of other kids playing in the sand beyond. He sent Beth off to join them and walked over to help the men. He laughed to himself at their typical gender role division, but he knew it didn't mean anything. After all, he and Bryan had been spending most of their time together taking care of the kids.

He hoped to change that part somewhat after tonight.

"Hey, guys," he said as he walked up. Bryan was bending to pick up something that John realized was a classic picnic basket, but he looked over his shoulder at John and smiled.

"Hey!" he said, moving the basket onto the blanket. "Glad you guys could make it." He glanced down at the bags in John's hands and nodded toward the blanket. "Just put your stuff down anywhere. We decided to go ahead and get the fire started before we eat, since we brought some hot dogs to roast." He put his hands on his hips and tilted his head. "How are your Boy Scout fire-starting skills?"

John laughed as he put his bags down on the blanket, fighting the urge to stare at Bryan's bare chest. "I hope that doesn't mean no one remembered to bring any matches."

"Nah, we like to show off our outdoorsy man skills," Davis replied. He bent to pick up the shovel and bucket and jerked his head off to one side. "C'mon, grab the wood and let's get this party started."

John and Bryan shared an amused look before each picking up one of the boxes of wood. Each held some split logs and a pile of twigs and branches, for kindling, John assumed.

"Don't worry," Bryan said as they walked over a few yards to where Davis had started flattening out an area for the fire. "We brought matches. Hell, I think Davis has one of those butane flame gun things. No rubbing sticks together necessary."

Unfortunately, John's mind took a different meaning out of Bryan's innocent words, and he almost stumbled as an image of rubbing his "stick" against Bryan's filled his mind. He caught himself and cursed under his breath. He had to get a grip on this or he was going to embarrass them all.

He managed to focus while they set up the fire, placing three logs in a triangle and a pile of kindling in the center, then watching as Bryan leaned three more logs together to make a pyramid. He sat back and nodded to Davis. "You do the honors," he said. Sure enough, Davis grinned and reached into a pocket on the leg of his cargo shorts, pulling out a long, slim instrument John recognized as a lighter designed for this kind of use.

"Cheater," John teased as Davis ignored him and squatted down, sticking the lighter into the middle of the kindling and pulling the "trigger" built into the side. A flame jumped out, and Davis held it in place, waiting until the kindling caught before moving to another spot and repeating his actions. He got three areas going before sitting back in the sand, crossing his legs and watching the fire grow.

John nodded as the flames took hold and, gradually, the three logs forming the pyramid started to smoke. "Good job, guys." He flashed Bryan a grin. "Guess we get to keep our manly man credentials for another day."

Davis made a sort of grunting sound that set them all laughing. "I think this calls for a beer," Bryan said, turning back toward the blanket. "John? You want one?"

"Absolutely." John knew he needed to take it easy with the alcohol tonight, but a beer or two would help keep him relaxed enough to have that talk with Bryan.

After dinner, he told himself as he watched Bryan's movements, smooth and easy, something John might have called graceful on a woman, but he wasn't sure whether that might come across as insulting. He shook his head ruefully. One more worry: saying the wrong thing, like he had the day they'd met.

When Bryan returned with three cans of beer balanced in his hands, he held them out to John first. "Here you go," he said, and John reached to pull the front can out from between Bryan's fingers. There was no way to accomplish that without touching him, but he braced himself against the sparks that zinged off his skin at the contact. He glanced up at Bryan to see if he felt it too, but his face was impassive as he turned to hand Davis one of the other cans. Bryan then sat down in the sand next to Davis, popped the top on his can, and took a long swallow, tilting his head back, the column of his neck stretching out, turning John's mouth dry.

Bryan caught his eye as he lowered the can and nodded toward the sand. "Have a seat and stay a while," he said, teasing, and John grinned as he took him up on the offer. He lowered himself to the sand maybe an inch or two closer to Bryan than he would have with any other guy, bending his knees and holding the beer can between them as he opened it.

"So what's next on the home fix-up agenda?" he asked, glancing between the other two men.

Davis rolled his eyes. "Ask the slave driver," he said. "And I'm not talking about my wife for a change. This guy"—he tapped Bryan's shoulder with the back of one hand—"has us on a tight schedule."

Bryan shrugged and shot John a smile. "One bedroom and bath at a time so we don't lose much income during the seasons," he said. "Smallest to largest. Two weeks each."

John's eyes widened. "Wow, that *is* fast," he said. "The bathrooms especially. But it makes sense," he added. "I'm guessing you'll be doing everything except the plumbing?"

Bryan nodded as he sipped his beer. "Luckily, the plumbing doesn't need much work," he said. "And we will take a week off here and there in there. We did the largest bathroom even before the kitchen, because it had a leak and it didn't make much sense to fix that and not just do it all. The others just need updating. We don't want to modernize everything, so we're keeping the claw-foot tubs, for one thing."

John smiled. "Yeah, my bathroom has one of those," he said. "The people who owned our house before Meghan did some updates. They took out a bedroom to expand the master bath and the one I use, so both have the old tubs but new, separate showers."

"We thought about that," Davis said. "And if we were remodeling to live there, we probably would."

"This just makes more sense for a B-and-B," Bryan added.

"Davis!" The three men turned to see Karen waving at him. "Could you come here for a minute?"

Davis grinned as he levered back to his feet. "Bet she needs me to keep an eye on Jeremy while she goes to pee," he said, laughing. "Perils of a pregnant wife."

John lifted his can in a toast. "I feel your pain," he said, smiling as he walked away. He turned his attention to Bryan to find him looking back with a quizzical expression on his face. "What?"

Bryan flushed and looked away. "Sorry," he said. "It just kind of surprises me sometimes, thinking that you were married before. I don't know why. Not like Beth wasn't the main reason we met in the first place."

If that wasn't the perfect opening, John didn't know what would be. He glanced over his shoulder to be sure everyone else was still a good distance away. "Listen." He leaned a little closer, keeping his voice low just in case. "Can we talk privately later? Like, after dinner? It's not anything bad," he said, off the look Bryan gave him. "At least, I don't think it is. Guess you'll have to be the judge of that."

He smiled and watched as Bryan's gaze dropped from his eyes to his mouth. They were close together now, and John felt his body reacting, heart rate and breathing picking up. He drifted forward without conscious thought before catching himself and leaning back. He cleared his throat and could see Bryan turning away, taking a sip of his beer. Trying to be casual, when John knew he was feeling the same things as John.

That talk couldn't come soon enough.

Chapter 13

A LITTLE while later, the entire group had gathered around the bonfire to roast hot dogs for dinner. Bryan handed out the extra-long skewers he'd brought, and John helped Beth get hers properly speared. She sat on the sand just in front of his crossed legs, and he leaned forward to support her small hand as they held the skewer over the fire.

To his left, he could see Davis helping Jeremy like he was, and to his right, Sarah's dad was helping her. A few other people had joined them, some John knew and some he didn't, all friends of Karen, Davis, or both. He realized sitting there how few people he knew on the island. He'd spent so much of the last four years keeping to himself, working and taking care of Beth, that he hadn't forged many friendships. It wasn't as if Meghan hadn't pointed it out every now and then, but it was only now, after making friends with Bryan and his family, that he realized how much he'd missed it.

Distracted, he almost let Beth's hot dog burn, but they managed to rescue it in time. John showed Beth how to get it off the skewer, closing the bun around it and pulling gently. She wasn't old enough to handle the hot skewer on her own yet, but she seemed excited to have been able to hold it while the hot dog cooked.

"There you go," John said, setting the plate with the hot dog on it to the side. "Give it a few minutes to cool off first, okay? Actually, why don't you help me roast mine while you wait? Then we can eat together."

Beth smiled and nodded, and John reached for another dog, threading it onto the skewer and resuming their previous position. He stared into the flames for a moment before he caught Bryan watching him from the corner of his eye and turned his head in that direction. Reflected flames danced in Bryan's eyes, and John smiled at him, slowly, deliberately, watching Bryan take in a breath in reaction. *Yeah,* he told himself. *This is going to be just fine.*

He returned his attention to his hot dog in time to keep from burning it. Once it was transferred to a bun, he handed Beth her plate, and they sat next to each other while they ate. John had brought carrot sticks in addition to the brownies, but they could have those a little later if they wanted. Right now he didn't want to move away from the group, especially not from Bryan. He could still feel the other man's gaze on him, and he was determined to enjoy every moment of anticipation for what might follow.

JOHN ate a second hot dog, this one roasted by Bryan when he made another for himself. Beth and Jeremy went back to playing in the sand with Sarah after their hot dogs were done, but the adults stayed around the fire, talking about everything and nothing. Bryan and John ended up side by side, John with his legs folded, Bryan sitting with his legs stretched out in front of him, hands braced in the sand behind him. He'd put his T-shirt back on, but the image of his smooth, bare skin never left John's mind.

The kids came running back over, and Beth threw herself into John's lap. "Jeremy said Mister Davis will tell us ghost stories!" She beamed at him, and John laughed and hugged her close.

"You're not gonna get scared, are you?" Beth shook her head vigorously, and John smiled wider. "Okay, then."

He expected Beth to settle down in his lap, but she crawled out and over to sit next to Jeremy, who'd plopped down right in front of his dad. Sarah and two other kids whose names John didn't remember gathered around too, and Davis started into some kind of convoluted tale that John couldn't quite follow. That might've been because he was sitting so close to Bryan, though.

Now's as good a time as any, he told himself. He leaned over far enough to bump Bryan's shoulder with his. "Want to go for that walk now?" He kept his voice low. Bryan's eyes glowed in the firelight, and he nodded.

They stood up quietly, and Bryan gestured down the beach for Karen's benefit so no one would wonder where they'd disappeared to. Neither bothered with shoes as they headed across the sand in the direction of the pier.

They walked in silence for a few minutes, in no hurry to get anywhere. Bryan took a stutter-step and kicked at the sand, sending up a wave in the path ahead of them. John laughed, and Bryan shot him a look.

"Never too old to play in the sand, my friend." He grinned and kicked up a spray again, and John took it as the challenge it was, sending up a plume of his own. Bryan took another shot and almost lost his balance, breaking into laughter as he caught himself, one arm windmilling with the effort to stay upright.

"Whoa there!" John reached out to steady Bryan on instinct, but he wasn't prepared for the shock of sensation that simple touch would give. He snatched his hand back, fingers burning like he'd touched the flames of their beach fire, but the burn spread into his chest when Bryan's laughter died away and he seemed to withdraw.

"Hey." John stretched his hand out again, this time touching Bryan's shoulder. "I'm sorry. I just…." He swallowed and let his hand slide away. "I'm not sure where to start."

Bryan studied him for a long moment. "Why not start at the beginning?"

John nodded. "Okay." He waved a hand toward the pier, and they started walking again, side by side, close enough that their arms nearly touched with every step. John still wasn't sure what to say, so he said the first thing that came to mind. "The day we met, you made an assumption about me," he said, but he didn't get any farther before Bryan interrupted him.

"Oh, hey, is that still bothering you?" He stopped and turned to face John. "Because you know I'm sorry about that, right?"

He put his hand on John's forearm, and John looked down for a moment before covering Bryan's hand with his. "It's fine," he said. "I know it was a misunderstanding, and I don't blame you in the least. That's not what I meant."

Bryan studied his face for a moment and seemed to find whatever he needed to convince himself that John was telling the truth. He looked down at their hands and his eyes widened, as if he were surprised to see how they were touching, and he pulled away.

"Sorry," he mumbled, turning back toward the pier.

John followed Bryan the few remaining yards to the tall wooden pylons holding up the structure above their heads. "What I meant was that I think I made some assumptions about you too," John continued as if he'd never stopped. "Some that weren't so obvious. And I think maybe we both need to clear the air a little. And yes, I have a reason, but I need to ask you something first."

They'd reached the pier, and Bryan stopped walking and turned back to face John again, his back to one of the pylons. "What's that?"

John stepped in close, sliding one hand onto Bryan's waist and bringing the other up to cup his cheek. "I don't think words would do it justice," he whispered.

He moved the last few inches to brush his lips gently against Bryan's, then drew back, watching Bryan's eyes. He saw surprise there, but more than that, he saw desire. Bryan's lips parted, and his gaze dropped to John's mouth, and John took it as the invitation it was.

He was less gentle this time, pressing his mouth into Bryan's, sliding his hand around to the back of his neck, holding him close. He felt one of Bryan's hands land on his hip and the other on his bicep, and he let his tongue slip forward, licking across Bryan's bottom lip before delving into his mouth. Bryan's taste exploded across his senses, and he heard himself moan softly. He took a half step forward, bracing one hand against the wood and using his body to press Bryan against it so he could kiss him more deeply.

Soft, wet sounds filled the air around them as they kissed. John didn't know how long it lasted. Time seemed to stop as long as Bryan's mouth was against his. He didn't want to end the kiss, but they still needed to talk, so he forced himself to draw away.

He took one look at Bryan's face—cheeks flushed, eyes half-lidded, lips red and wet—and dove right back in for more. He slid one hand down Bryan's arm as they kissed, tangling their fingers together. Bryan's other hand was on his back now, under his T-shirt, nails digging into his skin. John shifted his hips, and suddenly he could feel Bryan's erection, firm against his hip.

He broke the kiss with a gasp this time, pulling back to look Bryan in the eyes. He rolled his hips, sliding their cocks together through layers of clothes, and Bryan's eyes fell shut as his mouth dropped open on a low moan.

"Fuck." John untangled his hand from Bryan's and used the hand he still had braced behind Bryan to lever his body away. It felt like lifting the lid off a pot of boiling water. He could almost see the steam billowing out between them.

"Jesus." Bryan's voice was rough, wrecked, and John's body surged again in response. He took a step back on wobbly legs, and Bryan's eyes opened, dark and hungry as they met his.

"I...." John paused to swallow. "I don't regret that," he said, not wanting Bryan to think otherwise. "But I think maybe before we take this any further, we need to talk."

Bryan's mouth snapped shut, and after a moment, he nodded. Then he almost smiled. "I have to say," he said, his voice stronger but still raspy, "you sure know how to sweep a guy off his feet."

John laughed and held out a hand. "Come on," he said, smiling when Bryan slid his hand into John's. "Let's have that talk."

THEY picked a spot a couple of yards away from the pier, in a little gap among the sea oats, so they'd be out of sight of the rest of their party. They sat side by side, close but not quite touching.

John picked up a handful of sand and let it fall through his fingers. "So I suppose you're wondering why I asked you here," he started, and he grinned when he got the expected laugh from Bryan.

"Well, you've already surprised the pants off me, almost literally," Bryan shot back, leaning over far enough to bump his shoulder against John's. "Makes me wonder what else you have up your sleeve."

John sighed and brushed his hands together to knock off the remaining sand. "I talked to Karen the other day," he said. "She didn't know I had anything like this in mind. I barely knew it myself at that point. She didn't tell me any specifics." He turned to look at Bryan in the low light. "But she said you had some kind of tragedy in your past, and that you didn't like to talk about it. If we were going to be just friends, that'd be fine. But I think I've made it pretty clear I'd like more than that. And if that's the way we decide to go—"

"Then you need to know," Bryan finished. "You're right. Karen's right. You do. It's just…." He seemed to fold in on himself, pulling his legs up to his chest and wrapping his arms around them, looking so much like a child that John just wanted to hold him. He refrained, but only just.

"It's hard to talk about." Bryan's voice sounded distant, as if he were miles away instead of right next to John. "The short version is that my boyfriend and I got jumped when we were leaving a club in Atlanta. It was a few weeks after graduation. We both got beaten up pretty badly, but Eddie took the brunt of it."

He stopped and swallowed shakily, and John couldn't help himself, reaching over to lay a hand on the middle of Bryan's back. He wasn't sure it would help, but Bryan seemed to steady, leaning back slightly into John's touch.

"It was brutal," Bryan said. "I had a lot of bruises and some cracked ribs, a split lip. But one of the guys slammed Eddie's head into the pavement and then kicked him in the back of the head. He had a traumatic brain injury. He never recovered completely, and he never will."

"Shit." John slid closer, moving his arm to wrap it around Bryan's shoulders, watching for any sign that he was going too far. It never came. In fact, Bryan leaned into him, and John brought his other arm around to complete the embrace.

"It gets worse," Bryan rasped out, and John could tell he was fighting not to break down. "When we got jumped, I thought it was a bashing. They happen. Almost every gay guy has gotten beaten up for being gay or because someone thought they were gay. If not, they know someone who has. But with us, some other guys were walking by and saw what was happening, and they managed to grab one of them before he could get away. It was a guy we all knew, kind of a sleazeball, but gay. He took a lot of glee in telling them who set the whole thing up."

He stopped, and John just held him and waited for him to be able to go on. "And it was my fault," Bryan said finally, shoulders shaking. "It was this guy who'd been trying to get me to sleep with him for, like, two years, and I turned him down every time. And he got some of his buddies to jump us." He stopped again and took a shaky breath. "He told them he wanted Eddie 'out of the picture'. They beat him up because of me."

He couldn't talk anymore. He wasn't crying, but he was shaking from head to toe. John pulled him closer until Bryan's head rested against John's shoulder. "Shhhhh," John murmured into his hair. "It's okay. It's not your fault. It was the guys who beat you up, Bryan. It wasn't you."

He had no idea if his words were getting through, much less making a difference, but Bryan's shivers eventually slowed and stopped. He didn't move, though, except to slide one arm around John's waist and hold on like his life depended on it.

John didn't want to press him, but he thought maybe it'd be better to get through it all now instead of dragging it out. "What happened to Eddie?" he asked softly.

Bryan shivered again, just once. "He.... It was never the same," he whispered. "He had to go into assisted living, and I tried to be there for him, but his whole personality changed. It was like I didn't know him at all. We couldn't even talk, and he got.... He was violent. He never hit me, but he'd throw things or yell or hit the wall, and after what happened...."

He stopped, but John understood. "After the attack, you couldn't be around that."

Bryan nodded against John's shoulder. "I tried. I went to therapy. But after a while I just couldn't do it anymore." He took in a big gulp of air. "I left. I moved to Florida with my grandparents for a while, and then I moved here." His hand clutched at John's shirt. "I left him."

John ran a hand up and down Bryan's back, understanding now what made this so critical. The beating was bad enough, but at the root of the problem was Bryan's guilt.

"You did what you had to do," he murmured. "It wasn't anyone's fault. You couldn't change anything, and he couldn't change back into the man you fell in love with."

They fell silent, and John sat still and let Bryan recover. He knew the feeling all too well. Telling anyone about Liz for the first few years after her death felt like reliving it all over again, and it was still hard even now. And Bryan had not only lost his lover but had gone through a vicious beating himself. John couldn't imagine what he'd had to deal with.

Bryan finally took in a deep, if shaky, breath and blew it back out, hard. He moved to sit up, and John let him, although he kept a hand on his back. Bryan gave him a watery smile. "Wow," he said. "That…. I didn't think it would hit me that hard."

John smiled back. "It's understandable," he said. "You had two big traumatic events at the same time. Either one would be hard to handle, but both?" He shook his head. "I don't know that I would've handled it nearly as well as you have."

Bryan's eyes fell shut. "God, I keep forgetting what happened to you. You seem so strong and calm that it's hard to believe you might've ever felt like… like this." He waved a hand toward himself as his eyes opened and met John's. "Sometimes I feel like it'll always be this way."

John slid his hand up Bryan's back and let it rest on the nape of his neck. "It gets better," he said. "It doesn't go away. You haven't seen me on a really bad day."

Bryan studied John's eyes. "How did you…. I don't know how to ask this," he said, dropping his head. "You told me what happened, but you didn't say much about how you got through it?"

John let his hand slip away and fall back into his lap. He blew out a quick breath. "For a while I didn't think I would," he said. "I had a brand-new baby to take care of, and I could barely take care of myself. Some days I couldn't even do that." He shrugged and lifted his gaze back to meet Bryan's. "I ended up letting Liz's parents keep Beth most of the time. At first it was just to help out, but then…."

He broke away again, staring out toward the water. He knew he had to tell Bryan the truth, but he hated even thinking about those days, much less talking about them. He was trying to figure out how to say it when a warm hand slid onto his forearm and then down to grip his fingers. He looked back at Bryan and saw open, trusting eyes. "It's okay," Bryan said. "No matter what it is, I'm not going to run screaming."

He smiled, and John chuckled a little, grateful for the release of tension. He took another breath and dove in. "At first I thought it would just be once," he said. "Beth was with her grandparents, and I was home alone and climbing the walls. I left, and I ended up at a bar. A club. And I went in, and had a beer, and I looked around and found a woman who looked nothing like Liz. I danced with her, and bought her drinks, and...." He squeezed his eyes shut. "I took her home with me and fucked her in the bed I'd shared with Liz."

Bryan's hand tightened on his, and John kept talking as fast as he could. "I sent her home afterward, and I swore I wouldn't do it again, but a week later I was out again, in a different bar. I just stopped at the first one I came across, and it was a gay bar this time. So I picked up a guy and took him home and fucked him. And kicked him out.

"A few days later, I did it again. And then again. Men or women, I didn't care. I never went to the same place twice, and I never slept with the same person twice." His eyes flew open, and he caught Bryan's gaze. "Always safe. I swear."

Bryan nodded and brought his other hand up to cover theirs where they rested on John's thigh.

"I went on like that for close to four months," John said. "And I probably would've kept it up even longer, but Liz's parents had had enough. They were basically raising Beth by then. I had her maybe two nights a week. And one morning somebody woke me up pounding on the front door." He smiled then, the image still fresh in his mind. "It was Meghan. At six a.m. She drove half the night to get there from here, and I think if I hadn't looked like warmed-up shit, she would've punched me in the face."

Bryan snickered, and John smiled wider, but then it fell away. "She probably saved my life," he said softly. "She told me she knew I was in a hell of a lot of pain and that was okay but that I had a daughter to raise and a life to live, and I could either hole up and die and leave Beth an orphan, or I could figure out how to fight through the pain and rebuild my life." He shrugged. "It was her idea for us to move down here too. Get away from all those memories. It took a couple of months, but we did. And I've never regretted it."

Bryan nodded. "Like I said, I moved to Florida for a while after… after Eddie," he said. "With my grandparents. But they're pretty conservative and not too happy about having a gay grandson. They're not openly hostile, but it was uncomfortable. I went back to Atlanta and worked at a design store for a while, but it was like with you. Too many reminders. When Karen and Davis told me they were buying this place and asked if I wanted to help, I jumped at the chance."

John leaned forward and lifted his free hand to run his fingers down Bryan's cheek. "I'm glad you did," he said, keeping his voice low. "I think maybe it was the right thing at the right time. For both of us."

Bryan leaned into the touch, just enough that John could feel it. He took the invitation and moved in closer, touching his lips to Bryan's again. After a moment, he felt Bryan smile against his mouth and drew back, lips curving up in an automatic response. "What?"

Bryan smiled wider. "I was just thinking about what you said a little while ago," he said, "about how I made a pretty big assumption about you the day we met." He tilted his head and lifted an eyebrow. "I have to say, I don't think I've ever been happier to be wrong in my life."

John laughed and wrapped his arms around Bryan, pulling him in close and kissing him again. He slid both hands into Bryan's hair so he could tilt his head into the kiss. He felt Bryan spread his hands across John's back, and as their tongues met between their open mouths, Bryan let out a soft moan deep in his chest that set John's entire body on fire.

He forced himself to back away and look into Bryan's wide, dark eyes. "I've always been an upfront kind of guy." He could hear the arousal in his own voice. "So I'm going to be perfectly clear here. I like you. A lot. I want to follow this wherever it goes. But I don't want to rush you. Hell, I don't want to rush *me*, either."

Bryan grinned, and before John knew what was happening, he was on his back on the sand, Bryan lying half across his chest with his hands holding John's head, kissing him like his life depended on it. It was John's turn to moan, from surprise as much as from the taste of Bryan's mouth and the feel of his body. When Bryan broke the kiss, John stared up at him, stunned.

"I agree," Bryan said, his rapid breathing and flushed cheeks the only obvious sign that the kiss had even happened. "Slow and steady. We both have things to work out. But I gotta say, I really, *really* like kissing. So can we do a lot of that, at least?"

John laughed and lifted his hand to grasp the back of Bryan's neck. "All signs point to yes," he replied, and then they didn't talk again for a while.

Chapter 14

WHEN John and Bryan made their way back to the rest of the group, they got long, questioning looks from Karen and from Meghan, who'd arrived while they were gone, but no one else seemed to have noticed they were gone. The kids were wrapped up in whatever silly semi-ghost story Davis was spinning, and the handful of other adults were carrying on their own conversations.

John and Bryan sat down near the kids so they could watch and half listen. As they did, John had an idea, and he turned to Bryan.

"Hey," he said, keeping his voice low. "I'm supposed to go to Atlanta next week to work at the home office. You think…. I don't want to overstep my bounds or anything, but do you think you might want to go too? Maybe you could… go see Eddie? Talk to him a little? I don't know if it would help, but…."

He trailed off, uncertain now that he'd said it, but Bryan nodded a little. "I don't know either," he said. "But it might. And I haven't seen him in a while. I used to check on him pretty often when I was up there, but I haven't been back since I moved here." He shrugged. "It might make me feel better to know that he's doing okay."

Careful to shield the movement from the rest of the group, John reached over to lay one hand over Bryan's. "Just think about it. I'm taking Beth, but she'll stay with her grandparents most of the time. And they put me up in a corporate apartment that has two bedrooms, so your virtue will be safe." He lifted an eyebrow and dropped his voice an octave. "Or as safe as you want it to be."

Bryan laughed out loud, his head dropping back, and John smiled as he watched him.

"Daddy!" John turned to see Beth waving both her hands at him. "Come on, Daddy, we're gonna roast marshmallows!"

John squeezed Bryan's hand before climbing to his feet, brushing sand off his shorts as he walked the few feet over to Beth. He sat down cross-legged beside her and grabbed her around the waist, setting her off into giggles as he pulled her into his lap.

"Okay, now, do you want your marshmallows toasted or fried to a crisp?" he asked. From the corner of his eye, he saw Bryan sitting down between him and Davis, who had Jeremy in his lap.

"Burnt!" Beth tilted her head back to grin upside down at John.

"Burnt it is!" John answered. He smiled as Bryan passed along a skewer from Davis and then held out a handful of marshmallows.

"What about you?" Bryan asked. "Toasted or burnt?"

John grinned as he plucked two marshmallows from Bryan's palm. "Burnt all the way," he said. "Tasty, tasty carcinogens."

He speared one marshmallow, pushing it down far enough to make room for the next, and just like he'd done with the hot dogs, he held the skewer down so Beth could hold it next to his hands. "Now, when it catches fire, you'll have to let go, okay?"

Beth nodded, and John moved the skewer forward into the flames.

He turned his head just far enough to catch Bryan's eye, and they exchanged a smile as Bryan loaded up a skewer for Davis and Jeremy, who wouldn't hold still long enough for Davis to do it. Once they were roasting away, Bryan set up his own marshmallows, and just as he leaned forward to put his into the fire, John's flared up, orange charring the white confection to black. Beth's hands fell away from the skewer, and John drew the marshmallows off to the side, well away from her, so he could finish burning them and blow out the flames.

"There," he told Beth. "Perfectly blackened."

Meghan appeared on John's other side, smiling as she sat down, a plastic container in her hand. She popped the lid and held it out, showing John it was full of his mini brownie muffins. "Wonder how those would taste on these?" she asked, and John lifted an eyebrow.

"Intriguing," he intoned. It took him a minute to work out how to get the marshmallow off the skewer and onto the brownie without making a huge mess, but finally he was able to take a bite. As the flavors burst across his tongue, he smiled and gave a thumbs-up as best he could with both hands full.

Beth bounced in his lap. "Daddy, I wanna try!"

John brought the marshmallow-topped brownie down and held it for Beth to take a bite, her small hand closing around his wrist. She giggled as bits of burnt black flaked off around the edges, and John smiled down at her.

"Good?" he asked.

Beth bobbed her head up and down.

"Good." John popped the rest of the brownie into his mouth.

Bryan poked him in the leg. "Hey, you gonna share those or what?"

Meghan leaned across to set the container down on the sand between John and Bryan. "You gonna share the marshmallows?"

Bryan turned to grab another skewer, loading it up with marshmallows and passing it over to her. John got his second marshmallow onto a brownie in the meantime, and he and Beth shared it the same way as the first.

Several marshmallow-topped brownies later, Beth was drooping against John's chest. "Guess it's about time for us to be going," he said. He smiled at Davis and Karen, who'd settled in beside her husband to help corral Jeremy, who'd been jumping around as usual but was now starting to look a little sleepy himself. "This has been a blast, guys," John said. "Thanks for inviting us."

"Yeah, glad I could make it over," Meghan chimed in, leaning forward to wrap her arms around her knees. "We have a private dinner at the restaurant for staff and friends around midsummer, and I'd love it if you guys could come."

Karen smiled. "We'd love to!" she said. "Just let us know when. We've eaten at your restaurant several times, and it's great."

Meghan smiled wider. "Thanks so much," she said. She glanced at John, then at the half-asleep little girl in his lap. "C'mon," she said, climbing back to her feet. "I'll take the munchkin and let you gather up our stuff, since I don't know what you brought."

John smiled up at her and nudged Beth. "Hey, Bethy. Let's get you up and Meggie will get you home, okay?"

Beth mumbled and rubbed one eye, but she sat up, and John helped her stand, waiting until Meghan had a good grip on her hand before letting go. Meghan and Beth walked away, and John pushed to his feet, brushing sand off wherever he could manage. A shower would definitely be called for when he got home.

Bryan stood up next to him. "I'll help you with your stuff," he said, reaching for the container of brownies sitting nearby.

"No, leave those," John said. "If you guys don't finish them off, I'll pick them up tomorrow."

Bryan gave him an inscrutable look but then smiled and straightened up. "You're just trying to ply us with baked goods again," he said.

John grinned. "Figured me out, haven't you? I told you I'm not much of a cook, so baking it is."

"The way to a man's—" Bryan cut himself off and flushed lightly. John glanced down at Karen and Davis, still sitting in the sand. Davis wasn't paying attention to them, working on getting residual marshmallow wiped off Jeremy's fingers, but Karen's eyes flashed humor at him. She didn't have to say a word.

John glanced at Bryan and tilted his head toward the blanket where he'd left his things. "Let's get my stuff together," he said. He smiled down at Karen and Davis. "Thanks again for inviting us, guys. It's been a lot of fun."

Davis did look up then and returned the smile. "Glad you could come. We'll have to get together for a game sometime." He grimaced. "Assuming we can find the time around all the renovations."

Karen elbowed him lightly. "*You* agreed to the schedule, bub," she pointed out. She smiled at John. "We'll see you all soon?"

John nodded. "Count on it," he said.

He turned and walked toward the blanket, Bryan by his side. He heard Bryan chuckle. "Man, nearly gave away all our secrets there," he murmured, and John laughed.

"I think your sister already figured that one out," he replied.

Out of the corner of his eye, he saw Bryan smile and shake his head. "She was always the one figuring out Christmas gifts and the endings of movies," he said. "Hard to get anything past her."

John shifted just enough that their arms brushed together as they stopped next to the blanket. He leaned in a little closer. "You don't have to hide it from her, you know," he said. "Not on my account."

Bryan turned toward him, bringing their mouths within inches of each other. Bryan's gaze dropped to John's mouth. "Not on your account." He lifted his eyes to meet John's. "On mine. Just… slow, remember?"

John nodded. "Slow," he agreed. "We've got time."

Bryan's smile spread slowly across his face. "Well, not tonight, we don't," he said, voice back to normal. "Let's get you loaded up so you can get back to your family."

John laughed. "Trying to get rid of me. I see how it is," he said, squatting and reaching for the tote bag he'd brought with his and Beth's beach gear. "Got to get home to that other guy you've been keeping hidden, right?"

Bryan laughed again as he bent to help John, handing over the beach toys Beth and the other kids had been playing with earlier that were now scattered around the blanket. "I keep him so well hidden even I don't know he's there," he said.

Bag packed, John stood back up. He glanced over toward Karen and Davis, who were getting ready to go by then, Davis using the bucket of sand he'd dug out earlier to douse the remaining embers of their fire. "You think your family would mind if you walked me home?" John asked, returning his gaze to Bryan's face.

Bryan didn't hesitate. "Hey, guys," he called over. "I'm going to get the blanket and stuff and head on back with John, okay? We'll take the cooler over to the car on the way."

"No problem," Davis replied, not looking up from his task. "We'll finish things up here and be home in a few."

Bryan moved the remaining tote bag off the blanket onto the sand, and he and John got the blanket shaken off and folded haphazardly. Bryan laid it on top of the cooler, and in unspoken agreement, each of them grabbed a handle to carry it toward the parking lot.

Getting the cooler up and over the wooden walkway at the edge of the beach took a bit of work, but in a few minutes they'd set it down next to the Morrisons' small SUV, ready to be lifted into the back. "I have a set of keys," Bryan said. "But I didn't bring them tonight. The cooler's not heavy, though, and I'll help Davis get it inside when we get home."

John smiled and reached over to give Bryan's hand a squeeze. "They'll be fine," he said. "It's okay to be a little bit selfish once in a while, you know."

Bryan laughed, turning his hand to tangle his fingers with John's. "Oh, I can be very, very selfish sometimes," he said, moving closer to John. "Especially when it comes to sharing people. I can be kind of possessive now and then."

John felt heat flash through him at the look in Bryan's eyes. "I can deal with a little possession," he murmured, watching as Bryan's eyes dropped to his mouth again. John smiled. "Come on," he said, tugging a little at Bryan's hand. "Let's take the long way home."

THE long way, as it turned out, included a detour through the edge of the park where John and Bryan had first met, less than two weeks earlier. It seemed like so much longer than that to John. He felt like Bryan had been a part of his life for months, if not years. They walked hand in hand, not too worried about who might see them. The roads were quiet and the night was dark, offering them enough cover for something as small as holding hands.

John broke the silence. "So Davis mentioned your renovation schedule," he said. "Are you going to be able to get away for a week to go to Atlanta?"

Bryan shrugged. "The schedule's not that repressive. We can shift weeks around pretty easily, work on a different room or postpone without too much trouble. I'll talk to him tomorrow, but it should be fine."

John nodded. "Any reason you guys didn't do the guest rooms first?"

Bryan laughed. "The kitchen, mainly," he said. "Karen put her foot down. 'I've got to cook for these people! I need a decent place to do that before anything else!' Plus, that took the most time and messed up the house the most, so it just made sense to get it out of the way, even though that meant doing some room renos during the season."

John smiled. "Still need to recruit you to do our kitchen when the B-and-B is done. It's not terrible, but it's pretty outdated."

"Deal," Bryan said, squeezing John's hand.

They were at the house by then, and John pulled Bryan around toward the back. He could see a light on in Beth's window as they walked around the house and a shadow as Meghan moved by, getting Beth into bed. He stopped to the side of the back door, just outside the ring of light from the small lamp on the side of the house, and turned to face Bryan, sliding his free hand onto Bryan's hip.

"So," he said as he took a half step closer. "Can we call this our first date? Or does that have to involve an official invitation and some kind of somewhat formal event plan?"

Bryan laughed and leaned in. "I think yesterday was our first date, actually," he pointed out. "That was what you had in mind, wasn't it?"

John chuckled. "You've got me figured out pretty well," he admitted just before their lips met.

The kiss was soft and gentle, a perfect sort-of-first-date-ending kiss. Bryan brought his free hand up to John's bicep, wrapping his fingers around it. Their tongues touched just enough to send sparks down John's spine before he pulled back and smiled.

"Goodnight, Bryan," he said.

Bryan smiled wide. "Goodnight, John." He darted forward for one last quick kiss before backing away, only breaking their gaze when he reached the side of the house and turned to head for home.

JOHN'S smile followed him for the next hour as he got their beach things put away, straightened up a little, and got ready for bed. Meghan had disappeared into her room, and he could hear classical music playing, which meant she was reading, since otherwise she tended to go more modern with her choices.

John slid into bed feeling boneless, all the activity of the long weekend catching up with him. His mind raced through all the things he'd need to do the rest of the week: tweaking the preliminary reports for the following week while still handling his regular workload, getting his and Beth's things packed, making arrangements with her grandparents for when to drop her off and pick her up.

His thoughts flashed onto Bryan, and his cock twitched under the loose sleep shorts he wore. He'd already found himself fantasizing about the other man in the week since he'd realized his attraction, but now he had actual memories to supplement his mind's wanderings. He lay on his back and could almost feel Bryan lying across his chest, warm and firm, his mouth exploring John's. John loved kissing, and Bryan was damn good at it, but his body cried out for more, and John gave in.

John didn't masturbate often, but among the many things he was relearning was the simple indulgence of feeling pleasure. And after tonight, he needed a release.

He rolled out of bed and walked over to lock his door, normally left open for Beth in case she had a nightmare or got sick. On the way back to the bed, he dropped the shorts. Back on his back, he closed his eyes and pictured Bryan's face while he let his hands roam down his chest, thumbs brushing over his nipples, which were already hard peaks from anticipation. He pictured Bryan's mouth sucking on them and had to bite his lip to hold back the groan that wanted to escape.

He wrapped one hand around his cock, the other still teasing his nipples, imagining that it was Bryan's fingers that were gripping him firmly, stroking him slowly. He ran his thumb across the head, spreading the wetness from there down the shaft, his legs moving apart automatically.

John had been on the receiving end of anal sex just a handful of times, all of them back in college. He and Liz had played around with toys some, but his lost months after Liz died had been in part about being in control of something, anything, so he'd never let any of those men fuck him. Now, as he thrust up into the tight ring of his fingers, he let the other hand move down farther, fingers smoothing over his balls, brushing across his perineum, until they stroked over his opening. He imagined Bryan again, those long fingers pressing against John's hole, just the tip of one sliding inside, breaching the tight muscle. He let his own finger do what he imagined Bryan doing, and just the suggestion of penetration was enough to send a surge through his body.

When John had met Trent during his freshman year at Georgia, Trent had had a lot more experience, and he made sure John knew he liked sex both ways. John had his first turn bottoming a few weeks after they first had sex, and they both discovered just how much he loved it. Later, Liz had been an amazing and understanding lover, happy to be sure John had that experience with her as well, but after she died, John had thrown away the small set of toys they'd collected. He'd never regretted it, not even now, when all he wanted was the feel of a thick cock inside him. He didn't want silicone. He wanted the real thing.

He wanted Bryan.

He groaned as his finger pushed just a little farther, as his hand moved a little faster, his orgasm rising up from the base of his spine and exploding across his skin. His back arched, and warm come spurted over his hand and onto his stomach. He bit his lip again to keep from making too much noise. His mind spun and his body pulsed, his breath harsh in his chest, but he gradually relaxed, ears ringing as he floated back down.

Once his mind cleared, he rolled onto his side and up onto shaky legs, walking back over to the bathroom to clean up. He retrieved his shorts on his way back to the bedroom door, slipping them on before releasing the lock and heading back to the bed. He barely had the sheet pulled up before he was floating away.

Chapter 15

OVER the next three days, John got the coding tweaks he needed finished, put out a couple of fires caused by the same problem employee's inability to follow instructions the first time (that was going to have to be dealt with soon, which made him glad he wasn't the boss), and watched after Beth in the afternoons while Meghan was at the restaurant. He saw Bryan just once, when he stopped by after dinner Tuesday night to drop off the leftover brownies. With Beth still at the table right behind him, John couldn't do anything more than smile and thank him and confirm that they were still on for Atlanta.

"We'll drive up Sunday evening, if that's okay," he said. "It's either leave early or leave late, the way traffic goes up there. Beth's grandparents are in Conyers, so we can drop her off on the way into the city."

Bryan frowned at that. "Is my being there going to be a problem?"

John shook his head. "I told them the truth, mostly: that a friend of mine was coming along to keep me company and visit a friend of his." He shrugged. "We'll worry about long-term consequences later."

Bryan smiled and glanced over John's shoulder at Beth. When his gaze returned to John's, John could see what Bryan wanted to do in his eyes.

"Well," Bryan said. "I guess I'll get going. See you Sunday?"

John grabbed his hand on impulse, the movement covered from Beth's view by the door. "No," he said. "Come to dinner one night? Thursday or Friday?"

The frown was back. "What about Beth?"

John lifted an eyebrow. "I can behave myself if you can. And it's not like she doesn't know you already."

Bryan nodded once in acknowledgement. "Okay," he said. "Dinner." He grinned widely. "Hey, I think that might qualify as an actual date! Although maybe not with your daughter there...."

John laughed and let Bryan's hand go. "We'll count it anyway," he said. "We're pretty much making things up as we go along anyway, right?"

Bryan lifted an eyebrow. "Well, good," he drawled out. "Because I have a pretty good imagination."

John mirrored his expression. "I'm sure you do," he said. "We'll just have to put it to the test."

"Daddy!" Beth's voice drew John's attention. "Is Mister Bryan gonna stay and watch SpongeBob with us?"

John turned back to Bryan. "I promised her SpongeBob before bed," he admitted with a small smile. "I imagine you get your fill of that with Jeremy."

"You're not kidding." Bryan leaned in far enough to smile at Beth. "Sorry, honey, I've got to get back home. Maybe I'll see you later this week, okay?"

Beth nodded and smiled big. "Okay! Night, Mister Bryan!"

Bryan waved and took a step back onto the porch, returning his attention to John. "Night, Mister John," he said, laughter in his voice, and it took a huge amount of willpower for John not to do something he really, really shouldn't.

"Goodnight, Bryan," he said, letting everything he was feeling come out in his voice. "See you Thursday."

"I'll be here." Bryan grinned before blowing John a silly kiss.

John laughed as Bryan disappeared down the steps. He closed and locked the door and turned back toward the table.

"Let's go watch SpongeBob," he said, stepping over to pull Beth's chair back from the table. "And then we both need to sleep. Okay?"

"Okay, Daddy!" Beth hit the floor in a half run, headed to curl up in her favorite spot on the sofa. John followed, picking up the remote as he sat down and flicking the TV on to find the recording from earlier in the day. He started the show playing and settled back to let cartoon silliness carry him away, but Bryan never quite left his thoughts.

THURSDAY night, Bryan knocked on the back door at seven sharp. John had told him the time and to dress casually, that it wouldn't be anything fancy. John opened the door to find Bryan in loose khaki shorts, a polo shirt just snug enough to draw John's attention to his chest, and canvas sneakers.

John smiled and stepped back to wave him in. He frowned when he saw the foil-covered plate Bryan held. "Hey now, thought I said you didn't need to bring anything but yourself."

"Karen insisted!" Bryan held the plate up. "Chocolate chip cookies. She's been cooking or baking or cleaning something every day this week. Is it normal to start nesting so early?" He pulled a face that made John laugh.

"I don't think there's much in the way of 'normal' when it comes to pregnancy behavior," he said, taking the plate from Bryan and setting it on the kitchen counter. "Everyone's different. Liz couldn't stand pizza the entire time she was pregnant until the last two weeks, and then that's all she wanted. And she decided at eight months that she needed to learn to knit, of all things."

Bryan grinned. "How'd that work out?"

John groaned and shook his head. "I spent more time in yarn stores that month than you would believe." He smiled. "But she did get a small blanket made. It's what Beth came home from the hospital in...."

He trailed off as the memory kicked in. He'd been eerily calm, carrying Beth to the car with the blanket wrapped around her, strapping her into the car seat as if he'd done it every day for his entire life. Meghan had insisted on driving, and John didn't remember anything about the trip home. He only remembered walking into the house with Beth in his arms and starting to shake so hard he nearly dropped her.

Meghan barely had time to take her before he crumpled to the floor, sobbing. It had been the only time he'd cried until Meghan's early morning rescue months later.

Pushing away the memories, John nodded toward the table. "Have a seat," he said. "Beth's holed up with SpongeBob again. She's been on a tear this week. I think she's watched every episode of the entire series twice."

Bryan studied John's face as he sat down but eventually smiled. "I think I've seen every episode of the entire series twice myself," he said. "Spending so much time around Jeremy is one thing, but you have to remember, he's kind of an icon in the gay community too. It's mostly a tongue-in-cheek thing, but trust me, there's a lot of SpongeBob watching going on, especially with the college-aged guys."

John chuckled as he pulled out the plate of cold cuts he'd arranged a little bit earlier, figuring it was too hot to cook and sandwiches would be easy. "I'd forgotten about that. But yeah, now that you mention it, some of my gay friends in college seemed to be addicted to it." He laughed. "Of course, some of the same friends seemed to be addicted to certain substances as well, so hey."

Bryan grinned, watching as John set the cold cuts on the table. "Oh man, that looks great," he said. "You got all the good stuff, didn't you?"

"If roast beef, ham, and turkey are the good stuff, then yeah," John said, reaching for the two bags of bread in the basket on top of the refrigerator. "Got rye and some Kaiser rolls too." He put them on the table and turned back to the refrigerator. "You a yellow or brown mustard guy?"

"Either," Bryan said.

John opened the door and grabbed both, along with a jar of mayonnaise.

"It'll sound sacrilegious of me," Bryan continued, "but I put mayo and mustard on roast beef. I've never been a fan of horseradish."

John put the two bottles and the jar on the table and grinned. "I knew there was a reason I liked you," he said, tapping the lid on the mayo. "We'll just have to be sacrilegious together."

He grabbed the two bags of chips, one plain and one barbecue, from the counter and added them to the spread. "What would you like to drink? We have Coke and tea, I think some grape juice, and milk. And water too."

"Coke or tea, either is good," Bryan answered. "Save the milk for the cookies!"

John laughed, getting down three glasses and filling two with tea and ice and one with milk. "Let me go get Beth, and we'll eat," he said. He got two steps when he realized he'd forgotten something and stopped. He looked over at Bryan, who was biting back a smile.

"Plates in the corner cabinet, silverware in the drawer next to the fridge," John said, waving a hand. "Make yourself useful."

Bryan's laughter followed him into the living room, where Beth sat enthralled in front of the television. "Come on, Bethy, Mister Bryan is here and we're going to make sandwiches."

Beth turned her head slowly, as if trying to keep her eyes on the screen as long as possible, but John cut her off by picking up the remote and turning the TV off. She pouted at him for a second, but John reached for her hand. "Mister Bryan brought cookies for dessert," he said, and Beth brightened and scrambled up, grabbing John's hand and following him into the kitchen.

"Hi, Mister Bryan!" Beth called out as soon as she saw him, back where he'd been sitting a few minutes earlier, and she ran over to give him a hug.

Bryan let out a surprised laugh as he caught her, wrapping his arms around her. "Hey, Bethy," he said, bending his head to press a quick kiss on the crown of her head. "I'm glad to see you too."

John felt something in his chest clench and then loosen at the sight. He had to take a quick breath, but when Bryan looked up at him, he smiled.

Beth jumped down and climbed into the chair next to Bryan. "Daddy said you brought cookies!"

Bryan looked up at John, his eyes dancing with laughter. "Oh, so you just want me for my cookies," he said, directing the question to Beth even as he lifted an eyebrow at John.

"Yep, that's the only reason," John answered, pulling out the chair on the other side of Bryan, opposite Beth.

Beth dominated the conversation as they made and ate their sandwiches. She hardly paused to eat as she told Bryan all about all the SpongeBobs she'd been watching. She was delighted to find that Bryan knew the characters and their stories, and they carried on a serious discussion of how a snail could meow like a kitten—not to mention why you'd name a snail *or* a kitten "Gary"—and what made Squidward so mean so much of the time. John listened, torn between fascination at their interplay and a deep desire to drag Bryan upstairs and get him naked in a big hurry. He tried not to feel guilty about that. Truth was, he knew, little was as appealing as a potential partner who seemed to like your child as much as he did you.

By the time John and Bryan had their sandwiches and chips down to crumbs, Beth had managed to eat half of hers between her chattering and was starting to wind down. She was usually in bed by eight, which was fast approaching.

"Okay, Bethy," John said. "Two cookies and a little more milk, and then it's bedtime."

Beth pouted. "Wanna stay up with Mister Bryan."

John glanced over at Bryan, who turned his smile from Beth to John. "You can stay up long enough to eat your cookies," John said, standing up and reaching for Beth's plate and cup.

"I'll get the cookies," Bryan offered, rising from his seat and crossing behind John, who was reaching into the refrigerator for the milk. John felt a soft touch along his lower back, just above the curve of his ass, and turned his head to see Bryan shooting him a wicked smile that John had to return.

The smile stayed as John refilled Beth's cup and poured new ones for him and Bryan. Bryan was passing out cookies when John got back to the table with the milk, and Beth smiled around her first bite of cookie.

"Hey, Bethy," John said. "Mister Bryan is going to Atlanta with us next week."

Beth's eyes opened wide, and she stared at Bryan. "Really?" He nodded, and she bounced in her seat. "Are you going to Gramma and Grampa's too?"

Bryan laughed. "No, I'm staying with your daddy," he said. "I have a friend I need to go see. But I'll be riding up with you, and back next weekend. So we can talk in the car, okay?"

Beth nodded and took another bite. "Omkay," she said, and John smothered a laugh.

"Not with your mouth full, Beth," he admonished. "Remember to swallow first."

A choked sort of sound came from Bryan, and John glanced over to see Bryan biting his lip, his face turning red with the effort not to laugh. It took John a second to realize what he'd said, and he had to fight off a bout of laughter himself. *Oh, this is going to be interesting*, he thought, biting into his second cookie and trying to chew and smile at the same time.

HALF an hour later, cookies and milk gone, Beth was in bed and very close to sleeping. John and Bryan stood at the doorway looking at her. She'd insisted that "Mister Bryan" help tuck her in, and the way Bryan had blinked quickly in response told John how much he liked hearing that. He'd teased her and fetched Maxie from under the edge of the bed, and she'd given him a big, smacking kiss on the cheek in thanks.

John stepped back and pulled the door almost shut. "Come on," he said, tilting his head toward the stairs. "Let's see if we can find something other than SpongeBob to watch."

Bryan chuckled as he followed John back down toward the living room. "Hey, don't knock the 'Bob. Kept her occupied all the way through dinner, didn't it?"

John turned at the bottom of the stairs to face Bryan, who stopped on the last step, making him several inches taller than John instead of about the same height. John took Bryan's hand in his and used the other to draw his head down for a brief but lingering kiss.

"Thank you," he murmured against Bryan's mouth. "You have no idea how much it means to me that you like Beth."

He felt Bryan smile. "I have *some* idea," he said, kissing John back just a little bit longer.

John stepped back, pulling Bryan with him by the hand he still held. "I think the Braves are playing the Cubbies tonight," he said. "Want some popcorn or a beer?"

Bryan followed, smiling. "Beer would be good."

John squeezed his hand before dropping it and waving toward the sofa. "Make yourself at home and I'll be right back."

In the kitchen, he opened the freezer door and stuck his face in. He was laughing a little as he did, but man, he needed to cool down somehow. *Slow and steady*, he told himself again. Never mind that every cell in his body was screaming at him to drag Bryan upstairs to his room and lock them in for the night.

Closing the freezer, he retrieved two bottles from the refrigerator and twisted off the lids, carrying them back to the living room. Bryan had reclined in one corner of the sofa, legs stretched out in front of him, and had found the Braves game. He grinned at John as he took his beer.

"Braves up six-one in the fourth," he said. "Pretty good start, at least."

John smiled as he sat down. "I should check to see if they're in town next week," he said. "Maybe we can work in time for a game."

"Sounds great!" Bryan leaned his head back against the sofa, eyes on the screen. "I haven't been to a Braves game in…. Wow. I think since college, actually."

He went silent, his face falling, and John reached out to place his hand on Bryan's arm where it lay on the cushion between them. "Hey," he said, drawing Bryan's attention. "You know it's okay to talk about it, right? I mean, I understand. Maybe more than most other people would, in some ways."

Bryan studied John's face for a long moment before nodding. "Yeah, I guess you do," he said, his voice low. He flipped his arm and slid it up far enough for John's palm to rest against his. "How'd I get so lucky?"

A million responses ran through John's mind, but he chose the one most likely to lighten the mood. "Don't jump to conclusions," he said, interlacing his fingers with Bryan's. "You haven't seen me at anything approaching my worst."

Bryan slid closer and tilted his head to John's shoulder. "I could say the same to you. Although I think the likelihood that either of us will ever get back to the *worst* worst is pretty low at this point."

John smiled as he turned his head and lowered his chin to rest on top of Bryan's hair. "I'm glad I met you now. Because even a year ago? I don't think I would've been ready for any of this."

Bryan nodded. "I know what you mean." He let out a breath. "I can't promise I'm a hundred percent ready now." He lifted his head to look John in the eye. "But I can promise to try."

John kissed the tip of his nose. "That's all anyone can promise."

They settled back against the sofa, hands still entwined, shoulders brushing, drinking their beer and watching the game.

JOHN startled awake, not sure what woke him up. His neck had a major crick, and he winced as he lifted his head. Then he froze.

He was still on the sofa, but instead of sitting next to Bryan, just holding hands, he was leaned back into the corner of the sofa, and Bryan had curled into his side. John's arm was around Bryan's shoulders, Bryan's hand rested on John's stomach, and Bryan's head was pillowed on John's chest. His breathing was deep and even.

John looked at the TV. A movie he didn't recognize was playing, so the game was over, but he had no idea what time it was. Meghan wasn't home yet, so it couldn't be all that late, but he needed to wake Bryan up and get him headed home. John wouldn't be embarrassed if Meghan walked in on them—not like they were doing anything anyway—but he didn't know if the same would hold true for Bryan, and they needed to decide together when to confirm their relationship to other people.

Problem was, he really didn't want to move.

Bryan felt so good against his side, solid and real, and he didn't want to give that up. It had been such a long time since he'd had the simple pleasure of sleeping with someone. Not sex, necessarily, but the pure comfort of cuddling together, enjoying the feel of another person's body, sleep-warm and heavy. He hadn't had that since Liz, none of the liaisons after she died being anything more than physical release. He hadn't realized until now just how much he'd missed it.

He nuzzled his nose into Bryan's hair and breathed deeply, soaking in the smell of him, clean skin overlaid with a little of the day's sweat and topped off with just a touch of mint. He smiled. No cologne, it seemed, unless it had worn off by day's end—but then, Bryan had spent the day working in the house and likely showered before coming over. John liked that. He preferred natural to fragranced.

He brushed his fingers across Bryan's cheek. "Hey, sleepyhead. Time to wake up and head home."

Bryan blinked his eyes open, and he looked so confused for a moment that it was all John could do not to laugh out loud. He ran his hand into Bryan's hair. "We fell asleep watching the game. It must've been pretty boring, or else we were both pretty tired."

Bryan looked a little more awake by then, but he didn't move. "Mmmm," he said, turning his face until his nose pressed into the side of John's neck. "Was having a nice dream."

John shivered and slid his palm down the back of Bryan's head. "What was it about?"

Bryan froze in place and let out a brief chuckle, his breath warm on John's skin. "I don't remember," he said, lifting his head and meeting John's gaze, his expression sheepish. "I just remember that it was nice."

John leaned in close. "Was I in it?"

Bryan's gaze dropped to John's mouth. "I don't know, but I'd like to think so."

They kissed lazily, nothing pressing or forceful. John's body tingled, but he didn't feel the need to push forward. He was enjoying the ease of this, the anticipation. It felt like an old-fashioned courtship, although he'd be hard pressed to say which of them was doing the courting. Maybe both of them were.

They parted smiling, and John brushed Bryan's hair back from his forehead. "Gonna have to let you go," he said. "Meghan will be home soon, and I don't have a problem with that, but...."

"Slow," Bryan finished. "Your aunt walking in on us making out doesn't exactly fit the definition." He grinned as he pushed back and to his feet, and John watched him move, letting his gaze run down Bryan's chest for a moment before he stood up too.

"So," he said as they walked toward the door. "One-ish Sunday afternoon? That should get us to Liz's parents' place before six, so Beth will have time to settle down from the excitement before bedtime."

"Sounds good," Bryan said. "Anything specific I need to bring? Swimsuit, dress clothes, more homemade chocolate chip cookies?"

John laughed. "Cookies are always welcome," he said. "And not dressy, exactly, but there might be something like a nice dinner, so...."

Bryan gave a mock salute. "Got it. I'll be ready!"

John leaned in for one more light, easy kiss. "Now get outta here." He pulled the door open and waved Bryan out. "Gotta keep things all under wraps."

Bryan paused, one foot over the threshold, and turned back to face John. "That's not where I'd like to keep things."

He grinned and disappeared into the night, leaving John torn between laughter and desire—two of his favorite things.

Chapter 16

WHEN the main house phone rang Friday afternoon, John almost let it go to voice mail. But the landline rang rarely enough that it usually meant something important—when it wasn't a telemarketer—so he stepped into the hall to pick it up. He was surprised to see his mother's name displayed on the handset.

"Hello?" he answered cautiously. Rebecca McConnell almost never called the house, so he couldn't help thinking something was wrong.

"Hello, John. How have you been?"

Her voice sounded normal, smooth and somewhat regal, with a hint of a drawl, and John relaxed as he headed back into his office. "I've been well, Mom," he answered, settling into his chair. "Busy with work and looking after Beth, of course. How are you?"

John expected her to get right to the point of her call, and she did. "Also busy," she said. "I'm calling to ask if you and Beth would be available to come for dinner Sunday evening. It's been much too long since we've seen each other."

John blinked. It wasn't like his mother to offer invitations on such short notice. "Actually, Mom, we're leaving right after church tomorrow to head up to Atlanta," he said. "I'm needed for work, and we've already made arrangements for Beth to stay with Liz's parents."

Rebecca was silent for a few long moments before she spoke. "Would tomorrow night fit your schedule?"

Her formal tone set a small headache pounding behind John's eyes, and he forced back a sigh, reminding himself once again that she was his mother, even when she drove him crazy. "Yes, that would be perfect," he replied. "Will dinner be at seven, as usual?"

"Yes. We'll have drinks at six-thirty. Pamela will serve."

They said their goodbyes, and John let the lingering sigh out as he ended the call. Pamela was the private chef his mother used for special dinners, which meant the meal would come with formal service. He had nothing against formal dinners, but when he was visiting with his mother and bringing his daughter, he'd have much preferred something a little more relaxing. But then, his mother wasn't known for making him feel relaxed.

JOHN felt his mother's eyes on him from across the table, but he concentrated instead on getting Beth set up with her milk and napkin and cutting her chicken into pieces for her. In his peripheral vision, he saw his mother lift her glass of white wine and take a sip. It was her second glass, and he expected it to be her last. He couldn't remember ever seeing her drink any more than that.

His own glass sat untouched at the top right-hand side of his formal place setting. He'd opted for red during their brief pre-dinner drinks, knowing his mother wouldn't have anything stronger than wine and that beer would be out of the question. White had been served with dinner, however. With good china and crystal (at least a plastic cup had been allowed for Beth), cloth napkins and tablecloth, the formality of the service felt over the top for what amounted to a small family dinner. John should have been used to it by now, but as he often did, John wondered how things might be different with his mother if his father hadn't died.

His parents' relationship had always been a bit of a mystery to him. His memories of his father were that he was kind and loving, although more likely to throw a baseball around or take him fishing than to give him a hug. His mother gave out hugs much more often but otherwise stayed reserved, even aloof. He supposed the two of them balanced each other out, but after his father had died, his mother seemed to withdraw ever further into herself.

There was a good reason he rarely visited her. "Uncomfortable" didn't come close to describing it. But he wasn't going to deny his daughter her grandmother, as long as she didn't become hostile. So he finished with Beth's plate and turned to face his mother, smiling at her as he lifted his glass.

"How have your projects been going?" he asked. "Last time we talked you mentioned a charity event you were helping plan."

Rebecca allowed a brief smile as she cut delicately into her chicken. "Two, actually. The foundation gala is only a few months away, and of course we're well into work on the scholarship gala." She had supported a local history foundation and a college scholarship program for years, along with several others in the city, and John knew she worked tirelessly to make their events go off without a hitch.

John swallowed his bite of potato. "Well, if you need an escort, please be sure to call me. I haven't been to a good gala in years."

Another ghost of a smile crossed Rebecca's lips. They ate in silence for a few minutes, until Rebecca turned to Beth, her expression softening, reminding John why he didn't want to take her or Beth away from each other. "How are you enjoying the summer, dear?"

Beth looked at her wide-eyed for a moment before breaking into a huge smile. "It's fun! We go to the park with Jeremy and Mister Bryan or Miss Karen sometimes, and I watch TV and play, and we go to the beach and the restaurant to eat. And Aunt Meghan makes me lunch and reads to me sometimes when Daddy's working."

Rebecca turned back to face John, her expression cooling. "I'm sure your father appreciates Meghan helping out like that."

John pushed back the first retort that came to mind. He always seemed to end up defending Meghan against his mother's passive-aggressive insults. John couldn't even remember the last time the two women had seen each other.

"I do," he told his mother, ignoring the gibe. "She's wonderful with Beth, and an excellent cook, of course. The restaurant is doing very well."

Rebecca turned back to Beth as if he hadn't spoken. "And who are Jeremy and Mister… Bryan, did you say?"

"Mister Bryan and Miss Karen," Beth said, nodding. "Miss Karen is Jeremy's mom and Mister Bryan is her brother. Mister Bryan and Daddy are really good friends now. He came to our house for dinner the other night. He's funny!"

Rebecca raised a regal eyebrow and turned to look at John again. "He came to dinner?"

John steeled himself. "Yes, he did," he said. "And he'll probably come to dinner a lot, actually."

He didn't say any more, but he had a feeling his mother would pick up on the hint. He well remembered her reaction to his college boyfriend and then the mess he'd fallen into after Liz died. He could see her face tightening even as he watched.

"And what does his wife have to say about that?"

John let out the sigh that had been threatening since he first arrived. "He doesn't have one, Mother. He's gay." He half expected Beth to ask him what "gay" was, but one thing she'd learned at a very young age was that you did not interrupt adults at John's mother's dinner table.

Icicles formed in the air between them before Rebecca spoke again. "And you are friends?"

"Yes," John said. "And becoming closer friends."

The first cracks in Rebecca's façade appeared, as John had suspected they would once they embarked on this line of conversation. "And he is spending time with Beth?"

"Yes," John repeated. "He and Beth get along swimmingly. He's been wonderful with her." *And part of me already loves him for that*, he thought, but that was much further than he was willing to go at that point, especially with his mother.

Rebecca rested her fork and knife along the bottom edge of her plate. She adjusted the cuffs on her fine-gauge jacket and reached out to reposition her wine glass. John watched her. Even her fidgeting was formal. He waited for her next pronouncement.

"It's enough that you've taken up with something like... *that*." Her calm demeanor belied the subtle venom in her voice. She would not look at him. "But I simply cannot believe that you would parade that kind of unsavory lifestyle in front of my granddaughter."

John tightened his grip on his glass. "Beth," he said in a low voice. "Why don't you run into the parlor and get that book I brought for you out of your bag? Just sit and read in there, and I'll be there in a little bit. Okay?"

He could see how wide Beth's eyes were, but he didn't turn his head. "Okay, Daddy," she said, her voice small. She slid out of her seat and padded across the room to the door, disappearing around the corner.

John folded his napkin and laid it on the table next to his plate. "I don't ever want to hear you say anything like that in front of my daughter again." He kept his voice level, but anger lay under every word, and he knew his mother would recognize it. "I understand that you were brought up in a very conservative atmosphere, and I don't expect you to change your entire way of thinking. But I will not allow you to pass that along to Beth. She's my daughter, and this is my decision."

Rebecca laid her napkin on the table just as John had and rose to her feet. "I will not have this conversation," she stated. "If you are unable to listen to reason, then I have nothing further to say to you."

John's heart sank. He'd hoped that it wouldn't come to that. He tried once more. "Mother, please sit down," he said. "I know you're basing this on what happened after Liz died, but this isn't the same thing at all. I am very much rational and have thought this through. This is also my decision, and I would hope you'd respect that."

Rebecca regarded him steadily for a long moment before she spoke again. "I don't know where you went wrong, John," she said. "I don't believe you've ever recovered from Liz's death. I cannot condone your behavior or your choice to live your life in this manner. I hope that you will come to your senses soon, but until then, I don't believe there is anything else to say."

Defeated, but not about to give in even to keep the peace, John pushed his chair back and stood. "I'm sorry to hear you say that," he said. "I don't want to keep Beth away from her grandmother, but I will not have you teaching her intolerance. Please let me know when you're ready to discuss this rationally."

He didn't look at her as he left the room to collect Beth and head back home. He felt as if he'd just been through the most civil disowning in history, but he would've expected nothing less from his mother.

SUNDAY was hot. The thermometer hovered around ninety degrees by lunchtime, and John sweated through his T-shirt just walking to his car and back three times to load up. His suitcase and garment bag only took one trip, the other two spent carrying Beth's supplies. Her grandparents kept just a few toys on hand, since visits were so rare, so Beth and John had spent a couple of hours Saturday afternoon picking out some things for her to take along to play with. She also needed Maxie and her favorite blanket in addition to her clothes and a small package of "big girl" diapers. She hated them, but she sometimes had trouble with wetting the bed when she was away from home.

John's mind kept replaying the aborted dinner from the night before. He knew he shouldn't dwell on it, but it was hard not to. He'd known the risks before he'd laid a hand on Bryan, but his mother's reaction had been the first clear manifestation. He hoped it would be the last, though he knew that was a pipe dream.

Back in the house after carrying out the last load, John headed upstairs to take a quick shower and change clothes. He was tying his sneakers when he heard a knock on the front door, and Beth appeared in the doorway of his bedroom.

"Is Mister Bryan here?" She bounced on her toes with excitement, and John grinned at her as he stood up.

"I bet he is," he said, holding out a hand. "Let's go find out."

Beth grabbed his hand, skipping along beside him to the stairs. They climbed down together, and as soon as they hit the bottom, she started skipping again, pulling John along. He laughed at her exuberance but pulled her back just a bit so he could check to be sure it was Bryan at the door. It was, so he dropped Beth's hand.

"You can get the door, Bethy." She smiled at him, reaching for the door handle. It was just a little bit tough for her to open, but she used both hands and opened it a few inches, her head tilting up as she looked outside.

"Hey, Bethy," John heard Bryan greet her. "Are you ready to go to Atlanta?"

"Yes!" Beth pushed the door open and flung herself at Bryan, who caught her with a laugh as she wrapped her arms around his legs. Bryan untangled himself enough to squat down and give Beth a hug, and John's cheeks ached from smiling so widely.

Bryan looked up at him then, a gleam in his eye. "You ready to go too?"

John lifted an eyebrow in silent challenge. "Ready and willing," he replied, knowing Bryan would catch the double meaning in his words. Sure enough, Bryan held his gaze as he stood up slowly.

"Well, then," he said. "Let's get this show on the road."

THE first hour on the road, Beth barely stopped talking. She asked questions about things she saw out the window, chattered at Bryan about the episode of SpongeBob she'd watched while John loaded the car, and asked how much longer until they got there. She had coloring books and crayons, but she ignored them in favor of talking and bouncing in her seat.

An hour and fifteen minutes into the drive, she was fast asleep.

John checked the rearview mirror and saw Beth with her head tipped over against the headrest of her booster seat, her mouth hanging open and her eyes closed, Maxie held in one arm. "Never fails," he told Bryan, returning his attention to the road ahead. "Once the initial excitement wears off, she's out like a light. She'll wake up in a couple of hours, and we'll be getting pretty close to the Butlers' by then."

Bryan made a low sound of acknowledgement. "Tell me about them," he said. John glanced at him, surprised, but Bryan just looked at him steadily. "I want to know. They're Beth's grandparents. They're part of her life, so they're part of your life. And I want to know about your life."

John smiled, eyes back on the road. "Are you deliberately trying to make yourself too good to be true?"

Bryan chuckled and shrugged. "I figure it can't hurt." He reached across and poked John's thigh with his index finger. "Besides, not like you aren't in that same category. Trust me, even some of my old friends ran after what happened, but you...." He trailed off, and John slid his right hand off the steering wheel and reached over to clasp Bryan's hand.

"I told you, I've been there," he said. "I know what happened to me was different, but in a lot of ways, it was the same. So I get it. Not everyone will." He moved his hand back to the steering wheel. "So what do you want to know?"

Bryan shifted in his seat. "Well, I guess, just, what kind of people are they? Where are they from? Are they, well...."

"Are they going to be okay with you and me?" John finished the thought. "I think they will be. I mean, I don't think it'll be any more awkward than it would be with anyone else, considering that we do live in a red state. I'm their son-in-law, so it's going to be a little weird no matter what." He shrugged. "But they've always been pretty open-minded about things, even coming from the heart of the Bible Belt. They're from south Georgia originally. They moved to Conyers when Liz started college. Her dad transferred there because they had family in that area already."

Bryan glanced back over his shoulder at Beth, who still slept soundly, John could see in the mirror. "Was Liz an only child?"

John nodded. "One of the reasons we met, actually." He smiled a little at the memory. "It was a joint party with her sorority and my fraternity. They had this silly ice-breaker game where they divided us up based on how many siblings we had, and Liz and I ended up sitting next to each other. We started talking, and by the next weekend we were joined at the hip."

Bryan was nodding. "Sounds a lot like Eddie and me," he said. "We met at a mutual friend's birthday party. I got there a little late because I got held up at my job, and the only seat left was next to Eddie. We got to talking, and we were pretty much together from then on."

He grinned over at John. "And I doubt it was the *hip* exactly that you two were joined at."

John lifted an eyebrow. "Well, that general vicinity, anyway. We were twenty years old and hormonal. What would you expect?"

Bryan laughed. "No different from us at all, then," he acknowledged. "Let's just say I was glad I lived off-campus and had my own bedroom and a roommate whose girlfriend had her own place. Because we spent a *lot* of time there for a few months."

John bit his lip, a little reluctant to ask the next question that came to mind, but he thought maybe it was one of those hurdles they'd need to jump. "What was he like?" he asked, and held his breath as he waited for Bryan's answer.

Chapter 17

BRYAN was quiet for a minute before he spoke, and when he did, his voice was rough.

"Funny. That was the first thing I noticed about him. Yeah, he was cute, but there were a lot of cute guys around. Eddie had this… spark about him. When he smiled it was like the whole room lit up, and when he laughed, everyone did. He'd be silly or goofy and not worry about what anyone else thought. He could be snarky sometimes, but not in a mean way. And he could be serious too. I don't want to make it sound like he was flippant about everything. But what I remember about being with him above everything else was how much he made me laugh."

A slow smile had spread across John's face as Bryan talked. "Liz hated practical jokes," he said. "She wouldn't ruin them, but she wouldn't participate, and if you tried to pull one on her, she would get pissed about it. She just didn't think it was funny. But she loved to laugh, and she was really quick-witted. I had a hell of a time keeping up with her." He laughed. "I learned pretty fast never to get into a pun war with that woman."

Bryan tilted his head back against the seat, smiling. "Eddie loved practical jokes, but he only pulled them on people he knew liked them. Nothing worse than trying to make a joke and making someone mad instead. That happened once, on April Fool's Day. He locked his roommate out of the room when he'd gone to take a shower in just a towel. And he was stuck for hours because it was a Saturday right after midterms and almost everyone had left campus. Ben had done worse to him, but apparently he could dish it out better than he could take it."

John shook his head. "Sounds like he deserved it," he said. "But I imagine payback was hell."

"It was." Bryan laughed. "Total war for almost a month. Superglue was involved more than once. Hair was cut, or shaved, I should say. I thought they were going to cause serious injury before they called a truce."

He sobered. "After we… what happened, Ben was so upset. It was only a couple of months after the prank war, and he was afraid Eddie would remember it wrong and think they really hated each other or something. It took over a year before he went to visit."

John reached out, sliding his fingers around Bryan's, just wanting to offer a little comfort and support. Bryan lifted his thumb to rub along the edge of John's hand but didn't say anything, and they rode in silence for a while. Bryan leaned over to turn on the radio, stretching his right arm across his body to reach, never moving his left hand from John's. He searched until he found what sounded like an alternative rock station and shot John a grin.

"Close enough to Athens for college radio, I guess." He adjusted the volume to keep it as background and sat back, shifting so he was turned toward John. "What kind of music do you like? Nice, safe topic of discussion, right?"

John grinned. "As long as we don't have some kind of major disagreement and end up not speaking to each other." From the corner of his eye, he saw Bryan smile too. "I'm not a big music connoisseur," he continued. "I just kind of know what I like when I hear it. Pretty much any type you can name, there's probably something I like in there somewhere. Even something like opera."

Bryan was still smiling. "This is kind of my style," he said, nodding toward the radio. "Alternative, off the beaten path. Back in college I was all about the craziest avant-garde stuff for a while, but I managed to climb down off my high horse."

"It's kind of Athens law that you have to be a fan of R.E.M. and the B-52s," John noted. "And it's kind of college law that you have to like college radio-type music. Not so bad, really. College is for trying things on to see how they fit, right?"

"And shedding the things that don't," Bryan agreed. He dropped his gaze to his hands where they sat in his lap. "In my case, that meant some friends too. I didn't come out until college, and some of my old friends, and some new ones, weren't all that happy about it."

John nodded. "I lost a few when I started dating Trent. A couple of them tried to get back in touch after I married Liz. I guess they thought what they did was okay because it turned out I wasn't gay. As if it would've been okay if I *had* been?" He shrugged. "Don't have time for that stuff. If they'd apologized, maybe, but they acted like nothing ever happened."

Bryan sighed. "We were both pretty lucky, I guess. We both had some problems when people found out we liked guys. Or in your case, both. A lot of people go through a lot of shi—" He cut himself off and glanced back at Beth, who was still sleeping. John saw Bryan's face soften as he looked at her, and his heart gave a little flip in response.

"A lot of… really bad stuff," Bryan finished his thought, turning back to look out the window at the road ahead. "I had a couple of friends whose parents kicked them out or cut them off. One guy in my major was about five years older because he'd had to go out on his own when he was eighteen. His parents refused to have anything to do with him after he came out. He had a scholarship, but even then it took him that long to save up before he could start college."

He lapsed into silence. Then he laughed shortly. "Hell, even music comes back to the serious stuff," he mused. "Guess it's just that kind of day."

John reached over to take Bryan's hand again. "It's okay," he said. "Some days are just worse than others."

Bryan laced their fingers together, and John smiled.

LIZ'S parents lived an hour east of downtown Atlanta, in a subdivision old enough to have missed the cookie-cutter McMansion look. The house had a wide front porch complete with swing and comfortable rocking chairs and was surrounded by pines and magnolias. John associated a lot of happy memories with the house, even with the shadows of the bad lingering around the edges.

Just a few seconds after he pulled into the driveway, the front door opened and Jean Butler stepped out. She waved, smiling, and John waved back, popping his seat belt and turning back to smile at Beth, who was bouncing in her booster seat. As predicted, she'd woken up an hour earlier and had kept up a near-constant running commentary ever since.

"You ready to see Gramma and Grampa?" he asked.

"Yes!" Beth bounced more. "Can we go, Daddy?"

John glanced at Bryan, and the two men shared a quick smile. "How about we let Mister Bryan help you out of your seat while I say hi to your Gramma. Okay?"

"Okay!" Beth was back to her usual top volume, and John had to laugh again.

The two men climbed out, and John stepped over to greet Jean, who'd come down the steps to meet them. "Hey!" he said, smiling as he opened his arms to accept her hug.

She pulled him in close, pressing a kiss to his cheek. "It's so good to see you, John," she said, pulling back to look up at him. "It's been too long."

"It's always too long," he agreed. He half turned to look back at the car, just in time to see Bryan helping Beth down to the ground. Almost as soon as she was on her feet, she was running toward them, and Jean laughed as she bent to accept Beth's enthusiastic hug.

"Hi, Ladybug," she said, giving her a kiss on the cheek just as she had John. John felt a pang in his chest. The nickname had been one of her favorites for Liz too.

Jean straightened back up and smiled at Bryan as he approached, holding out her hand. "And you must be the fabled Mister Bryan," she said, drawing a surprised laugh from Bryan as he shook the offered hand. "Oh yes, little Miss Beth seems to be quite a fan. She told me all about you when she and her dad called the other day to tell me she was coming."

John felt Bryan's eyes on him, and his cheeks warmed. He hadn't mentioned that conversation to Bryan, but then, he'd been fixing lunch while Beth and her grandmother chatted, so he hadn't heard every word. "Well, little Miss Beth and Mister Bryan here have a lot in common," he said, reaching to run his hand over Beth's head. "An affinity for *SpongeBob SquarePants*, for example."

The low snort of laughter that escaped Bryan made both John and Jean smile wider. "Well, come on in, boys," Jean said. "William insisted on firing up the grill tonight, so I hope steak is okay with you for dinner."

John and Bryan exchanged a look, and Bryan shrugged. John had expected they might offer dinner, and if Bryan had no objections, he'd take it. Jean was an excellent cook, and William knew his way around a steak.

"Sounds great," John answered for all of them. "Bryan, could you help me with Beth's bags? Beth, you go with Gramma, okay?"

Beth nodded and reached for Jean's hand, turning her face up to look at her grandmother. "Can we go see the fishies?" she asked, and Jean laughed as she led her toward the house.

John turned toward Bryan, finding him with a wide smile on his face. "C'mon, pack mule," John said, reaching out to brush his fingers down Bryan's forearm. "Let's get Her Royal Highness's Matched Luggage inside."

Bryan followed John around to the trunk of the car. "*Spaceballs* quotes too? Man, you just keep getting better and better." He paused. "Or worse and worse, I'm not really sure."

John shot Bryan a look. "Says the SpongeBob aficionado," he retorted. He popped the trunk and lifted the lid, reaching for Beth's bags. Bryan waited until he'd unloaded and pushed the trunk closed before reaching for two of the four bags. He shook his head with a rueful smile.

"What *is* it with women and their luggage?" he joked. "And they're starting so young these days too!"

John chuckled as he picked up the other two bags and led the way toward the house. "At least Beth has the excuse of toys and such," he said. "Whenever Liz and I went anywhere, she always had twice as many bags as me. I mean, I know women have more necessities than men, but *twice* as many? Just seems excessive to me."

"Hey, talking to another guy here," Bryan pointed out. "You want answers, take it up with my sister." He paused, looking thoughtful.

"Although maybe wait until after the pregnancy hormones are done with her."

They were stepping inside by then, and John nodded down the hallway to their right. "Second door on the left," he said, standing aside to let Bryan go ahead of him. He knew what he'd see inside. The Butlers had set up the room for Beth during that first bad year, when she spent so much time with them, and all they'd done since was change out the crib for a "big girl" bed. The walls were painted soft green, and a bookshelf held small collections of books and stuffed animals on the lower shelves, within Beth's reach. John put the bags he carried next to the closet door and indicated Bryan should do the same. "Beth likes to help unpack, so Jean will do that with her later." He regarded Bryan for a moment. "You know, it occurs to me that I never asked if you're doing okay with this."

Bryan gave him a puzzled look. "You mean… the Butlers?"

John nodded, sliding his hands into his pockets and leaning to rest one shoulder against the wall. "It's got to be a little weird," he observed. "I mean, meeting the former in-laws is inevitable in a situation like this. But this"—he waved a hand between them—"it's still all so new. I don't want to rush you into something you aren't ready for."

Bryan smiled and took a step forward, running a hand up John's arm to his shoulder, where he squeezed lightly. "I'm fine, John," he said. "Really. Is it weird? Sure, a little. But Jean seems really nice, and it's not like we're going to go at it on their dining room table." He lowered his voice at the last, and one eyebrow lifted. His hand slid from John's shoulder to cup the side of his neck. "At least, I assume we aren't."

John had to bite back the bark of laughter that tried to escape. He pushed off the wall and reached out to pinch Bryan's side, using his surprised flinch to catch him off guard and steal a quick kiss. Bryan's hand was still on his neck, though, and when he moved away, Bryan pulled him back in for something a little more lingering.

They parted smiling, and John tilted his head back toward the door. "Let's go have some steak."

DINNER was excellent, as John had anticipated it would be. William had always been a man of few words, and this night was no exception, but he did have a few things to say about grilling. He was a charcoal man, never used lighter fluid, and liked his steaks rare, though he did (begrudgingly, John thought) cook up to medium well on request. "Well done" did not exist in his grilling vocabulary.

Jean's contribution of scalloped potatoes and fresh green beans left John eating until he thought he would burst, and only then did he remember dessert. Jean's baking outshone even her cooking, and there would be no way she'd have them eat without serving something amazing. Sure enough, as they were finishing their meal, Jean stood up and picked up her plate and Beth's before bustling off to the kitchen. She returned with a beautifully frosted red velvet cake, and John groaned. His favorite. Of course.

"Oh my God, Jean," he said. "If I'd known you had that hiding in the kitchen, I would've left more room for it!"

She smiled at him. "Don't worry, dear. I'll be right back with a plate and some tinfoil, and you and Bryan can take your slices for later."

She disappeared back into the kitchen, and John glanced over at Bryan to find him with a napkin in hand, using the classic lick-and-wipe method to clean a bit of something from Beth's dinner off her cheek. John's heart did a stutter-step in his chest at the sight. *Jesus.* If the guy was trying to make John fall for him, he had yet to make a single misstep along the way.

Bryan looked up at him and smiled, and it took John a great deal of willpower not to drag him out of there bodily and take him somewhere very private very fast. Instead, he took a deep breath and returned the smile, watching as Beth tilted her head against Bryan's arm. John's eyes were suddenly wet, and he looked away, blinking several times to clear his vision. Jean came back in with her plate and foil and started up a running commentary about her favorite desserts and how John just made the *best* pies, all while she cut several very generous slices of cake, arranged them on the plate, and covered the whole thing with a layer of foil. John was glad for the distraction to give him a chance to tamp down his emotions.

Finished, Jean picked up the covered plate and held it out to John. "I suppose you boys should get on the road before it gets dark. William and Beth and I will have our dessert, and we'll get her off to bed soon."

It was just six o'clock, and sunset was still more than an hour away, but John didn't argue, pushing back his chair to stand up. "Yeah, and we still have to unload when we get there," he said. He squatted down next to Beth's chair and smiled at her. "Do you have a goodbye hug for your daddy?"

Predictably, Beth flung both arms around John's neck, squeezing him tight. John slid one arm around Beth to return the hug, pressing a kiss into the top of her head as he pulled back and caught her eyes. "I'll call you during the week some, baby," he said. He usually called each day after lunch, although he didn't always catch them. "You be good for your Gramma and Grampa. I don't want to hear about you misbehaving, okay?"

Beth nodded solemnly. "I promise, Daddy."

He smiled and kissed her forehead. Pushing to his feet, he held out a hand to William, who'd stood up to see them out. "Great steak as usual, sir," he said. "Hope to have another soon."

William nodded. "Got all summer," he said. "Come back when you can."

John smiled and turned to Jean, who enveloped him in a hug before he could move. He laughed a little as he returned it. "It's so good to see you, John," she said. "We'll see you next weekend." She lowered her voice, although Beth and Bryan were saying their goodbyes by then, so it wasn't quiet in the room. "And I like your young man too."

John jerked in surprise. Pulling back, he looked at her face and saw a small but knowing smile there, tinged with just a little sadness.

"So do I," he admitted, just as softly, and she leaned up to kiss his cheek before turning toward Bryan.

"It was wonderful to meet you, Bryan," she said, holding out a hand, which he took. She wrapped her other hand around it. "We'll see you next weekend, and I hope you'll come back to visit us again soon too."

Bryan smiled. "Thank you, ma'am." He nodded to William before stepping back, letting John lead the way as Jean walked them out.

More goodbyes followed at the door, including Beth running up to hug first John's legs and then Bryan's, and Jean hurried back to fetch the plate of cake they'd nearly forgotten. Ten minutes later, they were finally back in the car, and they gave each other a long look before breaking into snickers.

"Sheesh," John said, starting the car. He stretched his right arm out, resting it on the back of Bryan's headrest, looking out the rear window as he backed out the driveway.

"Always seems to take a year, doesn't it?" Bryan's voice was suffused with laughter. "I heard a song once years ago from some variety show or something that was all about trying to take your leave after a get-together. It had lines like 'Did you get your dish?' 'I think I did', all the things you say when you're saying goodbye."

John chuckled as he turned back to the front and shifted into gear, heading back for the interstate. "I think I've heard that one, but I couldn't begin to tell you what it's from."

"We should make up our own," Bryan said. "'Leftovers, leftovers, take home your share,'" he sang, somewhat on key, to a tune that sounded familiar to John but that he couldn't quite place. Then he stopped and laughed. "Maybe we should leave the songwriting to the experts."

John laughed too. "Sounds like a plan."

AN HOUR and a half later, they'd gotten to the apartment complex, unloaded their bags, and flopped down on opposite ends of the sofa to catch their breath.

"Man," John said. "I guess it's cooling off out there, but it's so muggy you can't even breathe." He glanced at the clock. "Wow, can't believe it's barely after seven. I feel like I've been up for three days."

Bryan groaned. "Too early to go to sleep, too late to take a nap." He fumbled out with one hand on the side table, coming back with the TV remote. "Sunday night baseball, maybe?"

"Works for me." John mustered up the energy to stand up, kicking off his shoes and padding toward the kitchen. "I was promised Sweetwater, so we'll see if Adam came through."

He pulled the refrigerator door open and smiled at the two six-packs of bottled beer inside. "IPA and 420," he called out, naming the company's two pale ales. "Name your poison!"

"Either's fine," Bryan replied. "But it's been a while since I've had the IPA."

John pulled out two, bending to use the corner of the dishtowel hanging from the stove door to twist off the caps. He headed back for the sofa, seeing that Bryan had found the baseball pregame show but had it muted. He sat and held out a bottle.

"Thanks," Bryan said, smiling as he took it.

"A toast," John said, and Bryan raised an eyebrow. "To a productive week, in more ways than one." Bryan nodded his agreement as they clinked their bottles together.

Bryan turned up the sound on the TV, and they sat drinking their beer and watching the commentators give scores and highlights of the afternoon's action. John's eyelids were beginning to droop already from the day's activities and the alcohol starting to course through his system, but he didn't want to move yet. He was comfortable, and he had Bryan nearby… and hey, why was Bryan all the way over there, anyway?

John lifted his arm from the back of the sofa and waved his hand. "C'mere."

Bryan gave him a surprised look.

"What, just because we're off in Atlanta and not in my house, we can't cuddle a little? Do we need a chaperone?"

Bryan laughed and slid down the sofa and into John's side. John dropped his arm around Bryan's shoulders, and Bryan slipped his hand onto John's thigh, close to his knee, safely away from anything that might rush things too far ahead. John leaned over far enough to kiss Bryan just in front of his ear, and Bryan smiled and took another sip of his beer, eyes on the TV screen.

John settled in, sipping his beer and feeling Bryan's warmth against him, sort of watching the TV but mostly just letting his mind wander. He should have been unpacking and getting ready for the week, but he didn't much feel like moving. He should have been asking Bryan about his plans for the week, but he didn't much feel like talking either. Besides, it was still early in the evening, so they had time for all that later.

Bryan shifted next to him, leaning forward to set his half-empty beer on the coffee table. He turned and reached for John's bottle, too, and John let him take it, watching, curious, as he set it down next to his own. Then Bryan turned back toward John and cupped his cheek in one hand, and John had just enough time to crook a small smile before Bryan's mouth covered his.

Chapter 18

BRYAN'S kiss wasn't tentative, but it wasn't quite overpowering, either. It was deep, thorough, and incredibly arousing, but Bryan didn't push or demand anything except acceptance. John gave him that easily, opening his mouth, letting Bryan's tongue slide against his. He sighed and wrapped his arm around Bryan's waist, shifting to press their bodies closer together but keeping everything on that low level, not moving too hard or too fast.

Bryan's fingers brushed over the light stubble along John's jaw, and his thumb rubbed the edge of John's chin. The light touches sent tingles across John's skin, raising goosebumps like a cool breeze on a warm day. His body wanted more, the desire and arousal inside him begging to be set free, but he tamped it down. *Slow and steady*, he told himself. *This feels amazing. Enjoy every moment.*

Bryan backed away, the light pressure of his fingertips the hint John needed to follow suit. Their lips parted and their eyes opened, and John's heart did that little flip in his chest he'd come to associate with Bryan. Bryan's eyes were dark, trained on John's lips, and his thumb ran over John's mouth this time, wiping away the moisture.

"You're really good at that," John whispered, his lips moving against Bryan's thumb.

Bryan's eyes flicked up, and he met John's gaze with a smile. "I told you," he said, bringing his hand out to rest on John's shoulder. "I like kissing. A lot. And I tend to get pretty good at things I really like doing."

John tilted his head forward to brush his nose against Bryan's. "Lucky me."

Bryan kissed him again briefly before sliding out of his arms and reaching for their beers. "Here," he said, handing John his and settling back in against his side. "Let's finish our beers and then see about unpacking or whatever we need to do. I know you have to work early tomorrow."

John groaned, took a big mouthful of beer, and swallowed. "Did I ever mention I hate working in an office? Kind of silly for someone in my line of work, I guess. I think finding a way to work from home has been one of the best things I've done for myself. I like the flexibility and the quiet, and it's a huge help with Beth. She rarely goes to any kind of daycare."

Bryan nodded. "Yeah, that's one of the things Karen and Davis like best about the B-and-B. Jeremy went to pre-K this year, but otherwise he hasn't had to go to daycare since they bought the place."

John tilted his head. "Beth went to pre-K too." He shook his head. "Can't believe she starts kindergarten in the fall."

"They grow up so fast," Bryan teased, grinning, and John pinched his side in retaliation, jumping up before he could try to fight back.

"I'm going to get my stuff unpacked," he said, raising his voice as he walked into the kitchen to drop his empty bottle into the recycling can next to the trash can. "The bedrooms are pretty much the same, so grab whichever one you want." He wasn't about to suggest they share. That would *not* qualify as taking it slowly.

He turned around and jumped a little. Bryan was standing right there, trying and failing to fight off a smile. "Boo!" he said, and they lasted about three seconds before they both cracked up. Bryan held up his empty bottle, still laughing, and John hitched a thumb over his shoulder.

"Recycling," he said around the remaining laughter. As Bryan stepped to the side to go around him, John reached out, running his hand across Bryan's stomach, feeling the muscles twitch under his fingers. Bryan stopped, his head turning toward John, and the raw desire John saw in Bryan's eyes almost, *almost* cracked his willpower.

Instead, he let his hand fall away and took a step back. "Like I said, whichever bedroom you want is fine with me. I think they both have queen-sized beds still."

Bryan broke their gaze, turning to drop his bottle into the bin. He blew out a low breath and shrugged, glancing back at John. "Go for it," he said. "I'll be fine either way."

John hesitated for only a moment before heading back toward the door, where their bags still sat where they'd dropped them on the way in. He picked his up and started down the hallway, and in a split second decided to take the first bedroom. That way if Bryan wanted to sleep in, John wouldn't have to worry about waking him up on his way down the hall in the morning.

He was lifting his suitcase onto the dresser when a soft knock sounded on the doorframe. He looked over to find Bryan smiling at him, but he looked tentative. "You sure this is okay?"

John had to laugh. "Are we trying to out-polite each other or what?" He dropped his hands on top of his bag and nodded firmly. "Yes, Bryan, this bedroom is fine with me. And I'm sure the other one will be fine with you." He tilted his head, more serious. "And yeah, there's some tension here, and there probably will be all week. But that's okay. We'll deal with it. Okay?"

Bryan shook his head and smiled, at both of them, John knew. "Okay," he said. "See you in the morning?"

"Depends on how late you plan to sleep," John said. "I'll have to be up and out pretty early." He frowned. "I didn't even think about the car. Are you going to need it? I can get a cab or—"

Bryan stopped him with a hand held up. "No, I'm good. If I need it, I'll get up early enough to drop you by the office. But I'm spending tomorrow with a couple of college friends, and they can pick me up, so no problem."

John chuckled a little. "Overly polite again," he observed. He reached for the zipper on his suitcase. "Sleep well, and have fun with your friends tomorrow."

"You too, and I will." Bryan flashed a brilliant smile before heading down the hall, and it hit John hard enough that he had to pause to draw in a breath. He really was gorgeous, and John needed to watch himself this week. He didn't want to do anything to damage what was building between them, and he had no idea what kind of landmines might be waiting when Bryan went to visit Eddie.

JOHN walked into the office five minutes before eight Monday morning to a chorus of greetings from coworkers he hadn't seen in months. His last trip had been in January, so all the contact he'd had with them since had been long distance. He told everyone he was doing great, Beth was doing great, they loved living on Tybee, and no, they had no plans to move back to the "big city."

All in all, it took him a good twenty minutes to make his way to the small conference room near Adam's office that he used as his home base when he was on site. He'd just gotten his laptop unpacked and had started setting up his work area with the supplies that had been left for him when he saw movement in the doorway. He looked up to find Adam grinning at him, his hands on his hips.

"About time you got here," he said. "Enjoy the ticker-tape parade?"

John rolled his eyes and grinned. "I'm disappointed," he said, stepping around the table toward Adam. "No key to the city? No giant balloons? Where are the fireworks?"

Adam laughed and took the hand John offered, but he pulled him into a one-armed hug too. "It's good to see you, man," Adam said as they parted. He nodded into the room. "Setup gonna work for you?"

John shrugged. "Just fine. Just a week anyway." He grinned. "And you know I'll tell you if it's not."

Adam watched as John moved back around to his work area. "So, once you're settled and caffeinated, stop on by and let's get the list for the week knocked out," he said. "You free for lunch? Or are you meeting Bryan?"

John felt himself blushing but ignored it. "Free," he replied, not looking at Adam. "Bryan's visiting with friends today."

When Adam didn't immediately respond, John chanced a look up and saw him with an eyebrow raised and a small smirk on his face.

John rolled his eyes. "Get out of here, you." He made a shooing motion with one hand, and Adam laughed and disappeared. John shook his head, still smiling, and turned back to getting his space settled.

ADAM ordered sandwiches in for lunch, which they did most of the time when John was in the office. They shut the conference room door and spread out on the opposite end of the table from where John had been working, handing sandwiches, chips, and condiments back and forth.

A few bites into his sandwich, Adam put it down and took a sip of his water, which was almost all he drank, except beer, of course. He raised an eyebrow at John and wiped his hands on a napkin. "So did you get into his pants yet?"

John managed not to choke, but only just. Eyes watering, he grabbed a napkin to wipe at them. "Jesus, man," he finally said. "At least wait until my mouth is empty before you pull something like that out of your hat."

Adam was still laughing. "Sorry about that," he said. "But you haven't answered the question."

John rolled his eyes. "No, I have not." There was no use in trying to say it wasn't Adam's business. John was the one who'd brought it up with him to start with. "There are some issues there. More than I knew. We're…. I guess we're… seeing each other? I don't know how to describe it. But we're taking things slowly."

Adam nodded. "Issues? Or is that too personal to get into?"

John sighed, picking a piece of limp lettuce off the side of his sandwich. "There's an ex," he said. "And it wasn't a bad breakup or anything like that. They got…. They were jumped, and got beaten up pretty badly. And the ex never recovered. So they were forced apart by circumstances, not choice." He bit his lip, staring down at the chips spilling from the bag onto the table next to him. "That's part of why he came up. He's going to go see him this week."

Adam made an indistinct sound in his throat and lifted his bottle to take another sip of water. "That's a little awkward," he said, voice neutral.

John almost laughed. "To say the least." He lifted his head to meet Adam's steady gaze. "I have no clue how it's going to go. We both know he needs to do it. He still loves Eddie, and Eddie probably still loves him too. But Bryan isn't moving on, and he knows he needs to." He shrugged one shoulder. "I can empathize."

Adam nodded, chewing and swallowing the bite of sandwich in his mouth. "And how are you feeling about all this?"

John did laugh then, a small chuckle. "Still a little guilty. Still a little unsure. I'm trying not to let it show much. I'm farther along than Bryan is with all this. But mostly I'm okay. I'm treading carefully, but I'm okay."

"Bit of a tightrope."

"Not that bad," John replied. "Well, the part about Bryan seeing Eddie, yeah, that could blow up. But overall, it's been good."

John should've guessed what was coming next when a slow, wicked smile spread across Adam's face. "He a good kisser?"

John snorted. "None of your damn business."

"That'd be a yes, then," Adam observed, lifting the remaining half of his sandwich in a mock toast.

John shook his head and let it go. Not like he was wrong, anyway.

JOHN didn't make it back to the apartment until eight, having stopped to pick up a few groceries on the way home. To his surprise, the apartment was dark and empty when he stepped inside. He shrugged, figuring Bryan's friends had taken him to dinner, and carried his bags into the kitchen to unload. Sandwich supplies, eggs, and a quart of milk went into the refrigerator, coffee, chips, and cookies on the counter.

He'd also picked up a pizza for dinner, so he went ahead and put that in the oven before walking down to his bedroom to change into shorts and a T-shirt. One of the biggest downsides to working in the office was wearing business clothes. Ties weren't required, but the male "uniform" at the office was the standard dress slacks, shirt, and shoes, and while they weren't terrible, they weren't exactly comfortable, either.

Changed, John walked barefoot back to the kitchen, grabbing a beer out of the fridge and digging around for plates and something to slice the pizza with, surprised to find an actual rolling pizza cutter in one of the drawers. The pizza still had a few more minutes to go, so he went into the living room, put his beer and a couple of paper towels on the coffee table, and found the Braves game on TV.

He'd just slid two slices of the finished pizza onto a plate when he heard the front door open. "Hey," he called out. "I sure hope that's Bryan."

Bryan's laugh greeted him. "No, it's a figment of your imagination." He came around the corner, smiling widely, eyes bright, looking so gorgeous that John couldn't help himself. He closed the three feet of distance between them and kissed that smile. He did manage to keep the kiss light and easy, and Bryan returned it in kind, one of his warm hands coming up to rest on John's hip. He was smiling again when John drew away. "Hi, honey, I'm home?" he joked.

John grinned as he stepped back and waved at the pizza sitting on top of the stove. "Heated up a pizza for dinner, if you haven't eaten yet. And there's still beer in the fridge too. And a Braves game on TV."

Bryan nodded. "Had dinner already, but beer and baseball sounds like a plan." He ran his eyes down John's body, and John felt it like a caress. "Just let me go change clothes and make a pit stop."

John nodded, reaching for the fridge door. "Meet you on the sofa!"

THE Braves won, the beer and pizza were good, and Bryan's toes were warm against John's thigh. He'd sat down sideways on the sofa and pressed his feet against John's leg, and John had laid his hand over Bryan's ankles and left it there, even though it meant eating and drinking one-handed.

A warm lassitude sank over him the longer they sat there, and he might have drifted off to sleep if not for his body's continual reminders of his connection to Bryan. His reactions grew stronger with every minute they spent together, more so when they were touching, even as casually as this. It was a wonderful feeling, but it made the taking-it-slow thing pretty difficult to stick to.

Resolved, he lifted his hand off Bryan and pushed to his feet, then bent to pick up his empty beer bottle and pizza plate. Bryan stretched his legs out to fill the spot he'd left and smiled up at him. "Thanks for warming the sofa for me."

John laughed and pointed a pinky toward Bryan's bottle. "Hand me that and I'll get these tossed and put the pizza away. You need the car tomorrow?"

Bryan sat up straighter and reached for his empty bottle. "Yeah, if you don't mind. I'd like to go visit Andrew and Betsey, but they live up in Alpharetta."

John nodded as he tucked his bottle between his arm and his chest and took Bryan's from his hand, trying to ignore the feel of his skin as their fingers brushed. "I don't have to be in quite so early tomorrow, so if we could leave by around eight-thirty?"

Bryan was standing up by then too. "Sounds good." He linked his fingers together and stretched his arms out straight over his head, the hem of his T-shirt lifting and the waistband of his loose shorts dropping, opening up several inches of smooth, bare skin in between. John's mouth went dry, and he spun on his heel and marched into the kitchen before he gave up on all those well-intentioned resolutions and jumped Bryan right there in the living room.

When he'd finished up in the kitchen and gotten his libido under control, he came back to the living room to find the television off and Bryan gone. He walked down to his bedroom and glanced farther down toward Bryan's. The door was closed, but light glowed under it. He considered, for about three seconds, going down the hall to say goodnight, but he knew he was lying to himself. If he did that, he'd be doing a lot more than saying goodnight.

Sighing and shaking his head at himself, he went into his own bedroom, pushing thoughts of Bryan aside and focusing on getting ready for bed and getting a decent night's sleep.

Chapter 19

JOHN did sleep well, to his surprise, and it was a good thing, since he had to hit the ground running when Bryan dropped him off at the office Tuesday morning. They'd had just enough time to pick up breakfast and coffee on the way, and Bryan had given him a smile and squeezed his hand before he climbed out. The warmth lingered on John's fingers while he met with Adam and even held over while he dived into the list of report revisions Adam had compiled.

Focused on the coding, he jumped when Adam knocked on the doorframe. It took him a couple of seconds for his eyes to shift focus from the screen to real life. "Sandwiches are here," Adam said. "Holly is bringing them in now. You ready to eat?"

John glanced at the computer clock and was surprised to see that it was already one. He also realized he was hungry. "Definitely!" He stretched out his arms and twisted to release the tension that had built up in his back. "I didn't even realize it was lunchtime."

Adam laughed and moved into the room, pulling out the chair at the far end where he'd sat the day before. "I walked by a couple of times and you didn't even seem to be blinking. Are the changes that complicated?"

John shook his head and shifted down to the chair across from Adam. "No, I just tend to get engrossed in the coding and lose track of time." He grinned. "That's why you pay me the mediocre bucks, right?"

Holly came in with the box holding their sandwiches, and her eyes sparkled when she saw John. She'd been out with a sick child on Monday, so he'd missed seeing her until now. She wore her usual conservatively classic skirt, blouse, and pumps, her prematurely silver hair was cut into a short bob that suited her strong features, and as usual, her near-constant happy attitude made her shine.

"Well, if it isn't Johnny Buffett," she said, one of her myriad nicknames referencing his island lifestyle. "I can't promise you a cheeseburger in paradise, but I hear these club sandwiches are pretty close to heaven on earth."

John was on his feet by then, stepping around the table to give her a big hug as soon as she put the box down. "Good to see you too, Miss Golightly," he said, bringing out one of his own nicknames and smiling at her as he stepped back. "Thanks for making the arrangements for this week on short notice. And the Sweetwater did not go unappreciated, trust me."

Holly waved a hand. "You men always need someone to take care of you," she teased. She unloaded their sandwiches and drinks as she spoke. "How's that beautiful daughter of yours?"

Holly's own daughter was only three years older than Beth, even though Holly was ten years older than John. John smiled and reached for his sandwich. "She's still beautiful, and smart, and rambunctious, and a huge handful."

"And you love every second of it," Holly finished, making John laugh.

"You speak the truth," he said.

Holly grinned at him again, picking up the empty box in one hand and lightly smacking Adam on the back of his head with the other. Ignoring his soft "ow!" of protest, she headed for the door. "I'll shut this behind me," she said. "Try to keep the gossip down to a dull roar. *Some* of us are trying to get some work done out there."

She was gone, and John and Adam looked at each other for a long second before cracking up. "Another visit from Hurricane Holly," Adam said. He pulled the wrapping off his sandwich. "But I swear, you look up 'efficient' in the dictionary, and you'll find her picture. This place would just about fall apart without her."

John nodded and bit into his sandwich. Coolly efficient and a step ahead of everyone around her, Holly had been the support behind Adam almost from his first day with the company. John had no doubt that she'd move up the ranks right along with Adam, and John more than half expected Adam to be running the company by the time he was fifty.

Adam sipped his water. "Still behaving yourself, Johnny Boy?"

John rolled his eyes. "You know, for a happily married straight guy, you sure have an inordinate amount of interest in gay sex. Or lack thereof, in this case," he added, before Adam could give a predictable response.

Adam held out a hand, palm toward John in the universal sign for "stop." "No, no, no details, please," he said, grinning. "Just looking out for a friend."

John smiled. Despite all the joking and teasing, he knew Adam was sincere about that. Adam had helped see him through the darkest year of his life, and John didn't think he'd ever be able to repay him.

He turned the conversation to Adam's kids, watching him light up as he talked about them and nodding in understanding. The twins had just turned six, the youngest not quite three, so John had both empathy and sympathy to spare. He also found himself saying they should come to Tybee later in the summer to visit. "We have extra room, or if you'd rather, the bed-and-breakfast would be nice. I haven't seen all the rooms, but if they're anything like the kitchen Bryan designed, I have no doubt they'll be amazing."

Adam lifted an eyebrow at that. "Bryan's a designer?"

John shook his head, brushing his hands together to knock off potato chip dust. "He has an undergraduate degree in architecture but wasn't able to go on for his master's. He's been helping with the renovations and doing a lot of the design work. I think he may be considering switching to historic preservation instead, though. He seems to enjoy that aspect of it, so I told him I thought that might be a good fit for him."

Adam was silent for a few long moments. John looked at him and had trouble figuring out the expression on his face. "What?"

Adam almost smiled. "Just thinking Bryan's a lucky guy, that's all."

John wasn't sure whether to laugh or blush. "Watch it, Morgan," he managed. "Don't want people thinking things about you."

Adam did smile then, balling up his sandwich wrapper in his hands. "Don't really care what people think. I'd say the same thing if you were a woman." The smile turned wicked. "Although I guess then Bryan wouldn't be the one getting lucky."

"No getting lucky!" John gathered up his own trash. He paused and imitated the wicked smile. "Well, not yet, anyway."

Adam laughed all the way out into the hall.

THE apartment smelled like tomatoes and garlic when John got home from work just before seven, and he found Bryan in the kitchen, pulling a small pan of lasagna out of the oven. He looked up and grinned as John walked in. "Hey! Great timing. I wasn't sure when you'd get back." He nodded at the pan, setting it on top of the stove. "Grabbed a frozen lasagna and some garlic bread for dinner. Hope that's okay."

"Smells amazing." John waved a hand to indicate the white dress shirt he wore. "Just let me go change out of this so it doesn't end up with orange spots all over it."

When he returned from his bedroom a few minutes later, he found dinner waiting on the coffee table in the living-room set. Two plates of lasagna had bread sitting along the edge, two bottles of beer were open and ready, and Bryan was just putting down flatware and napkins. He smiled up at John, looking so sweet and open and beautiful that John had to kiss him. So he did, stepping up close and taking hold of one elbow, tasting his smile, a little deeper and firmer than the night before but still ending it before he got carried away.

They smiled at each other and sat down to eat. Bryan told John about spending the day with his friends, who'd been so glad he was coming to visit that they'd both taken a day off work just to spend time with him. The two of them had been very attentive while Bryan was recovering from the beating and had even made repeated efforts to help Eddie.

"They took me to visit him at least once a week," Bryan said. His voice was subdued, but his demeanor didn't seem withdrawn. "It was great about half the time and from bad to worse the rest. But they were amazing. I did a lot of crying on Betsey's shoulder. And when I...." He paused then and swallowed. "When I left, they were my biggest supporters. They got it, and I'm not sure anyone else did."

The unspoken *not even Eddie* hung there, and John reached out to run his hand down Bryan's back. "I'm glad you had them," he said. "Remind me to thank them sometime."

Bryan smiled at that and then shifted the topic, asking John how things were at work and about his friendship with Adam. John avoided talking about what Adam had done for him after Liz died, figuring then wasn't the best time to get into it, when the stories were so similar.

Dinner finished, the dishes taken care of, and an action movie they were ignoring on the TV, John sat on one end of the sofa and reached for Bryan's hand. He pulled Bryan in close, wrapping an arm around his shoulders and rubbing Bryan's knee with his free hand.

"So I haven't said this yet," he said, "but thanks for coming. This apartment is pretty big and boring when you're here alone. It's been great having someone here...." He stopped and moved his hand from Bryan's knee to cup the side of his face instead. "No. It's been great having *you* here. And no matter what happens, or doesn't happen, that's not going to change. Okay?"

Bryan smiled and rubbed his face against John's palm. John half expected him to start purring like a cat. "I'm glad I'm here too. This is nice. Just being able to spend the time together, no pressure." He pulled back a little, eyes widening. "You don't feel pressured for anything, do you? Because I—"

"No, no," John reassured him, sliding his hand down to rest on Bryan's shoulder. "Not at all. Just enjoying being here. With you." He let out a small smile. "And a little of this."

He leaned in to press his lips to Bryan's, and he heard a small laugh in Bryan's throat as he opened for the kiss. Their tongues brushed, just a whisper, and they drew back smiling.

"Sleep?" Bryan said.

"Sleep," John agreed.

They pulled apart and stood up, and John reached for the remote to shut off the TV before following Bryan down the hall. He stopped at his doorway just as Bryan turned in front of his and shot John a wide smile.

"Good night, John-Boy," he said, and John rolled his eyes.

"Yeah, never heard *that* one before," he said. "Watch out, or I'll start calling you Jim-Bob."

Bryan's laughter followed him into his room and, later, into his dreams.

JOHN woke to the smell of coffee brewing and… was that bacon? His stomach growled at him, and he rolled to his feet and padded into the bathroom. Business done, he pulled on the T-shirt he'd discarded during the night, too hot even with the air conditioning running, and headed down the hall to the kitchen.

He stopped in the doorway and tried not to stare too hard. Bryan stood at the stove, barefoot and wearing low-slung shorts and a snug T-shirt, lifting pieces of bacon out of a frying pan and onto a plate lined with paper towels. A bowl of what looked liked beaten eggs sat on the counter next to him, and the small table at the side of the room was set for two, right down to glasses of orange juice.

John took a step into the room, and Bryan's head popped up, his eyes wide. He smiled when he saw John. "Mornin', sleepyhead. I woke up way too early and couldn't go back to sleep, so I figured I'd make breakfast."

John had walked closer, ostensibly to get coffee, but he veered at the last second to lay a hand on Bryan's lower back and lean in for a kiss. Bryan returned it, making a happy sound in the back of his throat, and John smiled as he drew away.

"Morning yourself," he said, this time actually moving to get coffee. "You bought bacon and juice?"

Bryan shrugged. "Just walked across to the convenience store," he said. "Paid way too much, of course, but it just doesn't seem right to have eggs and toast without bacon. And might as well pick up some juice while I'm there, right?"

"Right." John sipped his coffee, strong and rich like he liked it, and turned to face Bryan, leaning his hip against the counter. "Need any help?"

Bryan shot him a quick glance. "You could push the lever on the toaster." He nodded to where the appliance sat in the corner, four pieces of bread sticking out of its slots. "Wasn't sure if you'd want one piece or two, so feel free to put one back if you like."

John reached out one hand and pushed the lever down, checking to be sure it was set on medium. "Two is nearly always better than one," he said, smiling when Bryan rolled his eyes. Bryan poured the eggs into the pan and started pushing them around with a long plastic spoon. John watched in silence before glancing over at the table. "Oh, guess we need butter or something?"

"Oh, yeah." Bryan gave him another look with a quick smile. "No jelly or anything, didn't think about that."

John shrugged. "Butter is great," he said, pulling open the refrigerator to retrieve the small tub of margarine he'd bought. "Or butter-resembling spread, at least." He waved the container in Bryan's direction, picking up his coffee mug and stepping across to put both on the table.

Bryan shot him another glance over his shoulder. "Go ahead and have a seat. I'll be over with the food in a minute."

John sat, and sure enough, his plate was filled very shortly after that as Bryan divided the eggs and bacon between them. He returned long enough to grab the toast and bring it over, and they were quiet while they buttered their toast and started eating.

John had known it was coming sometime, but he still didn't expect the next thing Bryan said.

"I want to go see Eddie tonight."

John stopped chewing and studied Bryan for a long moment. He knew the visit was a large part of the reason Bryan had come up with them, but he wanted Bryan to be sure he was ready, and he didn't want him to feel any pressure.

John swallowed. "If that's what you want to do, I'll do whatever you need me to."

Bryan grabbed his hand across the table, squeezing tight. "I just need you there with me," he said softly. "The rest we'll have to figure out as we go."

Chapter 20

JOHN pulled into a parking space and shut the car off. He turned to Bryan, who stared at the building, transfixed. John reached out to take his hand, and Bryan jumped.

"Sorry." John rubbed his thumb along the side of Bryan's. "You sure you're ready for this?"

Bryan turned his head to face John, and he seemed to relax when they were looking at each other. "Yeah," he said, his voice rough. "I mean, I don't know if I'll ever really be ready, but I need to do this."

John nodded and squeezed his hand before letting go and climbing out of the car. He walked around to meet Bryan as he got out on the passenger side.

Bryan pushed the door shut, pulled in a deep breath and blew it out, and nodded once. "Let's go," he said, and together, they walked inside.

They had to stop and sign in at the front desk, clipping on visitor badges before they could go back into the resident halls. Bryan took John's hand again, lacing their fingers together, and John followed as they walked toward Eddie's room.

When they got there, Bryan stopped short and stared at the closed door. His fingers tightened on John's so much that John had to fight back a wince. "I don't know if…." Bryan turned his head to look at John, his eyes wet. "Are you sure this is okay?"

John stepped up closer and untangled their fingers, lifting his hands to cup Bryan's face. "This is what you need," he murmured.

"And because it's what you need, it's what I need too. Whatever happens in there"—he nodded toward the door beside them—"is between you and Eddie. You don't have to tell me anything. Okay?" Bryan nodded, eyes wide, and John leaned in to kiss him softly. "Take all the time you need," he said, sliding his hands away.

Bryan gave John one last look before turning to push the door open and disappearing inside. John stood there staring at the spot where Bryan had been before finally shaking himself out of his fugue. A row of beige plastic and metal chairs sat against the wall nearby. He took a seat there, careful not to let himself watch the door, and waited.

John hated hospitals and anything resembling them. Not that many people were fond of them, but he'd spent far too much time in them, getting bad news. His dad had lived in one for half a day after his car accident, and Liz had walked into one healthy and never come back out. While this wasn't technically a hospital, it had the same clinical, sanitized feel, and it sent a chill down John's spine.

He studied the generic art print hanging on the wall across from him. It was better than most, at least, a reproduction of one of Monet's *Water Lilies*, mundane but classic. The expanse of blues with a few pops of yellow was soothing, likely selected for that reason.

John didn't feel very soothed.

He knew why Bryan needed to do this. He'd never come to terms with leaving Eddie behind, and he had to if he wanted to move out of the limbo he'd been in. John knew Bryan liked him, was attracted to him, but he could also feel the wall there between them. John was working to break through from his side, and he wanted to help Bryan do the same. He hoped tonight would help them take another step in the right direction.

JOHN didn't try to keep track of time as he waited. The hallway was quiet, with the occasional resident or staff member walking by. A middle-aged woman and a teenage girl that must have been her daughter came out of a room farther down the hall, and the woman gave John a small smile as they passed him headed toward the exit. He nodded in acknowledgement and watched them go.

He couldn't help thinking of Beth. The girl was maybe ten years older than her, and she had her mother right there with her. Beth would never have that. Even if John remarried, it wouldn't be the same. And if he and Bryan were together, it would be a whole different world.

Beth did have Meghan, he reminded himself. She'd been half mother and half big sister to Beth over the past five years—not to mention taking care of John as he crawled out of the well of grief he'd been drowning in—and John knew that wouldn't change, even if one or both of them settled down with a partner, of whatever sort. Beth would be fine. He would be fine.

Bryan would be fine.

John was pulled from his thoughts when the door to Eddie's room opened. Bryan stepped out, one foot still in the room, and turned his head in John's direction. His eyes were red but dry, and he smiled a little. "Hey," he said in a low voice. "Why don't you come meet Eddie?"

John was surprised, but he nodded and stood up. Wiping his palms on his thighs, he walked over to stand in front of Bryan. "Everything okay?"

Bryan nodded. "C'mon." He tilted his head behind him, and John followed him into the room.

The space was small but neat, with a twin-size bed, a wide dresser, and two comfortable-looking chairs. Eddie stood just in front of the chairs, and John ran his gaze over him quickly. He was a few inches shorter than Bryan and slighter, but wiry, not frail. He had dark blond hair and brown eyes, and a pink scar that ran from the point of his right cheekbone back into his hair, leaving a bald patch a half-inch wide that extended about an inch beyond his hairline. His eyes didn't quite seem to focus, and when he smiled, it was a little lopsided.

"Eddie," Bryan said. "This is my friend John McConnell. John, this is Eddie Brown."

John smiled and stepped forward to shake the hand that Eddie offered. "It's very nice to meet you, Eddie. Bryan's told me some really good things about you."

Eddie's smile broadened. "Thank you," he said, his speech slurred but understandable. He dropped John's hand and stepped back, lowering himself into one of the two chairs. John glanced at Bryan, uncertain, and Bryan nodded him toward the other. Bryan took a seat on the edge of the bed.

John sat and turned toward Eddie. He wasn't sure what to say, but Bryan stepped in.

"Eddie and I talked," he said, his gaze fixed on his ex-boyfriend. "He's doing really well here. They've been able to help him with a lot of things that I wouldn't have been able to do for him. And he has friends here, people he can watch TV with and play cards and talk." His eyes shifted to focus on John's face. "He likes it here."

Before John could react, Eddie spoke up, and John shifted his attention to him. "It isn't easy. I have bad days sometimes. Really bad days. They have me on medication that keeps me from doing...." He paused, as if searching for the word, but then shook his head. "So I don't get angry so much."

His head dropped, and he rubbed a hand across his thigh. "I got angry at Bryan a lot," he said. "I was really mean sometimes. And sometimes I still am. I try to stop, but I can't."

His voice shook, and Bryan reached out to touch his shoulder. "It's not your fault, Eddie," he said, and Eddie shook his head.

"I know it's not." He looked up at Bryan, and John could see his pain written all over his face. "But I hurt you anyway. And I don't want to hurt you anymore, Bryan. I don't want to hurt anybody."

John's eyes pricked with tears as he watched the two men. He could tell Eddie was a good man, not that he would have expected less of someone Bryan clearly loved. He'd just been through something horrible, something that had left him unable to control his own body and mind. Bryan had been hurt by the attack itself, physically and emotionally, but while he'd been able to recover, Eddie never would.

John did understand that a part of Bryan would always love Eddie, no matter what. They'd been torn apart through no fault of their own, victims of trauma and loss, and each of them had left some pieces behind. They couldn't be together, but they needed to stay in each other's lives in some capacity.

Bryan had slid off the bed and crouched in front of Eddie, his hands on top of Eddie's, holding them tight against his legs. "I know you didn't mean it, Eddie." His voice, thick with emotion, cracked, and he had to swallow before he could go on. "You loved me. You still do, I know. And I love you too."

Tears spilled out of Eddie's eyes. "You have to let me go, Bryan," he said. "You *have* to. If you don't, you'll die inside. And I can't watch you die like that. Please don't make me."

John's vision blurred from the wetness in his own eyes. He brought up a hand to swipe at them, wiping away the moisture, and when he refocused, Bryan had both arms wrapped around Eddie, kneeling in front of him on the hard floor, their foreheads resting together. He murmured something too low for John to hear, and Eddie let out a sound that could have been a sob, a laugh, or anything in between. Bryan turned his head far enough to press a long, lingering kiss to Eddie's cheek, right at the apex of the scar. He sat back on his heels, sliding his hands down Eddie's arms to tangle their hands together again.

He looked over at John and gave a tremulous smile. "Eddie had something he wanted to say to you."

John looked at Eddie, who stared at Bryan wide-eyed for a few long moments before turning toward John. "You love him?"

In his peripheral vision, John saw Bryan jerk. Apparently he hadn't been expecting that. Neither had John, and he chose his words carefully.

"I like Bryan very much," he said. "I care about him. I...." He glanced at Bryan and then back at Eddie. "I think maybe some things should be said in private first. But I can promise you, Eddie, that I'd do anything not to hurt him. No matter what."

He stopped, not sure if that would be enough to reassure Eddie, but from the way his shoulders relaxed, it seemed to have done the trick. "He can still come see me?"

The hope on Eddie's face warmed and broke John's heart at the same time. "Of course," John said, smiling. "We'll both come sometimes if you want. I'd like for you and me to be friends. Okay?"

Eddie smiled that lopsided smile again. "Can you play checkers?"

John laughed. "I haven't played in years, but if you want to play, I'll relearn how." He shrugged. "Maybe Beth and Jeremy would want to learn too."

Eddie's smile dimmed. "Beth is your d-d-d...." He stopped and blew out a frustrated breath, and John saw Bryan squeeze his hands. "Your little girl?" Eddie finished, and John nodded.

"She's five years old," he said. "She can come visit if you want. I think you'd like her."

Eddie regarded him seriously. "I don't want to hurt her."

"You won't," John said. "We'll all be careful. Okay?"

Eddie started to smile again and turned to Bryan. "I like him," he said. "He's okay."

Bryan barked out a surprised laugh. "I kind of like him too." He darted a glance over at John before returning his gaze to Eddie. "He's a really nice guy," he said, his voice soft. "And you know I'm not going to forget about you. Right?"

Eddie nodded, the movement a little jerky. "Me either," he said. He leaned forward until their foreheads touched again and closed his eyes. "Live, love, laugh."

John watched Bryan smile. "Live, love, laugh," he echoed.

After another long moment, Bryan kissed Eddie's cheek again and, wincing, climbed to his feet. "We'll let you go now, Eddie," Bryan said, rubbing at one knee. "I know it's getting close to bedtime."

Eddie leaned back in his seat, turning his head toward John again. "It was nice to meet you," he said. "I hope you can come visit me again soon."

John stood up and stepped closer to Eddie, reaching to squeeze his shoulder lightly. "I would love to come visit you again," he said. "Just as soon as I can. Okay?"

"Okay."

John stepped back then and glanced at Bryan. "I'll give you a few minutes."

Bryan nodded and gave him a quick, somewhat watery smile. John touched his arm for just a second before stepping back out into the hallway, pulling the door shut behind him.

He blew out a breath and leaned against the wall, feeling more drained than he had in a very long time. Eddie seemed to be a great guy under it all, and John's heart ached to think about what both he and Bryan had been through. Eddie knew he wasn't able to give Bryan what he needed, that he'd only end up hurting both of them. And he had a big enough heart to let Bryan go and give him the chance to live the life that Eddie could only dream of now.

John glanced around him, seeing the facility with new eyes. Despite the antiseptic atmosphere, it was clean and modern, not dirty or dingy like some long-term care facilities could be. Eddie's room was large for assisted living, and he seemed to be satisfied.

None of it made the place any less like a prison. Much like Eddie's own body.

John tilted his head back, staring unseeing at the ceiling. Losing Liz had felt like losing a limb or having his still-beating heart torn out of his chest. Bryan hadn't lost Eddie completely, but in some ways, it was even worse. *His* Eddie was gone, but he'd left behind a shell of the man he'd once been. They were caught in the middle, and neither of them could escape. Even now, after Eddie's plea to Bryan to let him go, John knew it wouldn't happen.

He also knew he could be okay with that. He could be Eddie's friend, and he could make a promise not to feel jealous when Bryan spent time with Eddie. He could help Bryan shoulder some of the burden of watching out for the man he'd loved, and he could be there for Bryan, whether he needed to talk about the past or forget about the present.

A hand touched his arm, and he jumped a little, turning his head to see Bryan smiling wanly at him. He hadn't even heard him approach.

"You ready?" Bryan's eyes were clouded, and John reached for his hand.

"Let's get you back to the apartment," he said. "I think maybe you could use a little decompression time."

Bryan let John lead him down the hall and outside. They walked to John's car, and Bryan stood silently while John opened the door for him to climb in. As John walked around the back end of the car to the driver's side, he thought fast and hard. He didn't know what Bryan needed now. Truth was, he didn't know him all that well. He knew a lot, and he could infer a lot more, but he needed to be careful. The last thing he needed was to make a big misstep and set back all the progress they'd made.

He slid behind the wheel and glanced at the clock display as he started the car. It was after eight-thirty, and they hadn't had dinner. He didn't look at Bryan, just checked behind the car and started backing out.

"I was thinking we could swing by the Varsity and pick up some chili dogs for dinner," he said. "Although maybe we should stop by a pharmacy for antacids to wash them down?"

"Whatever you want is fine with me." Bryan's voice was flat, withdrawn, but John let it go for now.

"I don't know," John said, pulling out into traffic. "The Varsity's kind of out of the way. Maybe tomorrow night for that. How about if we stop by Jason's and just pick up some sandwiches? Any preference?"

"Not all that hungry."

Bryan's hands lay limp in his lap, and John reached over to rest one of his on top of them. "It'll be okay, Bryan."

He waited, not sure if that was the right thing but needing to do something. He felt something release in his chest when Bryan turned his hands over and wrapped them around John's, holding on tight.

JOHN left Bryan in the car while he stopped to get sandwiches. It took longer than he would've liked, but the deli was one of his favorites, and he knew the food would be good. Twenty minutes later, they were headed back to the apartment, arriving not long after. Once they were inside, John put the sandwiches and chips on the kitchen table and got bottles of water from the refrigerator. Bryan sat down, but he didn't make a move toward eating.

John unwrapped his sandwich, and when Bryan still didn't reach for his, John unwrapped that as well. "I know you don't feel like it, Bryan," he said, "but you need to eat something. Okay?"

Bryan nodded and picked up half the sandwich, taking a bite, chewing, swallowing, and repeating. He didn't seem quite aware of what he was doing, but he ate almost half the sandwich before putting it down and wiping his fingers on one of the paper napkins printed with the restaurant's logo. John watched him, and Bryan picked up the bottle of water and drank a few sips before putting that back down too. He pushed his chair back and stood up, and without a word, he walked down the hall, and John heard his bedroom door close.

John put down the last quarter of his sandwich, his appetite evaporating. He wiped his hands and drank his water, leaning back in his chair, staring down the hall, and wondering what he should do. If anything. Maybe Bryan just needed some time alone. Maybe John being there would be too much for him to deal with right now.

He decided he'd leave it for now. He cleaned up the remains of their dinner, wrapping the second half of Bryan's sandwich and putting it in the refrigerator in case he wanted it later or for lunch the next day. He thought about turning on the TV for a while, but he was pretty drained from their trip to see Eddie. And if he felt this tired, he couldn't imagine how Bryan felt.

He pulled out a fresh bottle of water to take to his room with him for the night and flipped off the kitchen light, walking down the hall toward his room. He didn't see a light under Bryan's door and thought about going to check on him. It was a toss-up over whether that would do more bad than good at this point, though, so he went into his own room.

Changed and cleaned up for bed, John climbed under the covers and reached for the book he'd brought with him. He tried reading but had trouble concentrating. Sighing, he reached for his phone. Sometimes when he was traveling, he and Meghan would send text messages back and forth in the evenings, after she got home from the restaurant. It was late enough that she might be free.

You around? The usual first volley sent, John picked up the remote from the bedside table and turned on the TV, flipping through channels without seeing much until his phone vibrated some minutes later.

Everything okay?

John shook his head. If only she knew. *Rough night. Visited Eddie. It's bad, Meggie.*

He watched the next day's weather forecast while waiting for Meghan's reply. *Ouch. Sorry. Anything I can do?*

John shook his head and started typing out a response. *No idea. No idea what I can do. Bryan went into his room & closed the door. Don't know if I should interfere.*

The next text took a few minutes to arrive. *He wanted you there with him tonight. What makes you think he doesn't want you there now?*

John hadn't thought of it from that angle. Bryan had kept John with him the entire evening, except for the short time he spent alone with Eddie, until he'd disappeared into his room. *But what if he doesn't? I don't want him to feel obligated to say he's okay just because I'm here.*

If he felt obligated toward you, do you really think he'd be sharing so much of this?

John chuckled, shaking his head. *How'd you get so smart?*

The next answer came quickly. *Somebody's gotta be the brains of this outfit.*

Still smiling, John put the phone down on the bedside table as he stood up. He walked out into the hallway and down to the end, pausing outside Bryan's room to take a deep breath before he knocked.

"Come in." Bryan's voice was still flat, but at least he answered.

John opened the door and stepped inside, pushing it almost closed behind him. Bryan lay on his side on the bed, sheet pulled up to his chest, staring at the wall. He didn't look at John, who walked over and sat on the edge of the mattress in front of him, not waiting for an invitation. He reached out to brush his fingers over the back of Bryan's hand where it lay on top of the sheet.

"How are you feeling?" Not the most brilliant opener ever, John knew, but it was something.

Bryan shrugged but didn't respond. John started to move back, give Bryan a little more space if he needed it, but as soon as he shifted, Bryan's other hand grabbed for his, and he pulled. John followed, off-balance physically and emotionally at the sudden shift but trying to follow Bryan's lead. Bryan rolled over, yanking the sheet out of the way, tugging John down behind him, drawing John's arm over him to hold John's hand against his chest. John tried his best to keep a careful distance between their bodies, but Bryan was having none of that, scooting backward until his body fitted against John's, legs bent together, hips aligned.

As soon as he was settled, Bryan let out a long breath and relaxed into John. John smiled, half gratified and half amused, feeling more than a little bit like an oversized teddy bear. He shifted to get more comfortable and let his eyes fall shut. He didn't know if he'd sleep or how well, but he'd rather lie awake all night than leave Bryan alone in his bed now.

Chapter 21

JOHN woke disoriented, with no idea where he was, but he felt warm and comfortable, as if wrapped in a layer of cotton and down. It took a moment for his brain to catch up with the rest of him, and he realized he was lying on his back, Bryan curled into his side with John's arm around his shoulders. Bryan's hand rested over John's heart.

John smiled down at the younger man. He was glad Bryan had been able to sleep, and if that was in any part because he'd had John holding him, then all the better. As for John, he'd slept great. He felt well rested and relaxed. It had been so long since he'd slept with someone else, in the literal sense, that he would've expected it to be difficult. But here he was, awake after a good night's sleep, with the sun shining in on them.

Sun. *Shit*. John twisted his head around, almost wrenching his neck in his effort to see the clock on the bedside table. Relief washed over him when he saw it was only a few minutes until seven. Sunrise was so early this time of year that it often startled him if he woke up before his alarm. He didn't have an alarm at all in here, and as comfortable as he was, he easily could've overslept. He still had time, though, not being needed at the office until at least eight.

He turned his head back toward Bryan, watching his face in the early morning light. Bryan remained deeply asleep, features relaxed, lips parted. His hair stuck up on one side where he'd been lying on it earlier, before they'd shifted to this position. John lifted his free hand and ran his fingers through the tangled strands lightly, trying to tame them.

Bryan moved, and John froze. He hadn't meant to wake him, but he couldn't seem to stop touching him. He watched as Bryan opened his eyes, blinked a few times, and then jerked a little, his hand lifting off John's chest.

John couldn't help a small chuckle. "Good morning," he said, his voice still raspy from sleep. Bryan's gaze flew up to meet John's. "I hope you slept well."

Bryan's smile was like a sunrise, brightening his face and warming John's heart. "I did," he said, voice rough around the edges. "I can't remember the last time I felt this well rested."

John pressed a kiss against Bryan's temple. "That makes two of us." He shifted back. "Much as I'd love to stay right here, I do have a couple more days of work to get through. If things keep going well this week, I should get to knock off early tomorrow." An idea formed as he was speaking, and he looked down into Bryan's eyes. "Why don't we plan on dinner tomorrow night? Have a night out before we head back south, celebrate me making it through the week."

Bryan chuckled. "Are you asking me out?"

"I guess I am," John said, grinning. Another thought struck him. "I think they might still have Friday night beer tastings at Sweetwater. We could start there, then get dinner. Sound good?"

Bryan nodded and pushed himself up to sit. "I'll call today to check it out," he said. "I can make the dinner reservations too, if you want. Any preferences?"

"Whatever looks good to you is fine with me."

Bryan gave him a sidelong glance. "What looks good to me is you," he murmured. "Where I'm looking at it doesn't matter so much."

There was no way John couldn't kiss him after that, so he did. He let himself explore a little, tongues stroking together, but he pulled back before he got too carried away.

"I almost forgot," he said. "We were going to try to get in a Braves game too. You want to do that tonight?"

Bryan chewed at his bottom lip. "Honestly, I think I'd rather stay in and veg in front of the TV," he said. "Last night was…."

He trailed off, and John reached for his hand. "Rough," he finished. "I know. Decompression is good. But if you need to talk...."

Bryan smiled. "I know," he said. "And thanks."

John leaned in for another quick kiss before releasing Bryan's hand and climbing off the bed. "I'm going to shower and get ready for work," he said. "You need anything? I can get you something for breakfast before I leave, if you want."

Bryan opened his mouth to reply, but it widened into a big yawn. Both of them cracked up.

"Um, maybe I'll just veg most of today too," Bryan said, his cheeks pink. "I *will* take care of tomorrow night, though. And maybe pizza for dinner tonight? Or didn't you mention the Varsity?"

John nodded. "I'll call when I leave work to get your order and go by to pick them up. Appropriate to eat while we watch the ballgame, right?"

Bryan grinned. "Right." He curled back onto the bed on his side, arms wrapped around the pillow John had slept on. "Have a good day."

"You too." John gave him one last smile and pulled the door shut behind him, walking down the hall toward his room. He still felt pretty drained himself after the previous night, but he knew the idea of spending tonight and tomorrow night with Bryan would keep him going.

THE last two days at the office went much more smoothly than John had expected, or maybe it just felt that way because of the release of tension after Eddie. As promised, he brought back chili dogs and the Varsity's signature Frosted Orange drinks for dinner Thursday night, and he and Bryan ate in front of the Braves game, wincing as they watched their team get pounded by the Cubs. They shared a few sweet, easy kisses before bed, like the ones they'd had earlier in the week, but they slept in their own rooms.

Bryan was still asleep when John left for work Friday morning, and he didn't disturb him. Tension release or not, it still had been a tough week. And he had a pile of work waiting for him when they got back to Tybee, especially since he'd put it off for the trip.

Friday flew by, and John was surprised when Adam stopped in the doorway to his temporary office. "You planning to hang around all weekend?"

John looked up, wide-eyed, and then at the clock on his computer. 4:14 stared back at him, and their brewery tour started at five-thirty. "Shit," he said, saving the file he was working on. "I'm supposed to be—"

He stopped himself, chewing on the corner of his lip as he shut down his computer. He looked up again when Adam gave a snort of laughter, and found the man leaning against the doorframe, arms crossed over his chest, shaking his head and smirking.

"You know, you really don't have much of a poker face," he said.

John gave a rueful smile and stood up, reaching for his briefcase. "Yeah, yeah, you just keep telling yourself you've got it all figured out," he said. "I'll just keep doin' my thing and keepin' my mouth shut."

Adam laughed. "No kissin' and tellin'? I'll just have to let my imagination run wild, I guess."

John raised an eyebrow as he walked around the edge of his desk, stopping in front of Adam. "Does your wife know you're having gay sex fantasies?"

Adam waved a hand in dismissal. "Hell, she'd probably love it. How many men are into lesbian porn? Only stands to reason women would be the same way, right?"

John chuckled and shook his head. "The things we talk about, I swear." He grinned. "Well, I am off. No tellin' if there'll be any kissin'. Talk to you on Monday?"

Adam nodded and stepped forward, surprising John with a full-on hug. He could remember two times that Adam had hugged him, both around the time Liz died. He didn't question it, though, just returned it.

When Adam pulled back, he was smiling, but his eyes were suspiciously bright. "Go have fun," he said. "You deserve it."

John swallowed back a rush of affection for his friend and gave him one more smile before heading down the hall.

Outside, the sun was still bright, but a light breeze kept it from being oppressively hot. John didn't even break a sweat getting to his car, and as he headed back to the apartment, he debated taking a shower. A quick one, he decided. It would be their first real date, and he wanted to give it everything he had.

When he stepped into the apartment, he heard water running in the second bathroom and smiled. Apparently Bryan had had the same thought. John headed to his bedroom, dropping his briefcase next to the closet and reaching in to pull out the khakis and dress shirt he'd brought along. He laid them out on the bed and added clean socks and underwear before stripping off his work clothes and heading for the shower.

A quick wash and shave later, he was buttoning his shirt when a knock came at his door. He walked over and pulled it open, smiling at Bryan, who wore an outfit much like his only with a green shirt instead of his blue.

"Hey," Bryan said, returning his smile. "You about ready to go? Not to rush you, but it's after five, and I know you wanted to do the tour."

"Just about done." John left the door open and fastened his last button, crossing in his socked feet to the closet to retrieve his loafers. He half turned to face Bryan as he slipped his feet into his shoes and let his gaze run down Bryan's body and back up to his face, which had flushed from the scrutiny. "You look great, by the way."

Bryan's smile was as shy as John had ever seen it. "Thanks," he said. "You look pretty great yourself."

The compliment spread warmth through John's chest. He stepped back across the room to slide his hand into one of Bryan's and lean in to brush their lips together. Leaning back, he grinned. "Let's go have some beer," he said, and Bryan grinned back.

The short brewery tour was interesting, and they laughed as they took turns tasting several different beers, including a seasonal variety called, appropriately enough, Road Trip. After browsing through the merchandise but not buying, they headed to dinner. Bryan directed

John away from the industrial area where the brewery was located and into a commercial neighborhood, where they ended up at a small Italian restaurant. "I've never been here," Bryan said, "but the reviews were great, and the menu looked amazing."

John smiled at him. "I was here once, many years ago. Not with Liz," he added. "I brought my mom here for her birthday. We loved it. You made a great choice."

Bryan's eyes had softened. "You always take your mom out for her birthday?"

John shrugged, a little self-conscious. "Sometimes," he said. "She doesn't really need things. The birthday thing just kind of became a tradition, even before I met Liz."

Bryan reached for his hand. "You're a good son."

John really *was* embarrassed then, considering what had happened during his last dinner with his mother. "It's not a big deal, just dinner."

Bryan shook his head. "It's more than most people do for their parents." He squeezed John's hand. "You're a good man, with a good heart."

John didn't know what to say to that, so he just squeezed Bryan's hand back and tried to smile again. "Let's eat," he said.

They climbed from the car and headed inside, choosing a table on the patio since the temperature wasn't too hot. It turned out to be an excellent decision, as the evening gave them a beautiful sunset. Low, scudding clouds reflected red and orange from the sun's dying rays, lighting up the sky like a lava flow. They couldn't stop watching the colors change, barely looking away long enough to place their orders and take their drinks when they arrived. It wasn't until their antipasto appetizer arrived and the fire had faded to pinks and purples that they turned their attention to their food, each other—and a different kind of fire.

John could feel things building throughout dinner. They talked about their favorite places in Atlanta, restaurants they'd liked when they'd lived in the city; they told embarrassing stories on themselves and their friends. It could've been a typical first date, except John already felt so comfortable with Bryan that it felt more like two old friends catching up with each other's lives. The primary difference came with the undercurrent of anticipation, a frisson of electricity that made his skin tingle and his fingers itch to touch.

He pushed it down as best he could. They were in no rush. They'd reached some resolution during the week, helped Bryan farther along the path to accepting that his Eddie was gone and that it was okay for him to move on without him. But they had time. John would rather wait and be sure than move too fast and destroy what they'd been building.

On the other hand, he also remembered what Bryan had said the night they'd first kissed, on the beach under the pier. *I really, really, really like kissing. So can we do a lot of that, at least?*

John bit back a grin. Yeah, they could do that. Because he really, really, really liked kissing too, especially when Bryan was the one he was kissing.

BOTH too full to even think about dessert, they headed back to the car, walking close together but not quite touching. Not that it would have mattered here in Midtown Atlanta, where gay couples were a hell of a lot more common than they were on Tybee. But John was still feeling his way, figuratively speaking. Well, literally speaking too, for that matter, a thought that made him smile. Bryan saw it from the corner of his eye and lifted his head to look at John, curious. "Something funny?"

John smiled wider and shook his head. "Just a stray thought, nothing major." They were at the car then, and John opened the door for Bryan, waving him in. Bryan lifted an eyebrow as he got in, stopping with one foot still on the ground and looking up at John.

"Mister Chivalry," he said, laughter lacing his voice. "I always kind of wanted a knight in shining armor." His gaze ran down John's body like a caress, drifting back up until he was looking into John's eyes, smile still strong. "I guess khakis will work, though."

John felt his cheeks warm even as he laughed and closed the door once Bryan had pulled his leg inside. Walking around the front of the car to his side, he thought again about what they'd both said about taking things slow. He was finding it more and more difficult to stick to that plan. Bryan was, in a word, irresistible, and John wanted him, mind and body.

They were quiet on the ride back to the apartment. The Braves were on the radio, and as he drove, John half listened and half watched Bryan from the corner of his eye. Bryan had his head leaned back against the seat, turned in John's direction, eyes half-lidded, but he didn't seem to be focusing on anything in particular. A small smile played around his lips, and he looked as relaxed as John thought he'd ever seen him, even counting when he was asleep.

"What time do we need to leave tomorrow?"

John almost jumped at Bryan's voice, he'd grown so accustomed to the comfortable silence. He took a breath and shrugged. "Around eleven, I guess, since we're supposed to be there for lunch." He glanced at the dashboard clock. "It's still early, if you want to go out somewhere for a while?"

Bryan shook his head without lifting it from the headrest. "Not in the mood to party tonight," he said. "Rather just head home."

Bryan's voice held just a note of tension, and John frowned in response. He hoped the night hadn't been too much for him. It stood to reason he'd still be a little raw about everything, but he'd seemed okay the night before, their evening together relaxed and easy, topped off with sweet kisses. John hoped he hadn't let too much of what he was feeling show. He knew Bryan was feeling a lot of the same things, but the last thing he wanted was to pressure him to do something about it.

A few minutes later, John pulled the car into the designated spot in front of the building and shot Bryan a quick smile. "Don't move," he instructed with a smile before climbing out of the car and striding around the back end to Bryan's door. He opened it and held out a hand, which Bryan took even as he laughed up at him.

"My hero," Bryan cooed, and John grinned back. He tangled their fingers together and pushed the door shut before leading the way inside, and Bryan stayed close, their arms brushing above their joined hands. John had to let go to get the door open, but he took Bryan's hand again immediately, leading him inside before turning to lock the door behind them.

Just as he finished, he felt a tug on his hand where he was still holding Bryan's, and he was pulled into the hallway to the right of the door, toward the bedrooms. "What—"

He didn't get a chance to finish. Bryan pulled him in close, wrapped his free arm around John's shoulder, and kissed him, hard.

John heard himself whimper when Bryan's tongue stroked into his mouth. He slid his arm around Bryan's waist, more to steady himself than anything else, and Bryan tilted his head and kissed him harder, deeper, tongue driving in. More important, though, he untangled his fingers from John's and brought that hand around to the small of John's back and then slid it lower, using his grip as leverage to grind his body against John's. John's cock reacted automatically, blood rushing in, and John moaned into Bryan's mouth.

They'd been taking it slow, but slow seemed to have flown right out the window.

Chapter 22

JOHN took two steps forward, until Bryan's back hit the wall, and laid his body against Bryan's, hands cupping Bryan's head as they kissed. Bryan's fingers gripped the back of John's shirt as if he were trying to keep from falling, and the way his body trembled, John thought that might not be far from the truth. Their tongues slid against each other, and low moans and whimpers blended with the wet, slick sounds of their kisses.

John tore himself away from Bryan's mouth, focusing on Bryan's eyes with effort. "Tell me now," he said, his voice a low groan, his hands in Bryan's hair. "If you don't want this, if you're not ready for this, *tell me now.*"

Bryan's mouth hung open as he gasped for air. "*Yes*," he rasped out, pushing his body forward, pressing himself against John. "God, *please*, yes, I want this, I want *you*—"

John cut him off with another kiss, impossibly harder and deeper, his hands sliding down to tug at Bryan's shirt, pulling the tail out of his pants. John ran his hands under the soft fabric and across the smooth skin of Bryan's back, feeling the muscles bunching and flexing as they moved against each other. Bryan's cock lay hard against John's hip, and John shifted to line his up next to it. Then it was his turn to have his knees buckle. *Oh God*, it had been so long since he'd had this, from anyone, so long since he'd had someone else's body pressed against his, hot and ready. And to have it be Bryan, sweet, funny, beautiful Bryan, made his heart pound and his skin tingle and his mind go fuzzy.

Bryan's hands were pushing at his chest, and John drew back, concerned that Bryan had changed his mind. But Bryan smiled at him—smirked, really—and pulled him through the doorway of John's room. He stopped just inside and turned to lean against the wall, pulling John close and starting to work open the buttons of John's shirt.

"I like this color on you," Bryan said in a conversational tone, running his fingers across the smooth blue fabric. "It's very flattering. But I think right now I'd prefer just the color of your skin."

John blinked, wondering when the tables had gotten turned on him, but he wasn't arguing. He let Bryan undress him, shirt and slacks and even socks and shoes, but before Bryan could reach for his boxers, John grabbed his hands, lifting them up to shoulder height and pinning them lightly to the wall. He leaned in close, mouth a whisper away from Bryan's.

"What do you want me to do, Bryan?" He could feel his own breath bouncing back off Bryan's skin. "Do you want me to touch you?" He shifted his hips, pressed them against Bryan's, and Bryan's eyes fluttered shut. "Do you want me to suck you?"

Bryan moaned and tried to catch John's lips with his, but John moved to the side, bringing his mouth close to Bryan's ear. "Bryan," he murmured, voice low and rough. "Do you want me to fuck you?"

Bryan jerked and whimpered, and for a second John thought both of them were going to come in their underwear. And that wouldn't do at all.

John released Bryan's hands and started working on his clothes, getting his shirt unbuttoned and pushed off his shoulders by the time Bryan recovered enough to help. Bryan undid his own pants and shoved them down over his hips, letting them fall to the floor and kicking off his shoes as he reached for John.

They kissed messily, hungrily, Bryan stepping out of his khakis as they half stumbled toward the bed. John wrapped one arm around Bryan's waist and turned to lower him onto the mattress, following close behind, propping himself up with his other hand so he could hover over him as they kissed. Bryan wasn't having that distance, though, bringing up one leg to hook behind John's waist and pull him down until they were skin to skin, only the soft cotton of their boxers between them. John slid his hand into Bryan's hair, running his fingers through the soft strands. Every touch seemed to set his nerve endings on fire. He hadn't felt like this since Liz, warmth and comfort underlying the raw passion, adding layers and layers of feeling, amping up every sensation until he burned with it.

He tore himself away from Bryan's amazing mouth to press kisses across his jaw and onto his neck. Bryan shuddered when John ran his tongue over his Adam's apple, gasped when he scraped his teeth along the tendon at the side. Bryan's hips bucked up, and John ground down in response. He wanted to touch Bryan everywhere, wanted to taste him, but after so long without and so much anticipation, he didn't know how long he'd last.

He brought his head back up to catch Bryan's gaze and reached down to hitch Bryan's leg higher on his hip. He rolled his hips forward, pushing a gasp from Bryan's mouth. Bryan's lips were red and wet, eyes dark and wide, and John cupped Bryan's head with both hands.

"Want this." He rolled his hips again. "Want to watch you come."

Bryan moaned, and John felt his other leg come up behind him as Bryan crossed his ankles at the small of John's back. John thrust down, the angle perfect to slide their cocks together through the thin layers of fabric. It felt dangerous somehow, with a tinge of innocence, as if they were teenagers making out in one of their parents' living rooms, just beginning to explore life and love and this thing between them.

It felt like they were starting over, and maybe they were.

John slid one arm under Bryan, hand spreading wide across the middle of Bryan's back. He ran the fingers of his other hand into Bryan's hair and kissed him again, keeping up the slow, steady rocking of his hips. Bryan met his every move, sliding his fingers up John's back to clutch at his shoulders, his body rising and falling on the mattress in counterpoint to John's rhythm.

John wished they could stay like that all night, twined together, completely in sync. Their bodies had other ideas. Bryan shifted one leg, and the position John thought had been perfect shot up another few levels. He tore his mouth from Bryan's with a groan, dropping his head to rest in the crook of Bryan's neck, and started thrusting against Bryan in earnest. He could feel his climax building from the base of his spine, and the low noises and harsh breathing coming from Bryan drove him higher.

"Oh God." Bryan's words came out on a gasp, and John growled, turning his head to suck at the side of Bryan's neck. Bryan keened and jerked, and John felt warm wetness against his stomach. He thrust hard one last time and ground down against Bryan, hissing and then groaning as his orgasm slammed into him and he emptied himself in spurt after spurt.

JOHN floated down from somewhere near the ceiling to find Bryan had his head tucked into the crook of John's neck, his hot breath fanning across John's skin. John shifted his hips, and they both hissed at the friction, sensitive after their climaxes. John didn't care, though. He kissed his way down the side of Bryan's face until Bryan tilted his head far enough that John could reach his mouth. John kissed him deeply, not soothing or caressing but demanding, thrusting his tongue into Bryan's mouth like he wanted to thrust into Bryan's body.

Bryan took a few moments to catch up, but soon he was right there with John, hands pressing into his back, hips grinding against him. John could feel Bryan's cock waking back up right alongside his as they touched, stripping away their come-soaked boxers, the last barriers keeping them apart. Bryan rolled toward John, and John let him lead him over onto his back, Bryan straddling him on hands and knees. Bryan lowered his body down on top of John's, aligning them from hips to knees, and he kissed John again, stroking his tongue against John's, the movement of his hips sinuous, sinful. John moaned as their reawakening cocks brushed together.

Bryan left John's lips and mouthed his way down John's neck, licked across his chest, sucked on one hard nipple. John whimpered and cupped the back of Bryan's head, holding him close while he nipped and lapped at the rigid flesh, sending shockwaves of pleasure out along John's nerve endings. He moved to the other side and repeated the exquisite torture until John was gasping, his hips moving constantly.

Bryan lifted his head to meet John's gaze, and he wrapped one hand around John's cock. "Want this," he rasped out. "Want you inside me. Want to feel you everywhere."

John groaned and pulled Bryan down for a kiss, driving his tongue deep, feeling like he wanted to climb inside Bryan's mouth and never come back out. Bryan tore himself away and reached for the bedside table, pulling out the lube and condoms John had stashed there. John's eyes widened. "How did you—"

"I'm nosey," Bryan said, grinning. "I didn't read anything into it that I didn't already know. But I wanted to be sure we were covered just in case."

John knew he was blushing. "Me too," he said. "I didn't want you to feel like—"

Bryan kissed him to shut him up. "I don't," he said. "I want this, John. I'm ready."

John smiled. "You've got whatever you want. However you want me."

Bryan's gaze raked down John's chest to his cock, the head curved up toward his stomach, precome leaking onto his skin. He lifted his eyes back to John's, a wicked grin creasing his face. "I think I want you just like this," he said. "Hope you're okay with a bossy bottom, 'cause I wanna ride you."

John groaned again. "God, *yes*." He wrapped both hands around Bryan's hips. "Take what you want, Bryan. Anything. I'm ready."

Bryan dropped the bottle of lube on the bed and tore into the condoms, pulling one out and rolling it on quickly, tossing the others aside. He retrieved the lube and moved as if to coat his own fingers, but John caught his hand. "Let me," he said. "Please."

Bryan paused but then nodded, pouring the liquid over John's fingers instead of his own. John reached down and rubbed little circles over Bryan's hole, waiting for him to relax before sliding in the tip of one finger. Their gazes locked as John worked Bryan open, and the small part of John's brain still capable of higher reasoning thought it might just have been the hottest thing he'd ever done, watching every small reaction on Bryan's face as John prepared him to take in John's cock for the first time.

John had three fingers thrusting into Bryan's body when Bryan grabbed the bottle of lube again, pouring more out into his palm and spreading it over John's cock. He moved forward, and John followed his lead, pulling his fingers free and grabbing Bryan's hips as Bryan guided him home. John hissed at the tight pressure when the head popped inside, and Bryan moaned and shuddered. John could tell he was hurting, but Bryan sucked in a breath, blew it back out, and relaxed around him, pushing down another inch. He did the same thing again, and then on the third time, he slid all the way down, until his balls were nestled in John's pubic hair.

"Fuck."

"God."

John couldn't have told anyone who said what, but their gazes locked again as Bryan breathed through the last of the burning stretch. When he moved, lifting up just a fraction of an inch and dropping back down, it drove gasps out of both of them. He repeated the movement again and again, each stroke a little longer and faster than the last, until he was gliding up and down in a firm, quick rhythm. John kept his hands on Bryan's hips but didn't guide him, just rode along with him. Bryan's head dropped back, and he moaned toward the ceiling.

"You feel so good," Bryan ground out. "Never want you to leave. Don't leave me."

The choice of words cut through the haze of arousal, driving a cold spike through John's heart, but he couldn't stop. This was inevitable. *They* were inevitable, and they both needed it to be now.

Bryan thrust down harder, faster, one hand wrapping around his own cock, stroking at the same speed and rhythm as the movement of his hips. John was sucked back under the waves, mind shutting down and body taking over. Bryan's sharp gasp and faltering movements drove John right to the brink of climax, but it was the feel of Bryan's body clamping down around him that gave him the final push over the edge. His fingers dug so hard into Bryan's hips that he wouldn't have been surprised if he left bruises behind, but that fleeting thought barely formed before he was coming, head thrown back, back arching up into Bryan as he poured out inside his body.

John collapsed back into the mattress, and Bryan fell on top of him. John brought up shaky arms to wrap around Bryan's back, holding him there, loving the feel of his sweat-slick skin. Bryan turned his face into the side of John's neck, his breath coming out in warm, quick bursts. His hands lay flat against the front of John's shoulders, elbows bent out to the side, and his legs rested on either side of John's.

After what seemed like both forever and no time at all, John's shrinking cock slid out of Bryan's body, and they both sighed at the loss. John knew the condom was probably making a mess, but he couldn't summon up the will to care. He was slick with sweat and sticky with come and lube, with the heavy weight of another man lying on top of him, and he hadn't felt so comfortable in years.

Bryan shifted, lifting his head, and John looked down to find his eyes open and warm but a little wary. "Um… wow," Bryan said, and John smiled.

"Yeah," he said, kissing Bryan's forehead. "That was pretty damn wow."

Bryan snickered and shifted in John's arms. "Kind of a mess now, I think," he said. "Kind of sleepy too. Clean up and pass out, maybe?"

"Sounds good to me." But John wasn't letting Bryan go yet. He slid one hand to the back of Bryan's head and pulled him into a long, deep kiss, slow and easy, trying to say everything that he hadn't yet been able to put into words. They parted smiling, and Bryan slid off the bed, reaching for John's hand to lead him into the bathroom.

JOHN woke up when he rolled over and his arm hit cold sheets instead of warm body.

He lifted his head and looked around, only half expecting to see the bathroom light on or some other sign that Bryan would be right back. The rest of him was already pretty sure what was going on. He hadn't imagined Bryan's words while they were having sex. He'd been expecting some kind of fallout, and sooner rather than later.

He did need the bathroom, so he pushed to his feet and padded across the room, not bothering with a light as he relieved himself. He'd stayed in the apartment often enough that the dim glow from the city lights outside was enough for basic navigation. He washed his hands and walked back through the bedroom, stopping to pull on the shorts and T-shirt he'd worn to bed the night before.

As he stepped into the hallway, he could see a flickering bluish light coming from the living room. He debated for a second before flipping on the hall light to give Bryan warning that he was there.

Bryan just turned his head in John's direction, as if he'd been expecting him. He was wearing shorts and a T-shirt, too, and he sat curled up at the far end of the sofa, feet on the cushions and knees pulled up to his chest.

"Couldn't sleep?" John kept his voice neutral, trying to avoid anything that might sound like an accusation.

Bryan shrugged one shoulder but didn't say anything.

Slowly, John moved to sit on the opposite end of the sofa, keeping his distance. He glanced at the TV, which was showing an infomercial for some product he didn't recognize. He turned his attention back to Bryan, who was staring at the screen now but didn't seem to be focusing on it.

John waited a couple of minutes, just watching him. He was just on the verge of asking if he wanted to talk about it when Bryan started to speak.

"Eddie was the first man I had sex with." His voice was flat. Monotone. "I'd done some fooling around, blowjobs and things like that, but with Eddie, I wanted everything. He'd had sex before me, but it didn't matter to him that I hadn't, and when I finally said I was ready, he talked me through the first time. We'd been pretty much even on everything up until then, but he wanted me to... to be inside him first. And we did, and it was amazing."

His gaze drifted away from the TV, but he didn't look at John. "It took three more weeks before I let him in. I felt so guilty because we'd try and I just couldn't. And every time he told me it was okay, we didn't have to, ever, not if I didn't want to. But I did, I wanted to *so much*. I just couldn't get out of my head."

His eyes drifted shut. "The first time hurt more than I thought it would. I was too nervous. But Eddie took his time, talked me through it again, and by the time we finished, I loved it. I wanted to bottom for him all the time. We traded off after that, and every time it was *so* good."

Bryan lowered his forehead to his knees. His words were muffled, but John understood them. "The attack happened four months later."

John wanted to say something, wanted to take Bryan in his arms and just hold him, wanted to go back in time and erase the attack, even if it meant losing Bryan, because it would mean he wouldn't be hurting like this. The thought jarred John. He knew he cared about Bryan, but he hadn't realized until that moment just how deeply it ran. He cared enough that he'd be willing to give Bryan up if it would take away his pain.

That wasn't an option, so all he could do was try to help him through it.

Chapter 23

JOHN slid across the sofa, reaching for Bryan's arms where they were wrapped around his legs, pulling them away. Bryan's head snapped up, and John dropped one arm to lift Bryan's legs over his, maneuvering them until Bryan was half in John's lap with one arm around John's waist, John's arm around his shoulders. John tangled together the fingers of their free hands.

"It's okay," he murmured once they were situated, holding Bryan's gaze. "I know it's hard. You don't have to pretend it isn't, not with me."

Bryan's eyes were wide and wet. "Why are you so okay with all of this? You lost Liz. You haven't been with anyone in years either. But you're not falling apart."

John tilted his head until their foreheads touched. "It's different," he said. "We can't compare the things that happened to us. Both were bad. But your experience was a lot different from mine, and you haven't had as long to deal with it. And then this week just added another layer."

After a moment, Bryan nodded. "I think… it was good, talking to Eddie," he said. "It helped a lot. But I woke up and you had your arms around me and I felt so damn good, and all I could think was how unfair it was that I could have that and Eddie couldn't."

John ran his hand up and down Bryan's back. "It *is* unfair," he said. "It's awful, and I wish it weren't like that. But it is, and all you can do is make the best of it. Be there for Eddie when he needs you, and live the rest of your life the best way you can."

Bryan lifted his head so he could study John's eyes. "You're just making it more unfair." John could hear just a note of humor coming into his voice. "How do you always know the right thing to say?"

John smiled. "I don't. I just do the best I can. Sometimes I get lucky."

Bryan was smiling now. "I think we're both pretty lucky." He tightened his grip around John's waist, pulling him closer. "And maybe… we can both *get* lucky?"

John smiled into their kiss, but he kept it soft and ended it quickly. "Hey." He untangled his fingers from Bryan's and brought his hand up to push Bryan's sleep-mussed hair off his forehead. "You know you don't have to prove anything to me, right? If you want to just go back to bed and get some more sleep, I'm perfectly fine with that. Not that I'd turn you down if—"

That was as far as he got. Bryan had John flat on his back on the sofa, body heavy and warm on top of him, kissing him as if his life depended on it. All John could do was hold on as Bryan pushed at their clothes, got them both half-undressed, and wrapped one hand around their stiffening cocks.

"I don't know about you," Bryan murmured against John's lips. "But I sleep a lot better right after I have a really good orgasm."

John could only moan, his entire awareness focused on what Bryan's hand was doing. He clutched at Bryan's back, needing to hold him close but wanting to let him take what he needed, riding the waves of pleasure, cresting higher and higher. When his climax crashed over him, over them both, he felt washed clean, all the uncertainty and pain drained away.

Tangled together on the sofa, they slept.

BRYAN was gone when John woke up, but he'd cleaned John up, the sticky come gone from his stomach and his clothes rearranged. John smiled to think how hard he must've been sleeping for that not to wake him up. He rolled onto his side and saw a note tented on the coffee table. *Slept like a baby, gone for coffee*, it read, and John kept smiling as he sat up, scratching the fingers of one hand through his hair.

He considered, not knowing how long Bryan had been gone, but decided the coffee would still be there after he showered. He would've loved to share the shower, but he glanced over at the clock and saw it was after eight already, and they were supposed to be at the Butlers' to have lunch and pick up Beth by noon. They still had to pack, load the car, and drive an hour, so they couldn't afford to get *too* distracted.

Fifteen minutes later, showered and half-dressed, John was brushing away the morning breath when he heard the apartment door open and close. He smiled around the toothbrush, enjoying the warm feel he got just from knowing Bryan was nearby.

Mouth rinsed, he'd just wiped away a bit of foam when a knock on the doorframe drew his attention. Bryan stood leaning against the wall, smiling at him and looking way too gorgeous in cargo shorts and a Braves T-shirt, sneakers on his feet. His gaze raked John's bare chest. "I was going to offer you breakfast," he said, the tone of his voice deceptively innocent. "But I have to say, you look good enough to eat."

John dropped his towel on the vanity, stepping over to wrap his arms around Bryan's waist and pull him into a kiss. He was careful not to press their bodies too tightly together, not wanting to start something he couldn't finish, but Bryan's hands gripped John's biceps, and the moan he let out when their tongues brushed almost broke John's resolve.

Reluctantly, John broke the kiss, tilting his head to rest their foreheads together. "Much as I'd love to keep right on doing that," he murmured, "we have to get packed and head out before much longer. The Butlers are expecting us."

Bryan nodded, and John grinned as both their heads moved together. "I just want to...." Bryan trailed off. "Thanking you doesn't seem right, but it doesn't seem like enough, either. You've been so careful with me through all of this—"

"With both of us," John interrupted, lifting one hand to cup the side of Bryan's neck, thumb stroking along his jaw. "We've both got damage we're still dealing with. I'm sure we haven't found all the landmines yet. But I think we're worth it. Don't you?"

Bryan's smile lit up his face. "I do." His eyes widened, and he snickered. "Um, strange choice of words," he said, and John laughed as he got it.

"One step at a time," he said. He kissed Bryan again briefly. "Now let's have that breakfast. I don't know about you, but I kind of worked off dinner hours ago."

"More than once," Bryan pointed out, lifting an eyebrow. He took a step back, running one hand down John's arm to grasp his hand and pull him toward the kitchen. "I may have gone a little overboard. Buying food on an empty stomach is never a good idea."

John caught sight of the table and had to laugh. A plate holding what looked like one of every type of pastry in existence sat in the center, with two large paper coffee cups next to it. "Well," he said, bumping Bryan's shoulder with his own, "at least we won't be hitting the road hungry."

Bryan slapped him lightly on the stomach. "Watch it, or I might not share."

They were both grinning as they sat down and started breakfast together.

PACKING and loading was quicker than John had thought it would be. They didn't have to worry about cleaning up the apartment other than taking out the trash, so they took care of that and packed the remaining bottles of water and cans of soda to take with them. John gave everything one last check, and they left the apartment together, stopping on their way out to drop the trash bag into the compactor and leave the keys with the leasing agent on duty.

They were on the road before eleven. John navigated the light Buckhead traffic and got them onto the interstate in just a few minutes, and then he slid his right hand off the steering wheel and reached over to grab Bryan's left hand where it rested on his thigh. They stayed like that most of the way to the Butlers', their conversation light and relaxed. John knew it wouldn't be smooth sailing for them all the time, but after the past few days and with limited time alone left on their trip, he didn't want to delve back into any sensitive subjects if he could help it.

John was laughing at Bryan's spot-on SpongeBob impersonation when they pulled into the driveway at the Butlers'. William was walking up the slight incline toward the house from the mailbox and turned at the sound of the car, lifting a hand in a small wave before he continued on his way. John and Bryan hadn't discussed rules about displays of affection in front of the Butlers, or Beth, but neither of them touched the other as they walked toward the house, and John had a feeling Bryan would follow his lead. He decided to hold off for now. Everything was still so new, and they should be on firmer footing before bringing his former in-laws into things.

William was holding the door for them when they got there and gave them a nod of greeting when they got inside. "Beth and Jean are in the kitchen working on lunch," he said. He wasn't much of a smiler, but John knew from experience that was no reflection of his attitude.

"Thanks, William." Before John could say anything else, a small body came barreling around the corner and attacked his legs, almost bowling him over. John laughed and reached down to peel Beth's arms free, squatting so he could hug her properly. "Hey, Bethy," he said, running a hand down the back of her hair. "I missed you."

"Me too, Daddy." She pushed back, her eyes shining. "We got to go see the big fishes! And Gramma and me made cookies and we're making lunch too."

John smiled. He knew about the aquarium already from their phone call earlier in the week, but as usual, Beth's excitement had kept her flitting from subject to subject, and John never got much detail out of her. "Your granddaddy said you were making lunch. You want to go help Gramma finish?"

Beth nodded and dashed away, and Bryan chuckled from beside John. "I guess she means the aquarium?" he asked William.

William nodded and ambled over to his recliner. John and Bryan followed, sitting at opposite ends of the sofa.

"Joined the aquarium when it opened." William spoke as if no time had intervened after Bryan's question. "Jean's idea. She loves 'em. Everywhere we go, she wants to go to the aquarium. It's a nice one. Beth liked it."

John had grown accustomed to William's economy of words when he spoke. Getting him to string that many sentences together at once was an accomplishment. "Thanks for taking her," John said. "I wish I'd had time, but they're always adding new exhibits, so maybe next trip up we can make it over." He shot Bryan a quick smile. "Maybe the zoo too. Haven't seen the pandas in a while."

Bryan grinned back at him, then looked at William. "Mr. Butler, I don't think anyone's told me what kind of work you did? I know you're retired now."

"Phone company," William said. "Started with them when I was right out of high school. Stuck with them through everything. Worked as a tech until my knees gave out. Then I was a manager."

Bryan nodded. "Lots of changes over the years," he said. "Hard enough just keeping up with the names on the bills. Can't imagine going through all that from inside the company."

William shrugged. "It was what it was. Don't much matter now. Everybody's got a cell phone."

A noise came from behind John just before arms slid around his shoulders and he got a kiss on the cheek. "So glad to see you, Johnny," Jean said. She smiled at Bryan. "You too, honey. Now you boys come on and have lunch while it's fresh."

John and Bryan exchanged a smile and stood up, following Jean to the dining room next to the kitchen. The table had been set with everything just crooked enough to make it clear who'd done the bulk of the work. A plate piled with sandwich halves sat in the center of the table with a bowl of potato salad on one side and a plate of sliced tomatoes on the other. Jean disappeared into the kitchen and returned with a tray holding five glasses, four of tea and one of milk. She passed them around and put the tray aside before taking her seat opposite William, who'd moved from his recliner to the head of the table. John and Bryan sat opposite each other, and Beth climbed up into the chair next to John.

"Let us pray." William's voice drew their attention, and John bowed his head, watching from the corner of his eye as Beth did the same, folding her hands together. "Lord, we thank thee for thy bounty, which gives us strength. Bless us as family and friends. In your name we pray, amen."

"Amen." John heard Bryan echo the closing and looked up to give him a smile. William's blessings were always short but still formal, the language a remnant of his Southern Baptist upbringing. He and Jean had moved to a different denomination, but some things had been so ingrained by then that they'd likely never change.

Conversation over their chicken salad sandwiches was light, centered on what Beth and her grandparents had done during the week, with a little about the friends Bryan had visited. John said his work had gone well but didn't go into detail, since it would bore everyone else if he did. Bryan didn't bring up Eddie, and John wasn't about to broach the subject. Neither of them mentioned anything about what had happened between them.

Lunch finished, John stood up to start helping clear the table, seeing Bryan do the same, but Jean waved them off. "No, no, I know you need to get on the road back home. It's a long drive, and I don't want you out too late."

John had to fight off a laugh at that, not just because it was early June and the sun wouldn't set until well after seven but because Jean still mothered him after all this time. It was a nice feeling.

Beth's things packed up, goodbyes said, they were back on the road half an hour later. Bryan had offered to drive, since John had done all the driving so far, and after a moment of consideration, John agreed. He'd never been a good passenger, but he could always ask to switch if he got uncomfortable—or carsick, which had been known to happen.

The first hour went much like the trip up had, with Beth chattering away about her week and the things they saw out the windows before she fell asleep. John grinned over at Bryan, who smiled out toward the windshield.

"Did you use that trick when she was a baby?" Bryan asked. "Drive her around until she fell asleep?"

John sobered. "I... I didn't spend a whole lot of time taking care of her when she was a baby," he admitted. "The Butlers did most of that."

Bryan's hand wrapped over his where it lay against his thigh. "God, John, I'm sorry, I didn't think. I didn't mean to bring any of that up."

John shook his head and flipped his hand over to interlace their fingers. "It's okay. No, it's not a good memory, but it doesn't hurt like it did for a long time. I came out of it okay, and so did Beth. She doesn't remember any of it, and I'm getting better at living with it."

Bryan squeezed his hand. "I know it's a cliché to say time heals all wounds," he said. "But it's true. Doesn't mean there won't be any scars left behind, though."

John tilted his head back against the headrest and turned his face toward Bryan, studying his profile. "Even scars fade eventually," he said. "Time helps. So does having someone to share the burden."

Bryan's lips lifted into another smile. "Yeah." His thumb rubbed the side of John's. "It really does."

JOHN didn't know when he dozed off, but he woke to see they were approaching Savannah already. Yawning, he rubbed his fingers across his eyes and straightened up in his seat.

"Morning, sleeping beauty." Bryan's voice was teasing. "You hardly even snored."

"Shut up," John groused, but with no heat behind it. He looked back to find Beth still out. "She's slept the whole time?"

"She woke up for a few minutes about an hour ago," Bryan said. "But I told her to go back to sleep, and she did."

John laughed softly. "If only she always obeyed so well." He stretched his arms out in front of him and twisted at the waist to work out the kinks. "I can't remember the last time I slept in a car. I've always had trouble sleeping in cars or planes. Too hard to get comfortable."

"Well, you had an eventful week," Bryan pointed out. He shot John a quick glance. "We both did. But for some reason I got a really, really good night's sleep last night, and I'm feeling pretty energetic today."

He put just a note of suggestiveness into his words, and John reached over to run his fingers across the top of Bryan's thigh. "We're going to have to work out that whole privacy thing fast. Because I don't know how long I'm going to be able to keep my hands off you."

Bryan's smile widened.

Chapter 24

THEY pulled up in front of John's house a few minutes after six, and Bryan insisted on helping unload Beth's and John's things in addition to his own. Still a little groggy from napping in the car, John didn't fight him on it. In less than fifteen minutes, they had the car unloaded and Beth sent to wash up for dinner. John set the last bag down just inside the front door and turned to face Bryan, who was placing Maxie gently on top of the suitcase he'd carried in. The gesture made John's heart trip a little in his chest, and he took a step forward, laying one hand on Bryan's waist. Bryan's head lifted in surprise, and John kissed him.

"Thank you," he murmured against Bryan's mouth. "For everything."

He felt Bryan smile. "Thank *you*." He pulled back to look John in the eyes, his expression growing serious. "For everything, but especially for helping me get my life back."

John lifted his free hand to brush his thumb across Bryan's lips, watching as Bryan's eyes fluttered shut. John let his hands fall away and smiled at Bryan when he opened his eyes. "Got to get Bethy settled and start on the unpacking," he said. "You want a lift home?"

A strange expression John didn't quite recognize crossed Bryan's face, but it was gone a second later and he was smiling again. "No, I got it. Only a few blocks, and I could stand to work out the kinks from the drive anyway."

John almost had to bite his tongue to keep from making a comment about kinks. *Save it for when you can follow through*, he thought. "Okay," he said instead, reaching to pull the door open. "Tell the family I said hi, and I'll see everyone soon?"

Bryan nodded and started to walk outside, where he'd left his own suitcase at the bottom of the porch steps. He paused, though, and turned back to kiss John again, light and fleeting. "Bye," he whispered, giving John one last look before heading down the stairs, snagging his bag along the way. John watched him go with a small smile on his face, trying to ignore the urge to go drag him back and up to John's bedroom.

Give him time, John thought, stepping back inside and closing the door behind him. *It's a lot to take in. No rush.*

Still smiling, he picked up Beth's bag and headed for the laundry room to get her things started washing.

BETH slept through the night despite her nap, and John took her to Let's Be Shellfish for lunch after church on Sunday so she could chatter to Kai and Meghan about her week with her grandparents. John had been asleep by the time Meghan got home late Saturday night, but as he watched her move around checking on tables and the status of the kitchen, he noticed her throwing looks Kai's way. A lot of them, as it turned out. He glanced at Kai whenever he could see him without being obvious, and it seemed to be a two-way street. *Interesting*, he thought. *Have to have a little chat about that.*

Kai made macaroni and cheese for Beth, and on a whim, John ordered the same, knowing Kai would probably add shrimp or lobster to his. Both plates came out with a side of "red berries," and John's macaroni and cheese had lobster, as he'd suspected. John grinned up at Meghan as she set his in front of him.

"We need to talk, Meggie." He tilted his head toward the kitchen. "Seems maybe there's a little something I need to hear about."

The blush that colored her cheeks confirmed his suspicions. "I'm… kinda busy tonight," she admitted. "Tomorrow, maybe?"

John lifted an eyebrow. "I'm holding you to that." He reached for her hand and gave it a quick squeeze. "Happy for you. Really," he murmured, and her blush deepened before she pulled away and got back to work.

John grinned across the table at Beth, who was daintily biting into one of her berries. "Is it good, Bethy?" She nodded, still chewing, and John laughed and picked up one of his own berries, taking a bite. Sweetness flooded his mouth, and for a second his mind conjured up an image of holding a strawberry between his lips and having Bryan meet him in the middle, the rich flavors of fruit and man blending between them.

He swallowed and forced his mind away from that train of thought. No sprouting wood in the middle of his aunt's restaurant with his daughter sitting next to him. He reached for his tea and took a sip to finish cooling off his libido, which didn't want to cooperate. John couldn't blame it, having had such a sudden awakening after being dormant for so long.

Blinking a few times, he smiled as he watched Beth trade her berry for a spoonful of mac and cheese. "So what do you want to do this week, Bethy?"

Her eyes widened, and she swallowed her mouthful of food. "I wanna see Jeremy!" she said. "Can we go to the park? Can Mister Bryan bring him?"

John tilted his head to one side. "I don't know, Bethy. I'm sure you can see Jeremy. I'll call over and see if they're going to the park tomorrow, okay? But Mister Bryan and Mister Davis will probably be busy. They're still working on fixing up the house. You know Mister Bryan missed a whole week because he went to Atlanta with us."

Beth nodded, swinging her feet as she picked up another spoonful of food. "I like Mister Bryan. He's funny. Is he coming to eat with us again?"

John chuckled. "I hope so," he said. "We'll see. Like I said, they're gonna be really busy a lot of the time."

Beth nodded. "Can we go to the beach? We haven't been in *forever*."

Her dramatic emphasis left John forcing down a belly laugh. Two weeks certainly seemed like forever when you were five years old.

"Yeah, we can go to the beach one day," he said. "We might need to go early in the morning like we did before, so it won't be too hot."

"Okay!" Beth kept eating, and John joined her, enjoying the comfort of the restaurant and his family. It was good to be home.

JOHN called Karen Monday morning and found out she did plan to bring Jeremy to the park that afternoon, so John adjusted his schedule so he could take Beth out too. He smiled when Beth dropped his hand as soon as she spotted Jeremy and ran off to greet him. He walked over to where Karen sat, one hand on her stomach, and sat at the other end of her bench.

"How are you and the kidlet doing?" he asked, and Karen smiled at him.

"We are both doing really, really well. I'll hit five months at the end of this week, so we're over the hump." She rubbed her belly, the curve just starting to stretch the T-shirt she wore. "So to speak, that is. This hump still has a ways to go."

John grinned and leaned back against the bench, crossing his arms over his chest and letting his head drop back. The sun was high and hot, but a few scudding clouds were keeping things from being too steamy.

"How was your trip?"

John shot Karen a look. "It was… good," he said, cautious. "Got a lot done at the office, and Beth had a great time with her grandparents." He paused, a little seed of worry niggling at the back of his mind. "I guess Bryan's told you about his week?"

Karen shrugged one shoulder, her face turned toward the playground. "He and Davis hit the ground running yesterday and today, getting caught up on the house. I haven't had a chance to talk to him."

John nodded. "Yeah, I know the week put them a little behind," he said. "Most of the trip was good. I think… maybe he should tell you about the rest of it. Some of it was…. Well, I'm not sure how he'd feel about me saying anything to anyone. Even to you."

Karen nodded. "He saw Eddie."

John bit his lip, turning his head to look in the same direction she was, watching Beth and Jeremy smiling and laughing as they scrambled over the climbing set. "He saw Eddie," he confirmed. "We both did, actually. He seems to be a nice guy. I like him."

He realized Karen was looking at him then, and he looked back at her. Both of them were wearing sunglasses, so he couldn't see her eyes, but her question and the surprise in her voice told him what she was thinking. "He took you to meet Eddie?"

"Yeah." John was feeling that caution again, the concern in the back of his mind growing a little stronger. "We went Wednesday night. They talked for a while, and then the three of us talked. I won't go into details, but it.... It was tough, but it seemed to go well."

Karen kept her gaze trained on him for another long moment before her shoulders relaxed and she turned back toward the kids. "Okay," she said. "I just.... Okay."

John realized then that this might be the first real indication Karen had that Bryan could be serious about a relationship with John. Dating was one thing, but John knew having him meet Eddie was a huge step for all of them. And they'd taken it pretty early on, considering that even now it had been only two weeks since they'd first kissed and less than a month since they'd met.

It felt like so much longer than that to John, though. Bryan had slipped into his life seamlessly, as if he'd always been there. Being with him felt new and exciting but also familiar and comfortable. They could watch a ballgame and drink beer, or they could kiss and make love, and all of it just worked for them.

He found himself smiling. It had been less than two days since they'd talked, and already he missed Bryan. But he knew Bryan was busy, and he thought maybe a little decompression time would be helpful for both of them. So he'd give it another day or two before he called. Maybe he'd see if Bryan could get away to bring Jeremy to the park on Wednesday or Thursday.

He and Karen sat together for the next hour as the kids wore themselves out running around the playground. John told Karen that Adam and his family were probably going to visit and might want to stay at the bed-and-breakfast, which made her smile, and she told him of course she'd have a discounted rate for them. Karen asked if he'd baked any pies recently, and John laughed, promising to bring one for the next Sunday-night cookout.

When he and Beth headed home, after hugs from both kids, John couldn't seem to wipe the smile off his face. He couldn't remember feeling this happy, this content, since before Liz had died. He waited for the stab of pain to follow that thought, but it never came. There was a small ache deep inside, but the warmth of friendship and family kept it under control.

His life was changing in many different ways, and for maybe the first time, he didn't feel fear or guilt about it.

JOHN spent half the day Tuesday on the phone. One of the other programmers had made an unauthorized change to the report coding he'd done the week before, and it took four tries to talk him through fixing it. John sighed as he hung up the phone for the last time, rubbing the back of his neck and glancing at the computer clock. It was after three already. Meghan had left for the restaurant before ten, and Beth had spent most of her day in her playroom upstairs, acting out some elaborate story with what looked like every doll and stuffed animal she owned, or so John thought when he'd gotten a look when he went to get her for lunch.

John had a good hour of work left to do, so he dove right back into it, hoping his phone wouldn't ring again. He didn't fool himself into thinking he was indispensable by any means, but he had a natural knack for coding that made it easy for him and had a tendency to leave him impatient with others who weren't quite so adept. The programmer in question today was quite good in most respects, but debugging was his big weakness, and he'd been unable to find the error he'd introduced on his own.

John's comment to Adam popped back into his head: *That's why they pay me the mediocre bucks.* He grinned and shook his head. He was lucky to have this job, and he knew it. It paid well and gave him the flexibility he needed, and the fact that he enjoyed it and liked his boss made it a dream come true.

Even when it gives me a headache, he thought, rubbing his fingers over his forehead for a moment before turning back to the computer screen.

JOHN didn't finish work until after six, and once he'd gotten Beth fed and bathed and off to bed, he couldn't seem to settle down. He felt antsy and not at all sleepy, so he stretched out on the sofa to watch the Braves, who were playing in Denver with a late start time.

A little over an hour in, with the Braves up by four, John heard a key in the lock, and he turned his head toward the door at the sound of the handle turning. Meghan slipped inside, shooting him a quick smile as she set her bag down on the table next to the door.

"Not too late," he noted, watching her walk toward the far end of the sofa, where she kicked off her sandals before curling up on the cushions. "Not busy tonight?"

She shrugged one shoulder. "Above average but not crazy. We had two big parties that kept things hopping, but they were gone before closing. Got the last table out only ten minutes late."

John leaned his elbow on the back of the cushion and rested his hand against his fist. "So you gonna tell me what happened while we were gone, or do I need to tickle it out of you?"

Meghan snorted out a laugh. "Don't think you're getting details, buster," she retorted. "But, um." She bit her lip around a small smile. "So Kai finally made a move. And, well… I let him."

"Mmm-hmmm." John raised an eyebrow. "I take it this isn't a one-time thing?"

The blush on Meghan's cheeks deepened. "It already hasn't been."

John grinned. "You go, girl."

Meghan laughed again at that.

"Seriously, I'm glad," John said. "You deserve it. Kai's a great guy." He gave a mock frown. "He'd better stay that way too. I don't want to have to hurt—"

He cut himself off, popping his mouth shut as the implications of what he was saying hit him. *Ouch*, he thought. He realized Meghan was giving him a puzzled look, and he sighed. He needed to tell her his own story, albeit a redacted version.

"So, yeah, as you already figured out, you weren't the only one."

Meghan grinned wickedly.

"And no, I'm not going into details either. But it's.... You know something happened with Bryan."

Meghan nodded, her expression turning serious.

"He and his boyfriend were jumped and beaten up. His boyfriend never recovered. And while we were in Atlanta, we went to visit him."

"Oh, man." Meghan shifted closer on the sofa, reaching out to touch John's knee. "Was it bad?"

John nodded. "Yes, and... and no. I mean, Eddie's not going to recover. There's nothing any of us can do about that. But talking to him was good for Bryan. For all three of us, I think. I think Bryan's going to be okay with moving on now. And I made sure both of them know I'll do whatever I can to help both of them."

Meghan tilted her head. "And then...?"

John blew out a breath. "I knew I wouldn't get away with no details." He softened the gibe with a smile. "Yeah, there was.... We went to dinner Friday night, and he kind of surprised me afterward. I didn't think he'd be ready so soon, but he said he was."

He paused, not sure how much more to say, but Meghan squeezed his knee again. "Was it good for you?" she teased.

John barked out a surprised laugh. "It was.... Yeah. Damn good. And he did kind of freak out a little after, but we talked, and I think it's okay. I think we both still have a ways to go, but...." He looked Meghan in the eye. "I like him a lot, Meggie. I haven't felt this way about anyone in my life except Liz. And if I'm still feeling guilty sometimes over it, I can't imagine what he's thinking. Eddie may not be the same guy he used to be, but he's still here. Bryan wouldn't be Bryan if he didn't have some guilt."

Meghan nodded. "But you've talked about it, right? You're working on that?"

John tilted his head. "We talked Friday night, and a little on the drive, although I ended up sleeping most of the way back. I know we've both been playing catch-up since then, but once he's had some time to decompress, we'll talk some more."

Meghan frowned. "You haven't talked to him since you got back?"

John shook his head. "I figured I should give him some time to deal with everything. He went through a lot this week."

He didn't get any further before Meghan was waving a hand at him, palm out. "Wait, wait. So you fuck the guy"—John's eyes widened in surprise at her bluntness—"and disappear on him? What the *hell*?" She looked at him like he'd sprouted a third eye on a stalk. "What do you think you'd do if you were on the receiving end of that? You'd think you'd been fucked and dumped, is what you'd think. Most people would."

John's mouth opened, but no words came out. *Shit*, he thought. He'd been so fixated on giving Bryan time to catch up on work and space to think that he hadn't thought about any other implications of his silence. Of *course* he'd think something was wrong. They'd barely gone two days without talking since they'd met, even before they were more than just friends. Then they have sex, and the next day John disappears?

"*Shit*."

"Yeah." Meghan rolled her eyes and pushed to her feet. "Call the guy. Apologize. Kiss and make up. Do whatever you need to do, but I don't want to hear another word about this until you've straightened things out."

John was standing up too, digging his phone out of his pocket. He paused at the foot of the stairs. "Hey." He waited for Meghan to look at him. "Thanks for smacking some sense into me."

Meghan laughed. "The feeling's mutual. I finally listened to you, so it's your turn to listen to me. Now go!" She made a shooing motion at him, and he grinned and headed up the stairs.

Chapter 25

IT WAS late enough that John wasn't sure calling Bryan would be a good idea. He didn't want to start this off on the wrong foot by waking anyone up. So he started with a text first: *Can I call you?* He waited for the reply, trying not to be too anxious. Still, he couldn't help the sigh of relief he let out when the *sure* came back.

He picked Bryan's name out of his contact list and waited for him to pick up, reaching for his sneakers. He knew he didn't want to do this on the phone, so his mind raced until it settled on a likely spot: the park. He'd ask Bryan to meet him there.

"Hello?"

Bryan's voice sounded as tentative as John had heard it, and it made his heart clench in his chest. "Hey, Bryan," he said, keeping his voice soft. "Sorry to call so late, but there's something I…. I just really need to talk to you. Face to face, if I can. Can you meet me at the park?"

The pause was just long enough that John was sure he was going to say no, but to his relief, his answer was the same as by text. "Sure."

"Great!" John finished tying the laces on his sneakers. "I'll be there in just a few. Thanks, Bryan."

He ended the call and stood up, pausing long enough to grab his keys off his dresser. As he stepped into the hallway, he saw Meghan giving him a pointed look from the doorway of her room. He sent her a sheepish smile.

"I'll be back… sometime." He kept his voice low, not wanting to risk disturbing Beth. "And thanks again for the kick in the ass."

She grinned at him. "Anytime, Johnny."

He rolled his eyes at her and headed for the stairs. He was outside a minute later, half jogging down the sidewalk toward the park. As he got closer, he saw a dark figure already on the bench where he and Bryan had first met. He frowned for a second. Had Bryan already been at the park? That would be just about the only way he could've gotten there before John.

It didn't matter. John slowed to a fast walk, and in just a few more strides, he was standing in front of Bryan, who looked up at him with hooded eyes.

"Don't," John said, reaching for Bryan's hands. "Don't think what you're thinking."

He pulled Bryan up and wrapped both arms around him, dipping forward to kiss him, gentle as the breeze moving the salty air around them. Bryan's body was stiff at first, but after a few moments he melted into John, sliding his hands up John's arms, one hand wrapping around the back of John's neck and the other resting over his heart.

John broke the kiss just enough so he could talk. "I'm sorry," he said. "I shouldn't have disappeared like that. I thought you might need some time to decompress after everything, but I should've asked you what you needed. If you want me there, I'm there."

Bryan laughed a little. "I'm always gonna want you there," he said. "I can't promise I'll be the best company. It all feels like a fresh wound right now." He moved both hands to cup John's face, looking into his eyes. "But having you around keeps it from hurting so much. Best medicine I could ever ask for."

John reached for Bryan's hands, tangling their fingers together as he leaned forward for another kiss, deeper this time, their tongues coming out to stroke against each other. Bryan moaned softly, the sound washing over John like an ocean wave, emotion almost making him stagger with its strength. He brought their joined hands together behind Bryan's back, pulling him in closer, kissing him more strongly, and Bryan shuddered against him.

God, John wanted him so much. He tightened his grip, holding Bryan's hands together and using his arms to press Bryan tighter against him. Bryan broke the kiss with a gasp, his head falling back.

Well, now. *That* was interesting. John had held Bryan's hands down briefly Friday night, but this felt different.

John leaned forward and ran his tongue up the side of Bryan's neck to his ear, nipping the lobe. "You like that?" He slid his hands farther across Bryan's back, pinning his arms down more, and Bryan shuddered again. "Like a little restraint, do you?"

"Fuck." The word fell from Bryan's mouth in a whisper, but it had all the impact of a runaway freight train. John kissed him hard, slanting his mouth over Bryan's, and Bryan opened to him, meeting his every move, their tongues dueling wetly. John could feel Bryan hard against his hip, and he thought fast. He needed to get Bryan in private, and fast, but he had no idea how to make that happen. Neither house was a good option.

He tore himself away from Bryan's perfect, perfect mouth, leaving both of them breathing hard. "Want you," he rasped out. "So fucking much. But I don't know where…."

Bryan's eyes, clouded with lust, cleared slightly, and he smiled.

"YOU never told me about this," John whispered, a tone of joking accusation in his voice.

"Didn't need to until now," Bryan shot back. He let go of John's hand, which he'd been holding onto tightly since they'd left the park, and pulled out his keys, sliding them into the lock.

They stood outside a small building behind the bed-and-breakfast, which John had taken for a storage shed when he'd seen it before. Not so, he'd learned. It was a carriage house, originally built in the days before cars, but more important than its history was its purpose.

It was where Bryan had been living all along.

He'd explained in an economy of words as they hurried toward the house. "I stay in the house a lot of the time, when there's an empty room. The carriage house isn't in the best shape. But I spent a couple of weekends cleaning it up, and we moved one of the beds we were replacing in there. It gives me a little privacy, a place to get away and think when I need it."

John heard the words, understood them, but he honestly didn't care that much how it came about. All that mattered was having a private space they could share without worrying about disturbing either of their families. It wouldn't work all the time, considering it was still so close to the bed-and-breakfast, but for late evenings like this, it would be perfect.

Bryan had the door open and was pulling John inside, and he followed eagerly, wanting to touch Bryan everywhere. The door was closed and locked behind them in seconds, and Bryan dropped his keys on a small table next to the door and backed up to the wall next to it, drawing John along with him.

"You asked me if I like restraint." His voice was low and rumbling, and John could feel it deep in his chest. "The answer is yes. Nothing too rough, nothing like—" He stopped short, a shadow crossing his eyes, and John understood. "Not too rough. But a little hold me down, tie me up, take control…. Yeah. I get off on it."

He took John's hands and lifted them up to the wall over his head, letting go and crossing his own wrists there. John took the hint, twisting one hand around to hold both of Bryan's in place. He ran his other hand down the long line of Bryan's body, which was stretched tight with his arms held high, and felt the muscles twitch under his touch. Slowly, deliberately, he cupped Bryan's erection through the khaki of his cargo shorts, and Bryan sucked in a breath and shuddered.

"Is this what you want?" John's mouth was an inch from Bryan's when he spoke, and he traced his fingertips along the hard ridge of Bryan's cock. "Want me to take over your body, do what I want with you? What we both want?"

John had played games like this before, and he knew to be careful, even more so because of what Bryan had been through. But he didn't have anything serious in mind, only some light teasing. He had no qualms about going further if they wanted, but not without more than a handful of sentences being exchanged.

For now, though, it didn't matter. Bryan was writhing, pushing his hips forward, trying to get more of the light, teasing touches. John leaned his whole body against Bryan's, sliding his hand around Bryan's waist and onto his ass, yanking him close and grinding their hips together. Bryan groaned, and his head dropped back against the wall, and John lowered his mouth to the crook of Bryan's neck, sucking and biting at the tender spot, his hips still moving and his hand still holding Bryan's wrists to the wall above his head. His ears filled with the sounds of Bryan's harsh breathing and gasping moans, a symphony he knew he'd never tire of hearing.

He wanted more, more of Bryan, more of this feeling. Not just the arousal, the pleasure coursing through his veins, but the way his heart felt full and light at the same time, because Bryan wanted him. Just having someone like Bryan in his life would've been enough to make him happy, but he could barely contain the joy bubbling in him to know that, of anyone Bryan could've had, he'd chosen John.

John pulled back but brought both hands down to catch Bryan around the waist as he sagged against the wall, his knees gone weak. John knew the feeling, and he was pretty unsteady himself as he led Bryan over the few feet to the bed, pushing and pulling at clothes. Bryan went to work too, and by the time they hit the mattress, they were stripped bare, nothing but hot, smooth skin to explore.

John's mind filled with all the things he wanted to do to and with Bryan. It had been so long since he'd had a hard cock inside him, and for a moment he considered it, but Bryan had opened up a whole new world with his confession about wanting to be restrained. Tonight, John wanted to dominate, hold Bryan down again, loving the reactions he'd already gotten from him. But he did decide all of that could wait a few minutes while he licked and bit his way across Bryan's chest, sucking his hard brown nipples, leaving them wet with his saliva. He savored the salty taste of Bryan's skin as he ran his tongue down the groove between Bryan's tight abs, pausing to circle his bellybutton and then licking through the trail of hair below. Bryan's hard cock bumped John's cheek as he moved, but he left it alone, nibbling at Bryan's hipbone instead, pushing his legs apart, wrapping his lips around Bryan's balls.

Bryan shuddered and groaned with every new touch, panting, cursing under his breath, moaning out John's name. When his hands landed on John's head, John grabbed them and pinned them to the mattress on either side of Bryan's hips, lifted his head, and slid his mouth down around Bryan's cock.

Bryan's hips thrust up on what John would bet was pure instinct, and John followed the movement but shifted his position, bringing one arm across Bryan's hips to hold him still, never letting go of Bryan's hands. Bryan moaned and writhed, but John wasn't letting up any time soon, keeping him pinned in place while he laved the length of Bryan's cock from root to tip, mouthed his way back down, twirled his tongue in random patterns over the silken skin.

"God!" The word burst out of Bryan's mouth. "John, please, please, oh shit, *please*...."

John didn't have to ask what Bryan wanted. He knew. He took another minute to drive Bryan out of his mind before changing positions again, letting go of Bryan's hands so he could plant both palms against his hips and take his cock all the way in. He breathed past his gag reflex, fighting the urge to pump a victorious fist when the head tagged the back of his throat. *Just like riding a bike*, he thought, laughing silently at himself.

Bryan's hands were on his head again, twisting through his hair, pulling a little, but John ignored everything but the task in front of him. He started a pattern of long strokes, sucking hard all the way up until only the tip of Bryan's cock remained in his mouth and then gliding back down. Once Bryan was trembling underneath him, mumbling under his breath, John shortened his strokes, moving up and down an inch or so at a time, flicking his tongue against the underside.

Bryan's sounds got louder, his hip movements harder to control, and John laid one forearm across Bryan's body to hold him in place more firmly. That had the benefit of freeing up one of John's hands, so he slid it between Bryan's legs, fingers stroking across his balls and then probing farther back. He sucked Bryan's cock all the way down, at the same time rubbing firmly on the patch of skin between his balls and anus. He got the reaction he wanted: Bryan shouted in surprise, his back arched, and he cried out again as a warm, wet flood poured out into John's mouth. John swallowed as much as he could, gradually letting up on the pressure, licking away the remnants as Bryan collapsed against the mattress, looking boneless.

John sat back to look at Bryan, and the tip of his dick brushed the side of Bryan's knee. He jerked and hissed, having been so focused on Bryan that he hadn't realized just how close he was to the edge himself. He thought about jerking off right then, painting Bryan's chest with his come, but that wasn't what he wanted. He wanted inside, and he knew Bryan wanted him there. So he waited, not touching anything, just breathing, watching Bryan stir as his mind reentered the world. When his eyes opened, John smiled at him. "Good?"

He knew it was a silly question, and he was rewarded when Bryan rolled his eyes and mumbled something indistinct but, from the tone, clearly sarcastic. Bryan pushed up onto his elbows, and his gaze landed on John's hard dick. The urgency to come had faded some by then, so John wrapped his fingers around it and stroked, keeping his touch light.

"You want this?" He was a little surprised at himself. He'd never been one for a lot of dirty talk in bed, but something about Bryan made him want to throw all inhibitions aside and dive in headfirst. It helped a lot that it sure seemed to work for Bryan, whose cock was already showing renewed signs of interest.

"Yeah," Bryan said. His gaze flicked to John's face, and he gave a wicked grin before rolling to the side and pulling open the drawer of the bedside table. He tossed a bottle of lube onto the mattress near his leg, followed it with a condom, and flopped onto his back, dragging down a pillow to slide under his hips. "There you go, hot stuff." The challenge was clear in his voice. "I'm ready whenever you are."

John snickered and picked up the lube first, drizzling a few drops on the end of his cock before opening the condom and rolling it down, knowing the layer of lubrication would cut back on the friction a little so he could take his time. He slicked up his fingers next and reached down to circle Bryan's hole. Bryan sighed and spread his legs wider, bending his knees to frame John's body. John took the invitation and slipped a finger inside, crooking it up to find the spot inside that made Bryan jerk and moan. He worked him open one finger at a time, watching his every reaction, until Bryan's eyes met his again and he said one word: "Now."

John pulled his hand free and used it to guide his cock into place. He pressed forward steadily, not stopping until it felt like he'd bottomed out inside. He pulled back an inch and pushed in again, going in just a bit farther, then repeated the move. Bryan groaned every time, hands clutching at the sheets, and John started a shallow back-and-forth rock.

Bryan gradually found his rhythm, moving his hips in counterpoint. After a couple of minutes, John sped up, pushed a little harder, and Bryan moaned loudly, hands coming up, reaching for whatever part of John he could touch.

John had anticipated that. He grabbed for Bryan's wrists and surged forward, pinning Bryan's hands onto the mattress next to his shoulders. Bryan shouted in surprise and then let out a stream of obscenities, *shitfuck oh fuck fuck yeah fuck yeah*, as John started thrusting into him deep and hard and *God, so perfect*, John thought with what little brain power he had left. Bryan had almost no leverage to meet John's movements, but he tried anyway, feet sliding against the sheets, hips lifting, torso twisting. His moans were constant now, his head tilted back, and his body shuddered hard with every thrust.

Between the feel of Bryan's body around him, the sounds coming out of his mouth, and the picture of pure sex he made, John knew he wouldn't last long, no matter what tricks he might try. He didn't know if Bryan could come like this, if the friction of their stomachs against his cock would be enough, but John couldn't quite bring himself to release Bryan's hands so one of them could jerk him off. He didn't know if Bryan would have enough focus to do it, he was so far gone into a haze of ecstasy. Hell, John wasn't sure *he* could concentrate well enough either.

Instead, he tilted his hips down, changing the angle of his thrusts to rub their bodies together more firmly where Bryan's cock was caught in between them. Bryan got a lot louder then, so much so that John wondered for a second if they could hear him in the main house, but then Bryan's body tightened down around him and all thought flew right out of John's mind. He barely had time to register the look of utter pleasure on Bryan's face before his vision blurred and his own climax slammed into him hard, stealing his breath.

He came back to himself slowly, realizing that he still had a death grip on Bryan's wrists. He released them, and Bryan groaned under him but seemed only half aware of anything. John levered himself back and withdrew, tying off the condom. He leaned over toward the bedside table, happy to find a box of tissues that he could reach without having to stretch too far. He wiped off Bryan's stomach and then his own, wrapping the condom up in the tissues and dropping the whole mess and the box next to the bed.

Bryan didn't move the entire time, other than the rapid rise and fall of his chest. John reached up to draw his hands down, intending to check Bryan's wrists for bruising, but Bryan seemed to come alive then, wrapping his arms and legs around John, pulling his body down on top of him. John laughed, surprised, then shuddered when Bryan nuzzled into the base of his throat, the light stubble on his cheek scratching gently against John's skin.

"God," Bryan muttered. "God."

John tightened his embrace, rocking them both, soothing. "So good, Bryan," he whispered. "Everything's always so good with you."

He didn't remember falling asleep, but he never let Bryan go.

JOHN had his sunglasses on when he stepped onto his front porch, but everything still seemed several degrees too bright. That could have had something to do with the fact that he'd gotten less than three hours of sleep the night before, most of those in the form of naps between multiple rounds of sex with Bryan.

He'd slipped out of the carriage house just as the sun was peeking over the horizon, hurrying back home to shower and dress before Beth woke up. That was something they'd have to deal with soon: how to schedule time together around John's job, Bryan's renovation work, and Beth. Just being together wouldn't be that hard, but going on dates or having any real private time would mean some planning and negotiation.

John grinned. He knew they'd figure it out.

"Daddy, let's go!" John pulled himself from his thoughts to see Beth standing at the foot of the front stairs, her little hands on her hips and a frown on her face. "We're s'pposed to meet Jeremy and Mister Bryan already!"

John smiled as he walked down the stairs toward her, holding the straps of his backpack in one hand. "They're not going anywhere," he pointed out, holding out his free hand for her to take. "They'll wait for us."

Beth let out a put-upon sigh as only an exasperated five-year-old could. "Come on, Daddy!" She pulled on his hand, and John let himself be dragged along behind her. Despite his lack of sleep, he didn't feel tired, and even if he had, the prospect of seeing Bryan would've been enough to wake him right up.

When they arrived at the playground, half a dozen kids were already swarming the equipment, and all of the benches were taken up by guardians of one kind or another. John looked around, holding onto Beth's hand, and spotted Bryan off to one side, sitting cross-legged on the grass, leaning back on his hands with his face tilted up toward the sun. John's heart beat a little faster at the sight of him, lean torso stretched out, T-shirt pulled tight across his chest. It wasn't the only thing getting tight.

John forced himself to look away and smiled down at Beth. "You see Mister Bryan over there?" He nodded in that direction.

Beth's head turned that way, and she nodded fast.

"That's where I'm going to be, okay? You come over there if you need me."

"Okay, Daddy!" Beth dropped his hand and hugged his legs, and John laughed softly, running one hand over her hair.

"Go have fun, baby," he said, and she shot him that beautiful smile that looked so much like her mother's before letting go and running toward the playground. He watched her go, feeling his heart react again. God, she was growing up so fast.

"She's beautiful."

The voice startled John, and he jerked his head around to meet Bryan's smiling face. He'd walked up without John even realizing it. John felt his own face flush, and he smiled in return.

"She's amazing," he said. "I don't know what I'd do without her."

Bryan slipped his hand into John's, and John resisted the urge to look around and see if anyone noticed. They were standing far enough away from the others that no one could see even if they were looking. *And if they did, so what?* John thought.

"I'm glad you don't have to do without her," Bryan said. "I think she's amazing, and I like her a lot."

John squeezed Bryan's hand. "I know," he said. "One of the main reasons I started falling for you was that you were so great with her."

Bryan laughed softly. "Love me, love my kid?"

John stilled. He knew he shouldn't ask. He knew it was only a saying. He knew it was too soon. But he knew what he felt, and he needed to know if Bryan did too.

"Do you?" he whispered. "Love me?"

Bryan's eyes widened as if he'd just realized what he'd said. John half expected him to step back, make another joke, avoid the question. But he watched as Bryan straightened up and looked him straight in the eyes.

"Yeah," he said. "Yeah, I do."

John leaned in until their foreheads touched. "Good," he replied. "Because I do too."

Bryan sighed and squeezed his hand, and then he did step back. "C'mon," he said. "Let's see if we can steal a swing from some kids and have a little family-safe fun of our own."

John grinned as he followed Bryan over. The swings were less busy than the rest of the playground, and as they approached, a little girl climbed down from the one at the end and ran over toward the climbing set, where most of the kids were playing. John set his backpack down next to the frame and waved a hand toward the swing.

Bryan shook his head. "No. You go first."

John almost protested, but he couldn't even give himself a reason why, so he just smiled and sat, wrapping his hands around the chains, which had a thick plastic cover like a bicycle chain. Bryan came up behind him, hands landing just above his on the chains. "Want a push?" he asked, and John tilted his head back to smile at him upside down.

"Absolutely," he said.

Bryan wanted to kiss him, he knew. John felt the same way. But this wasn't the time or place for it. Instead, Bryan let his hands slide down, brushing his fingers over John's, and then re-grasped the chains close to John's hips. He pulled back a little and then let go, pushing at John's lower back. John swung out, and when he came back, Bryan pushed again, harder this time. Soon John was swinging freely, pumping his legs up and back, and he no longer felt Bryan's pushes. He looked to the side and saw Bryan had scored the swing next to his, pushing himself off, grinning over at John, his own legs sending him higher into the air.

John tilted his face up, enjoying the warmth of the sun and the cool of the breeze on his skin. His heart was light, and his mind was at peace. He closed his eyes and pictured Liz smiling at him, happy and content to see him happy, and he had to smile in response.

He knew it wouldn't always be this perfect. Nothing in life ever was. But for the first time in five years, he felt free.

SHAE CONNOR lives in Atlanta, where she works for the government by day and reads and writes about pretty boys falling in love by night. She's been making up stories for as long as she can remember, but it took her a long time to figure out that maybe she should start writing them down. Now, she usually has far too many stories in progress, but when she does manage to tear herself away from her laptop, she enjoys running, hiking, cooking, and traveling, not necessarily in that order.

Shae posts snippets, updates, and thoughts on writing and editing at her website, http://shaeconnorwrites.com. You can contact her at shaeconnorwrites@gmail.com.

Also by Shae Connor

http://www.dreamspinnerpress.com

Contemporary Romance from DREAMSPINNER PRESS

http://www.dreamspinnerpress.com

Contemporary Romance from DREAMSPINNER PRESS

http://www.dreamspinnerpress.com